"As I read *Seeds of Evidence*, I found myself wanting to jump into the pages and live out the story alongside Kit and David. With a perfect blend of suspense and romance, this is a thrilling and ultimately satisfying read!"
—Ann Tatlock, Christy award-winning author of *Promises to Keep*

"*Seeds of Evidence* is a gripping tale of two searches: FBI Special Agent Kit McGovern's quest to find the killer of a young Hispanic boy and her struggle to regain her faith. This action-packed tale will keep readers turning the pages—with primers on plant DNA and human trafficking thrown in as a bonus. And when a D.C. cop on sabbatical comes into Kit's life, she finds herself being drawn into what could be the antidote to the failed first marriage that still scars her."
—Howard Owen

"As a frequent visitor to Chincoteague Island, I was excited as I began this book. Following Kit McGovern and David O'Connor as they pursue justice for a young boy, the story and the island come alive. You can almost smell the water, feel its spray on your face, and feel the presence of the locals as Kit and David traverse the island in search of his killer. As Kit is determined to right this wrong, she also discovers some things about herself that will change her future. If you enjoy a good suspense novel you will not be disappointed with *Seeds of Evidence!*"
—Kathy Cosner

SEEDS OF EVIDENCE

Linda J. White

Abingdon Press fiction
a novel approach to faith

Nashville, Tennessee

For John and Kathy,
who persevere in faith

Acknowledgments

A novel is always a collaboration, the work of people with "gifts differing," who unselfishly contribute their talents to the final product.

Over the years, many current and retired FBI agents have graciously shared their expertise with me, teaching me everything from probable cause to pistols and prosecutions. I am so grateful for their generosity and their willingness to answer my many questions. A finer group of people would be hard to find.

Among those from the FBI Academy who contributed invaluably to my knowledge is the late Art Westveer, a former homicide detective who taught death investigations at the Academy. A kind and compassionate man, Art helped me "design" the beach child's body shortly before he himself was tragically killed in a car crash.

I'm grateful for my editor, Ramona Richards, and others at Abingdon Press who have helped make this a better book. And for my literary agent, Janet Grant, whose combination of dynamic creativity and business acumen continues to inspire and guide me.

My focus group, who took the time to read this manuscript in draft and offer feedback, saved me from many an error. My prayer group has undergirded me and joined in petitioning God for spiritual fruit from this work.

My family has been supportive, patient, and forgiving. My children—all grown now—Matt, Becky, and Sarah, tolerated my distractibility when I was working on scenes in my head. Becky's strong editing skills and Sarah's expertise in medicine and Spanish have found their way into my work. Larry, my husband, is at once my best critic and my best encourager. I would never have made that first trip over to the Academy if he hadn't dragged me, believing I had a story to tell.

Finally, I am thankful to my Lord Jesus Christ who pulled me out of a miry pit and set my feet on solid ground. Ultimately, it's all for Him.

1

THE BEACH IS TIME, LIBERATED. SAND ESCAPED FROM AN HOURGLASS, water freed from a pipe, wind unhindered by concrete or glass, Kit without a calendar or timesheet or meetings, her life measured only by the rhythmic pounding of waves and the sun's bold stride across the heavens.

The bright blue, cloudless sky prophesied the day would be hot. The morning sun warmed the side of Kit's face as she jogged. Each receding ocean wave cast a mirrorlike sheen on the wet sand. Ahead, a tiny band of sandpipers skittered, while behind, the waves washed away her tracks, slipping her past into the great, gray ocean.

At first, she thought the object she saw in the distance was driftwood covered by seaweed. Still, something about its shape roused her curiosity. She quickened her pace.

She saw a group of teens, four—no, five—of them, approach the object, then jerk back, shock evident in their action. Kit's heart jumped. She ran faster, her heels flinging up sand, her mind racing. Sweat broke out on the back of her neck. At the small of her back, the nylon fanny pack carrying her gun and FBI credentials—she was on duty 24/7—slapped her, urging her on.

The kids began shouting, jumping up and down, waving at her, and as Kit grew closer, she saw why: at their feet lay the body of a child.

"He's dead! Oh, God! He's dead!" a girl screeched. She huddled with her friends, their shoulders hunched, clutching beach towels like shields. The young men, two of them, stood arched over the body, peering at it like curious colts.

"Don't touch him!" Kit commanded. "Did you call 911?"

"Yes, ma'am." The boys shifted back.

Kit's eyes fell on the body. The little boy, clad in long, loose pants and a long-sleeved green shirt, was most certainly dead. One big roller of the incoming tide had deposited him up on the smoothly packed sand. Now, lesser waves lapped at him, fluttering his clothes, like fingers trying to grasp him and pull him away. It wouldn't be long before the sea reclaimed him.

Dread washed over her. She needed to secure the body. She didn't want to touch it with her bare hands; neither did she want it sucked back out to sea. She looked at the teens. They seemed frozen, unable to move. "Give me your towel," she said to a young woman, but the girl just hugged it closer to her chest. Nearby, a laughing gull planted his three-toed feet on a dune and chortled.

Another big wave hit, knocking Kit off balance and floating the boy's body. "No!" she breathed, watching the body drift. Germs or no germs, she had to do it. She grabbed the boy's shirt.

"Hold on! Let me help!"

Kit looked up. A thirty-something man with brown hair threw his surfboard down on the sand, put his iPod on top of it, and rushed to her side. "I got it." The man grabbed one side of the boy. Kit took the other, and together they gently moved the body to dry sand, beyond the reach of the waves. The teens shied away.

"Scrub off your hands," the man said as he rubbed wet sand on his hands and arms and dunked them in the surf. "Did you call it in?"

"He did," Kit nodded toward one of the teens. "Where'd you come from?"

"Up north."

"Did you see anybody up there?"

"No."

"Any boats?"

"Nothing."

Kit squinted and shaded her eyes as she studied him. Mid- to late-thirties, she figured, about 5'10", short brown hair, brown eyes, tanned, and fit. Very fit.

"Here comes your help." He nodded toward two four-wheel-drive pickups approaching from the south. "You OK now?"

"Yes. Thank you."

Kit looked down at the boy. His skin was pale, a sort of dusky gray. His large eyes stared into nothingness and his mouth hung open. Sand filled his nostrils and spilled out of the one ear she could see, and there were bruises on his neck. Ligature marks? Had he been murdered? Kit's breath caught. How long had he been dead? Already the flies were gathering. She wanted to shoo them away, to protect him from the ravages of natural decomposition. The body looked fresh. Would the water have preserved it?

By the time she looked up, the man had picked up his surfboard, and was walking on down the beach. "Hey! What's your name?" Kit called, but the man didn't respond, and the white wires running down from his ears told her his iPod had claimed his attention again. "That was a mistake," she muttered.

"Ew, gross!" A girl pointed. A seagull had landed on the boy's chest.

Kit reacted quickly. "Shoo!"

Behind the teens, the pickups jerked to a stop, and a man and two women in U.S. Fish & Wildlife Service uniforms climbed out. Kit's mind raced: her vacation. Two weeks of no responsibility. She could simply identify herself as an FBI agent, tell them what she knew, and walk away.

But before her lay a little boy . . . possibly murdered!

But Fish & Wildlife could investigate it. And why would the FBI get into a simple murder case?

Kit shifted on her feet. The sun blazed on her shoulders. An unidentified body, a child, no less. A child. A little Latino boy . . .

She didn't miss the half-smile on the man's face as the officers approached. She had on a bright blue two-piece swimsuit and athletic shorts. No T-shirt. Sweat beaded on her skin.

"Where'd that come from?" A stocky, plain-looking woman with close-cropped brown hair stopped in her tracks, about eight feet away from the body.

"Kit McGovern, FBI." She flashed her creds at the woman. "Are you the officer in charge?"

"Yeah. Brenda Ramsfeld, Fish & Wildlife."

"Kid fall off a boat?" The leering man strode up to the body and nudged it with the toe of his boot.

"Don't touch him!" Kit's anger surged. She turned to Ramsfeld. "Do you see the marks on his neck?"

"Like somebody killed him? Cool!" the man responded.

"We've never had a murder here," Ms. Ramsfeld said, glancing at her coworker, a woman with blonde hair.

The man laughed. "You've seen CSI, Brenda. You know what to do."

"You think he died here, on the beach? What about those kids?" Ramsfeld gestured toward the teens.

"They found the body washing up in the surf. I saw them."

"So maybe he was murdered at sea and dumped overboard," the blonde suggested.

"Quite possibly," Kit said, her heart jumping. If the murder didn't happen on land, the FBI could rightfully claim the case. Thoughts of vacation slipped away like sand. "The lifeguards didn't report anything?" she asked Ramsfeld.

"They're just now coming on duty. Besides, look at the way those waves are coming in."

Kit turned. The Atlantic was in fine form today, the three-foot gray-green waves coming in at a slant, breaking about five yards out, sending sea foam sliding up over the hard-packed sand in a gentle caress, then sliding back. She squinted into the sun, scanning the horizon, but saw nothing—no boats, no surfers, no dolphins. She turned back to Ramsfeld. "From the northeast?"

"Right. The littoral current would be from the same direction. So why would you think lifeguards to the south would have seen anything?" Ramsfeld's voice dripped disgust.

She still kept her distance, Kit noted, standing nowhere near the body. "So he probably did die at sea. The Bureau would have jurisdiction."

Ramsfeld threw up her hands. "All right, look. You want it, you got it." She shook her head. "Just my luck," she said, shooting a look toward the others, "something major happens and the Bureau gets here first." She put her hands on her hips. "I'm guessing you'll need the medical examiner."

"Right," Kit said, "and identification from those teenagers. And photos of the body. Do you have a camera?"

"You want photos with or without the ghost crab nibbling at his ear?" the creepy guy joked.

Kit glared at him. "Just get the camera."

The onshore breeze stiffened a bit, sending a spray of saltwater over the scene as a breaker crashed onto the beach. Kit

lips, tasting the salt. "Until the ME gets here, we'll
secure the scene."

's July and in an hour I'm going to have a beach full of
ationers. You're not expecting me to provide staff long-
rm, are you?" Ramsfeld said.

"If you could spare one person until they get here, I'd appreciate it." Kit hoped against hope it wouldn't be the man, who
returned with a small digital camera in hand.

Ramsfeld shot her a look, then she turned to her blonde
staff member. "Pat, you stay with her. Joe and I need to get back
to work."

◦━━◆━━◦

Kit took all the pictures she thought she'd need. Then, waiting for the ME van, she listened to Pat complain about the
way things had changed on the job since Brenda Ramsfeld had
become their chief. After a while, even Pat wearied of that talk
and wandered off, climbing the dunes in search of shade. After
she left, Kit had only the sand and surf and sun and one dead
little boy to keep her company.

She sat on a piece of driftwood, watching the tide come
into her beloved Assateague. A barrier island off the coast
of Virginia, Assateague cradled its smaller sister island,
Chincoteague, in the crook of its arm, protecting the humans
who lived there from the brunt of the ocean's force. Kit had
been coming to the area since she was a child, drawn by her
love for her grandmother who lived there.

Kit had been on the wild, wind-swept island in the fall
when snow geese by the thousands gathered on brackish
ponds, honking and calling, and in the winter, when the wind
whipped up sea foam and deposited it in mounds well beyond
the dunes. She'd been there in the spring, when migrating birds
came again, so many different kinds she couldn't keep track of

them, and the Sika deer fawned, and the wild ponies gave birth to their foals. And in the summer, when long days on the beach called her to an eternal perspective, the timeless pounding of the waves and the endless vista reminded her that her temporal troubles were but a passing phase.

She needed to hear that reminder again. That was why she'd come.

⚬━━◆━━⚬

The medical examiner, Dr. Scarborough, was a fifty-something, burly man with snow-white hair and a brusque, businesslike manner. His eyes widened slightly when he saw Kit dressed in a bathing suit and shorts, and she felt her face grow warm. Thankfully, he didn't say anything.

She watched while he took pictures with a digital camera, and then snapped on gloves and gently examined the body while dictating into a digital recorder. His assistant, a young, thin man dressed in khaki pants and a white shirt, looked on.

When he finished, Dr. Scarborough stood up and faced Kit, fixing his piercing blue eyes on her. "The boy was strangled. Autopsy will tell us whether that killed him or he drowned."

Kit's gut clenched. "How long ago?"

"As much as thirty-six hours."

"That long?"

"Cold salt water preserves the body. Again, the autopsy will narrow it down." The ME looked down at the boy again. "I see no other injuries, except for a few sea-life nibbles. He didn't bleed out."

"Why is he so gray?"

"All his blood has gone to the center of his body." Scarborough pulled off his gloves. "My preliminary finding: homicide by strangulation, twenty to thirty-six hours ago."

Kit drove to her rental cottage. Scarborough's words tumbled over and over through her mind. Someone murdered the boy. Strangled him. Sometime in the last thirty-six hours.

Who would kill a little boy in that way? By strangling him? She tried to imagine it. A mother? She couldn't see a mother wrapping a cord around a child's neck and choking him until he died. A mother's boyfriend? Much more likely.

So why didn't she protect him? Kit knew the answer to that without thinking. All too often women were too emotionally dependent on their men to protect their kids.

She showered, spread an aloe-based cream that smelled like coconut over her sunburn, then dressed in work clothes—khaki pants, a white shirt with a small, stand-up collar, and a Navy blue blazer, necessary, even in summer, to cover her gun. While she laced her highlighted, light brown hair into a French braid, her mind worked hard, calculating how she would sell her involvement in the case to her boss.

Sweat moistened her hand as she pressed her cell phone to her ear. At her boss's gruff "Hello," she described finding the child on the beach.

"I thought you were on vacation," Steve Gould responded.

"Yes, sir, but I think this warrants our attention."

"Why?"

"I think we're the best agency to investigate it."

"One kid? Who cares about one kid?"

She knew he meant that the FBI generally got involved in more complex cases. "If he were kidnapped, we'd care."

"He's not. He's dead."

"Yes, sir, but . . . but his body . . . his body was found on a federal reservation. We can assert jurisdiction."

"We don't want to."

"I want to."

Kit heard him sigh.

"Why, McGovern? Just tell me why."

Kit squeezed her eyes shut and pictured the little boy on the beach. She realized she was trembling. Why did she care so much? "It's all about justice, sir. Somebody wrapped something around this little boy's neck and choked him until he died. Who did it? We have the best resources to figure that out. Otherwise . . . otherwise I can almost guarantee this'll become a cold case."

She could hear Steve tapping on his desk. "This is the way you want to spend your vacation?"

"Yes, sir."

"Oh, for crying out loud," he grumbled. "Call the Assistant U.S. Attorney. If he won't prosecute, then drop it," he ordered her. "Otherwise, you have two weeks to convince me you're not wasting our resources."

As she hung up the phone, Kit wondered if her new boss was naturally tough or if he had heard the rumors about her. She was not a loose cannon! She didn't care what her old supervisor said.

❦

Kit drove to a vacation-property rental office in town. The agent, Connie Jester, was Kit's friend, Chincoteague born and bred, a sixth-generation islander who knew every native, transient, and come-here who had wandered over the high, arched bridge and ended up settling down. Her position made her a pipeline for a rich storehouse of information.

Kit told Connie about the body on the beach. "Well," the redhead responded, "that makes sense. When I heard the FBI was involved, I knew it had to be you. But aren't you supposed to be on vacation?"

Kit shrugged. "I can't just ignore a dead child." Momentarily, in her mind's eye she saw faces, Honduran faces, Salvadoran faces, faces from an adoption website. "Connie, what can you tell me about the local Latino community?"

"Oh, they come in at times, big groups of them, going over to the beach. Families, mostly, although there always seems to be a bunch of unattached young men."

"Where do they stay?"

"Most of 'em are day-trippers. When they do stay, they either camp or pile people in a motel room." Connie's blue eyes flashed. "You know, there are a lot of migrant workers on the peninsula, picking tomatoes and melons, green beans. Some of 'em stay on, working in the poultry processing plants or picking crabs. A few try their hand at making a living on the water, but that's something few natives can do, much less newcomers."

"Is it likely they'd go out on a charter boat?"

"Have you checked those prices lately?"

Kit bit her lip, buying time to think. In all the years she'd been coming to Chincoteague, she'd never been out on a fishing boat, never seen Assateague from the ocean. "Who's the commander of the Coast Guard station now?"

"Well, that would be Rick Sellers. Nice guy. From New York, but a nice guy, anyway."

Kit wrote his name down. "If a child disappeared, why wouldn't somebody report it?" she mused out loud.

"Running drugs," Connie suggested. "Either that or illegal. Nobody's gonna raise a flag when they're doing something wrong."

That made sense. Kit heard the sound of the office's door opening.

"Here's David O'Connor," Connie said. "He's a D.C. cop. Y'all ought to get along just fine."

Kit looked up. Coming in the door was the thirty-something man from the beach.

The man grinned as their eyes met.

"David took your grandmother's house for six whole months," Connie said. "That's why I couldn't give it to you."

Six months, Kit thought? What was he doing on Chincoteague for six months?

"It's a great place," he said.

Kit felt the color rising in her face. Her grandmother's house was now a rental property. She wished she had the money to buy it.

Connie smiled at him. "Kit here's a Fed."

"I met her this morning." Amusement crinkled the corners of his eyes.

"Why were you up on the beach so early?" Kit asked.

"You don't surf, do you?"

She blinked, put off by the response.

"Low tide came at 8:16," he explained. "That's the best time to surf. The waves break farther out, and they're bigger. I drove over to the island at six, hiked up a ways, surfed until low tide, hiked farther north, surfed some more, and was walking back when I saw you." He flashed another smile. "FBI, right?"

How did he know?

"I could tell by the suit," he joked.

Embarrassment sent blood rushing to her face. Kit struggled to regroup. "Not too many cops get six months off. You must be a special case." She lifted her chin. "I'll need your contact information."

"I was surprised you didn't ask for it before." David motioned to Connie who handed him a pen and he scrawled a phone number on the back of one of her business cards, then gave it to Kit.

"I'll be in touch."

"I can't wait."

Connie cleared her throat. "What can I do for you, David?" she asked brightly.

The two lapsed into a conversation about water heaters and kayaking.

Kit left. His attitude grated on her like sand. She walked to her car and sat for a moment, trying to shake off her annoyance. She had to lose the emotion and prepare for the conversations she planned to have next. She'd wanted to ask Connie about Brenda Ramsfeld, but she had allowed David O'Connor to deflect her from her mission.

She was still sitting in the parking lot in her personal vehicle, a green Subaru Forester, fiddling with her CD player, when David O'Connor emerged from the rental office. She clicked off her music and watched him as he opened the lift gate of his own SUV, a battered Jeep Cherokee with an orange one-man kayak and a blue surfboard on a rack on the roof. She saw him rummage through a gym bag, retrieve a dark blue golf shirt, and pull off the T-shirt he'd been wearing. That's when she saw the scar, an ugly round knot on his left shoulder blade, still a deep, angry red.

She'd seen that kind of scar before. It was a bullet exit wound.

2

KIT PULLED UP TO A PARKING SPACE OUTSIDE THE SUNBAKED FISH & Wildlife Service building on Assateague. The receptionist ushered her into a cool, inner office. "Thanks for your help this morning," she said to Brenda Ramsfeld.

The Fish & Wildlife chief responded with a grunt.

"What kinds of crimes have you seen lately?" Kit settled into the chair she'd been offered.

Ramsfeld stared at the pencil she held in her hand and pressed its point into her desk blotter. "Normal beach stuff. Alcohol, illegal bonfires, a couple of marijuana possession cases . . . nothing terribly interesting."

"How often do you patrol north of the swimming area?"

"Every two, maybe three hours."

"And who was on that patrol this morning?"

"Joe Rutgers. The guy who was with me this morning."

"I'll need to interview him."

Ramsfeld sat back in her chair. "He'll be thrilled."

Kit studied the woman. "You like this post?"

Ramsfeld let out an exasperated gasp. "No. I didn't want to come here. The higher-ups mandated the transfer. There's nothing here but birds and sand. Nothing. The body on the beach was the first interesting thing that's happened in months."

"Where'd you transfer in from?"

"The West Coast. I'm going back as soon as I can. And you know what? Handling that murder could have been my ticket."

But you really didn't want it, Kit thought. She handed the digital camera back to Ramsfeld. "I'll keep the SD card if that's OK."

"Yeah, I figured you would," the chief responded.

Kit waited in a private office while Joe Rutgers drove in from the beach. When he walked in, he had a silly grin on his face and smelled like salt and sweat and something else, Kit thought. "Sit down," she said, motioning to a chair across the table from her. "What time did you patrol north of the life-guarded area this morning?" Like riding a wave, she wanted to stay ahead of this guy.

"'Bout seven," Joe said.

Kit guessed he was in his forties. His brown hair showed flecks of gray and he had a scar across the bridge of his nose. "And what did you see?"

"Sand. Birds. Ocean."

"That's it? No people."

"Nope."

Kit flexed her jaw. "How far north did you go?"

He told her.

"The patrol takes about 45 minutes. You left the lifeguarded area around seven, and you didn't see anyone as you drove north?"

"That's right."

He should have seen David O'Connor. Kit looked straight at Joe. "And which dune is it that you stop behind to smoke your joints, Joe?"

20

The man's eyes opened wide in surprise. He pushed back his chair and wiped his hands on his thighs.

"Now, you want to tell me the truth? Because, as you know, lying to a federal investigator can get you more time than, say, simple possession."

A drip of sweat ran down the side of Joe's face. "All right. I didn't make it all the way up to the limit of the refuge. I took a break. I shouldn't have." He wiped his brow. "But it was so early . . . I didn't think it would matter."

"'You didn't think' is the correct answer." Kit wrote on her notepad. "From now on, Mr. Rutgers, I suggest you think carefully."

Should she consider Joe a suspect? Kit thought he was probably too lazy to kill someone. Still, his tacit acknowledgment that he'd been derelict in his duty would keep him on her list for now.

The town of Chincoteague had its own police department, then there was the Accomack County sheriff's office, and above that the state police in Melfa. Eventually, Kit would need to bring them all in; she'd begin, though, with Chincoteague Police Chief Jerry Daisey, another native islander.

The Chief was in his forties, a bit paunchy with sparse gray hair. Behind his walnut desk, a matching credenza held pictures which Kit presumed to be of his family—a slim, brunette wife, two kids, a boy and a girl, and a dog, a black Labrador retriever. On the wall hung some awards, including a diploma from the National Academy program at the FBI Academy.

"I appreciate your support, Chief," Kit began.

"Anything I can do. That's a shame, isn't it? Little boy like that. And right in the summer tourist season. TV reporters are gonna have a heck of a time finding motel rooms."

"I'd just as soon leave them out of it for now."

He laughed. "The kids have put it on YouTube already and Brenda Ramsfeld's been giving interviews since noon."

Kit's mouth drew into a thin line. She took a deep breath. "Chief, you know this community better than anybody. What do you think we're looking at here?"

The Chief shook his head. "From where that boy washed up, I don't think it has anything to do with this island or Assateague." He stretched back in his chair and looked outside the window for a moment. "My secretary says you know Chincoteague pretty well, been coming here since you were a kid."

"I haven't gotten back here for a few years and a lot of things can change in that time." As she said those words, images of the recent events that had so disrupted her life appeared in her mind. Yes, life can change in a heartbeat. She caught herself touching the finger where her wedding band used to be.

"You got that right," the Chief said, snorting. "Back in my granddaddy's day, people might get drunk, might get into a fight or something, maybe get caught with somebody else's wife down at the one true bar we had at that time. But nowadays, we see a lot more. Drugs, underage drinking, even caught a stripper some tourists brought in for a party a couple of years ago. We threw the book at them. Chincoteague's a nice place, a good place to bring a family, and we want to keep it that way."

"So you don't think we could connect the boy to Chincoteague."

"I doubt we could. There's a pretty big ocean out there, and a lot can go on." Chief Daisey cocked his head. "Why does the FBI care about one kid, anyway? Business that slow?"

No, business wasn't that slow, she thought as she walked out to her car. Between counter-terrorism, bank robberies, white-collar crime, serial killings, and public corruption, the FBI had plenty to keep it occupied. By all rights, she should be letting another federal agency handle this case. But she wasn't ready to let go of it yet. And even she did not know why.

Kit passed two TV satellite transmission trucks on the road as she drove toward the Coast Guard station. No doubt they were on the island to catch some on-the-scene footage for the evening news. The more the news media got involved, the worse it would be for her. God forbid the bigwigs at FBI Headquarters in Washington should catch a news report and decide to get involved.

She inched through Chincoteague's "downtown"—some shops and a hardware store, and the old Island Theater, which was, as usual, playing *Misty of Chincoteague* in special matinees. The book by the same name, written by Marguerite Henry, had made the island and its ponies famous. Generations of visitors had fallen in love with the place.

Kit figured Coast Guard Chief Petty Officer Rick Sellers was about her age. Blond-haired, blue-eyed, and pale as a ghost in the middle of summer, he apparently had the kind of fair skin that never tanned. Kit wondered how he managed in a job that kept him largely outdoors.

"Tell me more about this kid you found," Rick said, inviting Kit to sit down. "You found no identification?"

"None that we saw in the preliminary exam."

"You figure he drowned?"

"We'll know more from the autopsy."

"A Latino boy, about seven or eight."

"That's right."

Rick pursed his lips and frowned. "Don't know any kid that's been missing." He shook his head. "What can I do for you?"

"You can tell me about the crimes you deal with."

Rick laughed. He leaned back in his chair and propped the sole of his shoe against the edge of his desk. "Not much. Nothing happens here!"

"How long have you been stationed on Chincoteague?"

"Three years."

"No drownings?"

"Not in the waters we patrol."

"Drugs?"

He dismissed that idea with a wave. "We get a sailboat run aground about once a year, and a fishing boat runs out of gas now and then. Otherwise, the job's mostly moving the channel markers and waiting for the big storms to come up the coast."

Kit studied his face. It was narrow, like a fox's, and his blue eyes were quick. His laid-back persona seemed carefully constructed and maintained. Automatically, she glanced at his hand. No wedding band. "You like it quiet, I guess?"

"I got divorced a couple of years ago. That's all the conflict I'm going to need for a while."

Kit blew out a breath softly. "I hear that." She wrote in the small notepad she'd brought with her. "So, you all have no maritime interdiction efforts going on? Nothing targeting drugs or illegals?"

Rick snorted. "Around here? Look, there are people here who use, but we're not a major link on a transport line or anything like that. It's not that easy to negotiate the channel, for one thing. Lots of shoals where it meets the ocean."

Kit bit the inside of her cheek. "I haven't been out there."

"You've never seen Assateague from the water?"

"I've been over to Tom's Cove, but not out on the ocean."

"Then let's go!" He stood up.

"Now?"

"It'll take an hour and a half," he said.

Kit checked her watch. Just 5 p.m. Dinner could wait.

Rick pulled the Coast Guard boat out of the slip and into the Chincoteague Channel. The afternoon wind was dying down and the outgoing tide left the channel glassy and smooth. Kit looked across the broad reaches of water and marshland stretching toward the mainland. She saw egrets plucking minnows out of the shallows and a brown pelican do a dramatic dive after a fish. A couple of fishing boats dotted the horizon. On one of them, a woman held a bright pink umbrella as a shade from the sun. Kit inhaled deeply, savoring the comforting fragrance of the salt air and the marshes.

"The water looks so calm, but it's deceptive," Rick shouted over the roar of the Boston Whaler's engine. "Underneath, the currents are treacherous." He waved to a charter fishing boat coming back into port.

"You like being stationed here?" Kit asked.

He nodded. "It's all right."

They slid past a large marina and reached the southern end of the island, where Kit used to fish for flounder and sea bass. Rick pointed to the channel markers guiding them in an S-curve through the broad expanse between Chincoteague and Assateague. "These shoals are where people get in trouble."

"You can't just go straight?"

"Nope. You've got to stay in the channel or you'll run aground."

They zigzagged through the shallow areas. As they rounded the southern tip of Assateague, the onshore breeze picked up. Kit saw the Atlantic Ocean stretched out before them, an endless sheet of wave-tipped blue-green sea. The Coast Guard boat took the waves well, riding some, breaking through others, the salt spray rising in protest, then subsiding.

They turned north, with Assateague on their left and the vast ocean on their right. Kit's thoughts centered on the little boy. What in the world was he doing out on the water? "You get Latinos out here fishing?"

"I don't see many."

"Pleasure boaters?"

"Very few Latinos." He took a deep breath. "How long have you been an agent?"

"Five years."

"In Norfolk that whole time?"

"No, I just transferred there."

Rick looked over at her. "How'd you get involved in this case?"

"I couldn't walk away."

Motoring about a quarter mile offshore at about fifteen knots, Kit could see through binoculars that most of the beachgoers had dropped their umbrellas and gone home. On the ocean side, a few charter fishing boats were headed back to Chincoteague. Could one of them have seen the boat carrying the little boy? "Those boats ever go out at night?" she asked.

Rick shook his head. "Early in the morning, but rarely at night."

"The big commercial vessels stay farther out, right?"

"Yes. They don't want to mess with this area. They keep out in the Atlantic until they can cut in to Wilmington and Philly. Or they go on to New York and New Jersey. Or they've cut into the Chesapeake Bay, to the south, before they even get this far."

Kit looked down at the controls of the Boston Whaler. "Where would a boat like this fuel up?"

"Norfolk, Wachapreague, Chincoteague, Ocean City. That's basically it along the Delmarva Peninsula."

"You think marinas would notice a group of Latinos getting fuel?"

Rick smiled. "Oh, yeah." He cut the engine back as they approached the area offshore from where Kit found the boy's body. "How long do you figure the kid drifted in the water?"

"Initially, the ME guessed no more than thirty-six hours. The autopsy will be more accurate." She put her hand to her brow, shielding her eyes from the sun, which had begun its descent to the horizon. From the ocean, Assateague looked like the sandy spit it was, a white strip stretching from north to south, untamed, and unspoiled.

"And he was strangled, right?"

She raised an eyebrow. "You got that from the news?"

Rick laughed. "Heard it in town."

Kit let it pass. "The waves are breaking from the northeast. Is that the usual pattern?"

"In the summer. In winter or when a storm comes up, that can change."

"So the current would run south along the beach, right?"

"Yes, it would slip south. You've felt it when you're in the water, I'm sure."

Kit looked up toward the northeast. "So if he fell off a boat, we're talking up there somewhere," she gestured toward the vast ocean.

"Yep." Rick squinted. "That's quite a crime scene."

⚓

David O'Connor sat on the front porch of Kit's grand-mother's former home, in an old white wicker rocker, watching the sun slide toward the horizon. Tomorrow he would begin painting the house. He planned to go to bed early and get up early to avoid working in the heat. He had his shirt off, and was massaging some cream into the scar on his shoulder, stuff that supposedly softened the collagen fibers and improved mobility. It was hard, though, to reach the bigger scar on his back, and frankly he wondered if the cream wasn't just another one of his sister's snake oil compounds.

He capped the jar and pulled his shirt back on, then decided to walk across the street and over to the dock to watch the rest of the sunset. As he walked down the steps and the screen door slammed behind him, he automatically thought of his gun. Half the reason he'd come to Chincoteague was to get away from that, but old habits die hard, and he had to set his jaw to keep from turning around to retrieve it.

Walking through the motel parking lot he could hear kids playing in the swimming pool out front, and his mind turned again to the little dead boy on the beach. It's not your case, he told himself, but he couldn't help wondering how the boy got there, and where his parents were. Was he dead when he hit the water or did someone choke him then throw him overboard, still alive?

Shaking his head to dislodge those thoughts, he looked through the motel office window. He saw the front desk clerk, a young woman named Maria, waved to her, and continued walking through the parking lot and out onto the blue-gray weathered dock. A few small boats bobbed in slips near the shore and a couple of youngsters, two boys wearing Washington Nationals baseball caps, stood on the dock. One of them had a small line in his hand, the other a net. They peered excitedly over the edge and David knew they had a crab nibbling their bait.

The sun sat just above the horizon, a blood orange disk lending its dying light to the shimmering atmosphere. The marshes to the west, deep in shadow, looked purple now. David could still smell them. He was a long way from D.C.

When he stood at the end of the dock, he felt like he was in the middle of the water, surrounded and enveloped by the colors of the sunset and the deepening twilight. The waves beneath him lapped gently against the pier and birds swooped all around, looking for one last morsel of fish, their wings making soft whooshing noises in the air. As David breathed slowly, evenly, his soul reached out for the beauty before him.

The sunsets were why he'd taken the house on South Main Street, and in just the few days he'd been there, he'd not been disappointed. Every night seemed different; tonight, a symphony of deep red yielding to pinks and purples played out before him on the horizon and echoed on the water, first on the channel, then in the runs and sloughs beyond the marshes across the way. He saw waterfowl lift off from a marsh, and a large white bird land on a channel marker, and he heard fish plop as they jumped up to catch the insects that hovered over the water. He looked down at the dark, swiftly moving water, and for a second he imagined taking one step forward, and slipping into its embrace.

Muttering an oath he diverted his eyes. He could hear a boat coming up the channel. He stood still and watched it make its way north, its running lights defining its outline. It was a good-sized powerboat, something like a Grady-White or a Boston Whaler, with a small canopy. It cut through the water efficiently, undeterred by the strong currents. David watched as it pulled into the Coast Guard station just a few hundred yards away.

Then it was quiet again, except for the call of a night bird.

As darkness fell, he heard footsteps on the pier, and thought it was one of the crabbers, but when he turned and looked, the footsteps belonged to Maria, from the motel office. "*¡Buenos noches, señorita!*" he said. He found himself anticipating her smile. She wore a sundress with a white background and big splashes of bright flowers. Her thick, dark hair framed her face and fell to her shoulders.

"So how are you tonight, Señor David?" she asked in her thickly accented voice.

He responded in Spanish, telling her he felt tired from surfing and running errands and that he was going to go back to the house, read for a while, and go to sleep. She loved the fact he would speak to her in her language, and he was happy to please her. It seemed such a small thing.

"*¿Dónde comió usted esta noche?*" she asked. Where did you eat tonight?

He told her he hadn't eaten, and she frowned at him, pursing her lips, and began making restaurant suggestions. Finally he raised his hand, laughing, and told her he would just probably make a sandwich and then go to bed.

They chatted some more about her job, the beach, and her plans for the weekend. Off in the distance, toward the motel pool, he heard voices again, children's voices, and he looked at Maria, and casually asked her if she'd seen the story on the news about the little boy found washed up on the beach.

She said she hadn't, but David knew a television blared nonstop in the motel office, and certainly that story would get her attention. He didn't know where she was from, just that she was a Latina, and a college student working at the motel for the summer. "Some mama is missing her *niño*, yes?" he said to her, trying to stimulate her interest. "Wonder why they were out on the ocean?"

Her eyes flickered. "Probably fishing, like everyone else," she said in English, and David knew at that moment that there was more to it than she felt willing to share.

That night, he lay in bed for hours, staring at the ceiling, thinking about the boy, about Maria, and this FBI agent, Kit, and wondering how a world that could be so beautiful could also be so cruel.

3

THE MEDICAL EXAMINER HAD SCHEDULED THE AUTOPSY OF THE LITTLE BOY for 9:00 a.m. at the morgue in Norfolk. Kit planned to be there.

The cottage she'd rented from Connie Jester sat perched on the east side of Chincoteague Island, overlooking the Assateague Channel. From her deck, she had a view of the great, red-and-white-striped lighthouse and the bridge linking the two islands, and she could launch her kayak right from her yard. With the windows open, she could hear the shriek of herons and the plopping of fish in the water.

As dawn lifted its light over the horizon, Kit stood on her deck and ate a carton of yogurt. She inhaled the smell of the salt marsh. The cattle egrets and marsh hens stalked the shallows, catching minnows and alewives, the mainstays of their diets. She saw an osprey leave its nest in a strong, arching flight, and counted four different kinds of gulls flapping about the marshes.

She hadn't slept well the night before. Images of the beach child, and questions about him, plagued her. Who was he? Where had he come from? Where was his mother? And then, more broadly, did God really count the sparrows? Where was he when someone was strangling the Latino boy? Watching?

Kit had watched other autopsies but they had been performed on criminals, a young man shot robbing a store, and a drug dealer who'd overdosed. This would be the autopsy of a child, and his age and the circumstances of his death set her feelings on edge. She masked up, fully aware that doing so would in no way block the smells to which she would be exposed. When a morgue worker offered her a dab of Vicks VapoRub to dot beneath her nose, she took it. Then, notebook and pen in hand, she tightened her resolve and entered the room.

"Feel free to sit down if you want to. I'll narrate," the medical examiner said, looking up as she entered. Dr. Scott McGregor had already joked with Kit about their common Celtic roots, which only made her think about David O'Connor. She wondered again how he had been shot, and why he was on Chincoteague for six whole months.

Dr. McGregor had two people helping him, his regular assistant and one student. True to his word, he narrated as he cut, listing everything from the sand in the little boy's ears to the weight of his liver, from the contents of his stomach to the size of his skull.

Kit wrote it all down, although she knew she'd get it in official form eventually. She asked a pertinent question or two along the way, and requested clarification when the doctor said something she didn't understand. When they finished, she sat down with the doctor in his office. He lit up a cigar. "I know I'm not supposed to smoke in these government buildings," he said, "but sometimes nothing but a stogie will do."

She smiled her acquiescence and looked down at her notes. "Dr. McGregor, how long do you think the victim had been dead?"

He took a long draw on his cigar, and let the smoke drift from his mouth. "What's the ocean temperature off Assateague right now? 70? 71?"

She hadn't checked that, but her failure in that regard didn't slow the doctor down.

"Being submerged in water makes a big difference. Salt water, too. The rule of thumb is one day on the ground equals one week in the water equals one month underground. I found very little evidence of decomposition and only a little of predation or infestation, so my preliminary estimate is that death occurred within twenty hours of the time you found the body on the beach. Furthermore, the body had been on the beach less than half an hour before you got there."

"I think it had just washed up."

Dr. McGregor nodded, and went on talking about flies, crabs, and other agents of decomposition, and Kit found her mind taking it in like medicine, as necessary but not pleasant. She wondered how he could continue to live a normal life, with normal relationships, without seeing everyone as a future decaying corpse. "The cause of death will be ligature strangulation," he said.

Kit snapped back to attention. "So he was dead when he hit the water?"

"Right. No water in his lungs. Someone wrapped something—a cord or a rope—around his neck, killed him, and dumped him overboard."

"What about those marks on his wrists and his arms?"

"His right wrist looks like someone grabbed him like this," he demonstrated with his own hands, "like adults do sometimes. His fingernails are broken, which could indicate he defended himself, but could also just mean he's an active boy or that he's involved in manual labor."

"Like ag work?" Kit asked. "Could he be a farm worker?"

"At age eight? He's not supposed to be."

Kit tapped her pen against her leg, caught up now in possible scenarios.

"I'm ruling it a homicide," the ME said.

Kit's mind whirled. "How far would a body travel in the ocean in twenty hours?" she asked, trying to pinpoint where the boy might have fallen off of a boat.

"I'd suggest you ask an oceanographer about currents. Try the Virginia Institute for Marine Sciences over in Gloucester." He pronounced it "Glosster."

"I'll do that."

"Oh, Agent McGovern, one more thing."

Kit refocused on him.

"My assistant found some interesting things in the boy's clothing. You know how he had his sleeves rolled up?"

Kit nodded.

"There were some tomato seeds caught up in them. It's not very likely they would have been deposited there in the ocean. And you heard me when I said I'd found lots of tomato seeds in his gut, like tomatoes were a major source of food. Also, the kid had acorns in his pocket. Six of them. I'm thinking you might do well to have a forensic botanist take a look at those things. We'll bag them for you."

A forensic botanist. Kit pondered that idea. As she walked out of the ME's office, exhaustion swept over her, and she realized her entire body had been tense for hours. She pulled out her cell phone. The Assistant U.S. Attorney, Mark Handley, had told her to call him with the autopsy results.

"Look," she explained, sensing his resistance after she gave him the basics, "this isn't just a little boy. We found his body on a federal reservation. He was murdered. Why was a Latino boy out on the ocean? Why did someone kill him?" She took a deep breath. "I think we may be looking at something bigger than just one murder. Maybe it's trafficking in drugs. Maybe the kid knew something he shouldn't know. Maybe it's illegals, coming in by boat."

She waited during a long pause. Kit's heart drummed. Then the AUSA indicated he would conditionally accept the case. She could proceed. Kit hung up her cell phone. Overhead, a crow in a pine tree cackled.

⚬══✦══⚬

Where had the boy been dumped into the ocean? The ME had suggested the Virginia Institute of Marine Sciences might help. And the only problem with consulting with VIMS was the institution's connection with the College of William & Mary. And the only problem with William & Mary was its association with one Eric Allen Sandford, J.D. PhD, assistant professor of ethics at the school's Marshall-Wythe School of Law.

Eric was Kit McGovern's ex-husband.

They had met at the University of Virginia one spring morning when the gardens near the Lawn were in full bloom and all the world seemed to be in love. They were both pre-law, and like most UVA students, they loved Charlottesville, deep discussions, and Greenberry's coffee. Justice was their mutual passion, but their paths had taken different turns after graduation. Kit went on to get a master's in forensic psychology while Eric went to law school at George Washington University. When she accepted a job as a police officer trainee in the Fairfax Criminal Justice Academy, they had a salary they could live on and so they married.

Seven years of hard work followed. He didn't understand her decision to enter law enforcement rather than the law. Still, her choice of career certainly paid the bills and so he didn't complain. Then she applied to and was accepted by the FBI, went through the Academy, and was assigned to the Washington Field Office. He continued his education, first attaining a J.D., then going on for more graduate work in philosophy. It seemed to Kit he enjoyed studying the law more than practicing it, but she recognized his years as a student couldn't go on forever: his PhD in legal ethics was within reach.

By the time he finished his dissertation and attained that coveted degree, they had been married seven years. She was six months away from being thirty years old and well aware of her biological clock. She looked forward to having children, maybe even adopting as well, giving a child from Latin America a home.

If she'd sensed a growing distance in their relationship, she'd chosen to ignore it. Degrees in hand, he obtained a teaching position at William & Mary, the culmination of a long-held dream. And that's when he told Kit he really didn't want to be married anymore.

The shock of his announcement, and the trauma of the next year, left Kit reeling. Her entire world felt like it was tilting, like the *Titanic* about to slip into the sea. She tried to get her husband to go to counseling, tried engaging the help of their minister, even tried petitioning his family to help. And what about their faith? Christianity was part of the glue of their marriage . . . had he forgotten the tenets of their faith? Their vows? But Eric had made up his mind, and no one could talk him out of the split.

Her divorce was Crisis No. 1, and two years later, she still grieved the loss of their marriage and her hopes for a family. Someday, her minister told her, God would make everything right. That seemed little comfort to Kit.

She dealt with her feelings of rejection in her usual way: she sucked up her gut, put away her desire for children, and poured herself into her calling as an agent of justice in this life. She felt privileged to be with the FBI, but her passion, coupled with a complete disregard for political correctness, had precipitated Crisis No. 2, in which she'd taken an unpopular stand on a high-profile criminal case, pursuing a suspect her boss thought irrelevant. She was sidelined, forbidden to follow her instincts, and she had no choice but to back off. Then a reporter began asking questions along those same lines. Her boss accused her of leaking information, which she hadn't. Still, it was clear she had lost her boss's trust. When she found out Norfolk needed a scuba-certified agent, she had applied for the job and been accepted. Now, here she was, pursuing justice in Crisis No. 3, justice for a little boy delivered into her path by the pounding surf of the Atlantic.

And where was God during all this? She had no idea. She'd almost stopped asking.

⚜

Dr. Harry Light, an oceanographer at VIMS, had spent his career studying currents in the mid-Atlantic. He stroked his beard. "No one's ever asked me before how far a 54-pound body might be carried in typical August sea conditions off of Assateague Island," he said to Kit.

He walked over to the overstuffed bookshelves in his office, and began thumbing through a thick volume. "Let's see," he murmured. "We could create a 54-pound dummy, equip it with a transmitter, drop it overboard . . ."

"But sir," Kit said, "that wouldn't simulate a real human body, would it? I mean, a corpse begins emitting gases even in the early stages of decomposition, and wouldn't that make it rise and fall in the water?"

"Yes, yes . . . and then the currents at various levels . . . oh, posh," Dr. Light said, slamming his book shut. "I'm not sure we could get a good match."

"I'd be happy with a rough estimate."

The professor look relieved, calculated the average velocity of the currents in the summer in that area, scratched a number down on a piece of paper. "Try this," he said.

Kit started to leave.

"You've checked with the Coast Guard, right?"

"Yes, sir."

"So then you know about IOOS."

Kit stopped in her tracks. She turned around.

"The Integrated Ocean Observing System. Coast Guard uses it, along with NOAA. It tracks ocean currents by high-frequency radar. Invaluable for search and rescue, oil spills . . . gives quite a bit of data. Real interesting if you're into that sort of thing."

"Is it operational in the Mid-Atlantic?"

"Sure! MARACOOS, the Mid-Atlantic Regional Association Coastal Ocean Observing System, collects data for the whole area, from Cape Cod to Cape Hatteras."

"So like, if something is in the water, they could predict its drift?"

"That's right."

"Do they keep historical data?"

"Oh, yes. What I gave you there," he nodded toward the paper, "is an average of currents in the area. But they'll give you specifics for the date in question. You said you talked to the Coast Guard. Didn't they tell you?"

❦

Why hadn't Rick mentioned IOOS? Surely he knew about it! Kit jabbed her key into her car ignition.

Fuming, she called the administrative assistant for her squad, and got her to track down the Coast Guard's Mid-Atlantic Search and Rescue Unit which, it turns out, was in Norfolk. Kit went to that office, and within thirty minutes, had the probable range of latitudes and longitudes from which the child had been dropped, based on the ME's estimate of the time of his death, and the speed of the currents in the area within that time frame.

Of course, that area now was empty ocean.

And Rick? She'd confront him later. Why hadn't he told her about IOOS?

As Kit drove over the causeway leading to Chincoteague, she tried to spot her grandmother's house, a game she'd played since childhood. The buildings on the island's Main Street were stretched out like pearls on a necklace in the distance, far across the channel. Kit had found if she could find the large, barn-red house and count two to the left, that would be her grandmother's.

When she finally nabbed it, she saw the sun glinting off some object next to the house. Curious, when she got to the island, she turned down Main Street. What she saw when she got to the house made her jerk to the side of the street and jump out of her car.

"What are you doing?" she said, approaching the ladder leaned up against the siding.

David O'Connor had his iPod going and didn't even look down. Kit tapped on the ladder, then shook it. That got his attention. "Hey!" he said, climbing down, paintbrush in hand. He pulled his earbuds out.

"What are you doing?" she demanded. Her face felt hot.

He looked at the house, then back to her. "Painting?"

"Blue? Blue? You can't do that!"

He smiled like an amused parent. "OK," he said. "But you tell the owner."

"It's always been white!"

"I think you'll like it. It's almost the color of your eyes."

Kit flipped open her cell phone, turned her back on David, and called Connie.

"That's what the owner wanted," she told Kit. "Look, honey, David's doing a lot of work on the house in exchange for reduced rent. He's going to save that house, Kit."

Kit snapped her phone shut, her jaw still tight.

"Everything OK?" David said.

She raised her chin. She couldn't meet his eyes. "It's been a long day."

He glanced at his watch. "You want to go to dinner? I'm starving."

"No, thanks."

He shifted his jaw. "I'd like to talk to you . . . about your case."

"I don't discuss investigations."

"I've got some information I'd like to pass on to you."

"You can tell me here."

"I'd like to take you to dinner."

"I can't let you do that."

"You almost throw me to my death and now you won't eat with me?" His eyes were brown, and right now they were sparkling with humor. The declining sun played off the golden highlights in his hair and illuminated the light stubble of his beard. His mouth bowed upward in a slight smile.

Kit took a deep breath.

He took her hesitation as a cue. "How about Rita's in forty-five minutes?"

Rita's Restaurant on the east side of the island had one table overlooking the Assateague Channel left when they got there. "Lucky us," Kit said, but David just smiled and the look in his eyes told her he'd called ahead. How annoying!

He also knew the waitress, and when Kit said she'd have the flounder stuffed with crab meat he ordered the same thing. "That's good," he said. "I've had it before."

A pool of reserve kept Kit quiet. How should she take this man? She found him attractive and off-putting at the same time. His confidence disarmed her, but she couldn't figure him out. She sensed an undercurrent about him that she couldn't quite identify. Her ability to read character was pretty good; but then, if he was a cop, his was as well. What was he thinking about her?

"OK, so you seem to know these birds around here. What's that?" he asked, nodding toward the bright white bird that had just landed nearby.

"Cattle egret," she said.

"And those?" He pointed off to the right.

"Terns. And a fishing gull."

"And those little guys?"

"Swallows. They're actually eating mosquitoes as they fly. So we like them."

"How do you know all this?" he asked, smiling.

"I've been coming here a long time."

"Couldn't have been that long. How old are you?"

"I'm thirty-two. But I've been coming here for twenty-five years."

David whistled softly. "Twenty-five years is a pretty long time. I take back what I said." He smiled softly. "So what's Kit short for?"

"Katherine. Katherine Anne."

He nodded. "That's a good name."

Kit toyed with her fork. Her father's pet name for her growing up was Kitty.

"How long were you married?"

Her eyes opened wide in surprise.

"You keep touching your ring finger," David said, demonstrating. "I'm guessing your wedding band hasn't been gone for long."

Kit felt the heat of embarrassment in her face. "What do you do for the Metropolitan Police?"

"I'm a detective," he said.

"Homicide?"

He shifted his jaw. "Yes."

"So you could tell the boy had been killed?"

"I saw the ligature marks on his neck." He stretched back in his chair.

"How'd you know I'm in law enforcement?"

"How many women carry a gun bag on the beach?"

"It looks like a regular fanny pack!" she said defensively.

"Not if you know what a gun bag looks like."

Kit toyed with her silverware and debated her next move. "So how is it you can take six months off?"

David smiled softly. "I wanted to quit. My boss wouldn't let me. He pretty much made me take a break instead."

"Something happened?"

He shrugged. "You know how it goes." He shifted in his chair. "How long have you been an agent?"

"Five years. So what happened? Shooting incident?"

He ignored her question. "You like it? Being an agent?"

"I have a passion for justice."

"That's a good thing."

"Sometimes it gets me in trouble."

"I thought the FBI was all about justice. How could that get you in trouble?"

The lamp in the middle of the table flickered, forming shadows on the white tablecloth. "Politics," she said. "I pursued a lead in a case that wasn't politically correct."

The food came, interrupting their conversation and dissipating the tension. Kit felt like she'd just been in a tennis match. Serve—volley—volley—slam! Talking with David was an aerobic activity. She focused on her food. The flounder was tender and sweet, the crab perfectly cooked, and both of them ate in silence for a few minutes. Kit stole a look at him. She liked the way his eyes crinkled when he laughed, and she liked his bone structure. He had a strong jaw and a wide, open face. His neck was thick and his forearms were ropey with muscle. Their short conversation proved he was smart and aggressive, not bad qualities, normally, but she felt like she had to be on her game with him. She barely knew him. No way was she was ready to share the details of her life with him.

"This is really good," he said, lifting a forkful of flounder.

"So what were you going to tell me?" she asked.

David cocked his head.

"You lured me here saying you had information about my case."

"Did I?" He laughed. "All right then." He took a bite of salad, glanced out of the window, nodded and said, "Giant white bird, right?"

Kit turned her head to look at the creature outside. "Great egret. The only three-foot-tall, long-legged white bird on the East Coast."

He grinned. "I was close, very close." Then he told her about his conversation with Maria.

"You speak Spanish?" Kit asked him. She had learned a little in college, more when she and Eric were talking about adopting a child from Latin America, but she wasn't fluent.

David nodded. "She didn't open up. Maybe somebody's running drugs, maybe illegals, maybe it's something else. But here's the other piece of the puzzle. I talked to an old guy down at Smitty's. You know where that is?"

Kit nodded. Smitty ran a rundown bait shop down toward Cap'n Bob's, near the southern end of the island.

"I wanted to see about doing some fishing. This old guy was out on the ocean two weeks ago, around 11:00 p.m. He saw a boat loaded with people running up the coastline with its lights off. He said people were just hanging off the gunnels."

"The what?"

"The sides of the boat," David explained.

"What was he doing out on the ocean?"

"Jimmy? He said he was fishing."

"You think he saw a boatload of illegals?"

"Maybe." David gestured. "All I know is, you don't run up the coast in a boat loaded with people at night with your lights off unless you're doing something wrong. He saw the same thing last week, same place, same time. Then I remembered reading in the paper that there's been a drug interdiction operation on Rt. 13 lately. I'm wondering, is somebody trying to avoid that by going out on the ocean? So I'm going out there to see what I can see."

"What?" Kit said. "When?"

"Tonight. Jimmy rented me his boat and I'm going out."

"By yourself? That's crazy."

"The weather's good. We've got a three-quarter moon, which is enough to see by. And I do a lot of things by myself."

Kit's heart pounded. "I'm going with you."

"There might not be anything out there."

"I don't care. I want to go. Can you find a latitude and longitude if I give it to you?"

They agreed to meet at David's at 10:00 p.m. Kit went to her cottage and changed into work clothes, khaki cargo pants, and a dark-colored golf shirt, but she substituted boat shoes without socks for the boots she usually wore. She grabbed a light jacket, strapped on her gun, and tied her hair back in a loose ponytail at the nape of her neck. Then she drove to South Main Street, and pulled into the driveway of David's rental, her grandmother's old house.

⌖

The channel seemed quiet as they steered away from town in the twenty-two-foot Grady-White David had rented. It was a good boat, sturdy enough for the ocean, and Kit could tell by the way he handled getting out of the slip that he knew boats.

"Four years in the Navy," he told her when she said something about it. He also insisted she put on a life jacket. "I always wear one, especially at night," he said. "It's only smart."

Stars lay scattered across the clear night sky in a thousand points of light. The Grady-White easily handled the chop on the channel, and its engine sounded strong as they cut through the waves. Kit realized she was shivering with excitement. "You can't go straight down here," she said. "There are shoals. You have to follow the channel markers."

"Can you navigate?" David handed her the chart and a small flashlight.

"I've only been through here once." When she clicked it on, the light was red. That was better for night vision—if you used a white light, it would take you 15 minutes to readjust so you could see in the dark. Kit knew that, and the fact that he apparently did, too, added to her confidence.

Using the chart, Kit guided him through the channel markers through the shoal-laced water on the south side of

Assateague. As David cleared the confused seas at the confluence of Chincoteague Channel and the ocean, he swung the boat left. Kit sat next to him, bracing herself with one hand on the frame of the boat.

"Did they do the autopsy?" David asked, once their course was steady. "I didn't want to ask you in the restaurant."

"Yes," she said, shouting against the wind and the roar of the motor.

"What did they find?"

"Ligature strangling, like you said."

"How long before we found him?"

We? "He died within twenty hours." Off to her left a quarter of a mile or so, Kit could see the white sand of Assateague, and the white line of the breakers just offshore. Miles off to the right, she could see a brightly lighted ship. "What's that?" she asked, pointing to it.

"Cruise ship." He glanced at her. "It's for people who actually know how to take a vacation," he shouted, grinning.

She smiled, and the wind felt cold against her teeth. The blackness of the ocean spread out before her like ink spilled across a page. Only the strip of white sand of Assateague oriented her. The three-quarters moon shed just a little light, and she felt hidden and exposed all at the same time. She looked up at the stars, wondered what it would have been like for the old sailors, steering only by the heavens, drawn into the unknown by the wind and the sea currents.

David cut the engine back. He pointed toward Assateague. "We're about even with where the body washed up."

"How do you know?"

"I carry a GPS with me when I'm surfing. I marked it as a waypoint."

"So we're opposite that spot now?"

David swung the boat to starboard, and pushed the throttle forward. "Yes. Give me your lat and lon."

She yelled out the numbers of the spot the Coast Guard Search and Rescue had estimated as the approximate location that the boy's body entered the water. As Assateague fell further behind them, Kit glanced over her shoulder, as if keeping the barrier island in view would somehow make her less vulnerable. Ahead, she saw nothing but the vast sea and a star-studded sky, and she couldn't help but think of God, how big he was, and how small she felt.

After a while, David cut the engine back, left the helm, and picked up a fishing pole he had lying in the back. "We're here. Want to fish?" he asked her.

Kit hesitated. "Why are we doing this?"

David grinned. "Killing time, so we can see what we can see." He grabbed a minnow from the bucket he'd brought, impaled it on the hook, and dropped the line overboard. Then he handed the rod to Kit. "Hang on. If you feel a tug, jerk it hard to set the hook, then reel it in."

She rolled her eyes. "Yeah, I've done this before. What are we fishing for?"

"Whales." David laughed. He grabbed a pole for himself, repeated the process, and stood balancing in the boat, moving his rod, winding in line, and waiting. The vast darkness invited conversation. Soon they were trading law enforcement stories. Then he explained about the fish teeming below them in the deep ocean, and she pointed out constellations and star clusters.

They idled for a half an hour, fishing and talking and not catching anything, and as midnight rolled around she began to wonder if they should give it up. Then she saw David look once, then a second time, to his right. His expression changed, and he began winding in his line. "What's up?" she asked him as he laid his rod down in the boat.

"I thought I saw something."

Kit brought in her line and secured her rod. David turned the boat so they were headed straight into the waves. Some broke over the bow, sending spray back toward the helm. Kit shivered at the shock of the cold water.

"Yes, there," David said suddenly, pointing.

Kit could see it now, outlined against the horizon, a dark, fast-moving boat, running without lights. Their paths would cross if they both stayed their courses. David dropped the throttle back so they were barely making headway. "What can you see?" she asked.

The boat screamed northward, maybe one hundred yards away from them. David and Kit heard voices carried on the wind. Shouting. "What'd they say?" she asked.

"I can't make it out."

Suddenly, the boat's motor changed pitch, and the bow turned in their direction. David uttered a sharp expletive. "Get down, get down!" he said. He grabbed Kit and pushed her low in the boat and swung the vessel around. He jammed the throttle full forward and Kit lost her balance. She peered over the transom, saw muzzle flash and then heard the shot. "Stay down!" David commanded, as another shot sounded.

Kit's heart hammered in her chest. She unzipped her fanny pack and drew out her Glock. The engine of the Grady-White roared in her ears. She could see David crouching as low as he could get over the wheel. She peeked over the stern again and saw the boat pursuing them, then more muzzle flashes.

She couldn't line up a shot, not in that pitching boat, and not at that range. "Stay down and hang on!" David yelled.

"I'm not a kid!" she wanted to say, but realistically she could do nothing to help. She felt David change the boat's course, swinging it back and forth in irregular arcs, trying to be as difficult a target as possible. Then they hit a wave awkwardly and the Grady-White shuddered and faltered, wrestling with the sea. A wave broke over them, drenching them, and a sudden fear gripped Kit. Would they, too, end up as bodies on the beach?

4

KIT FELT THE BOAT'S HESITATION AS A LARGE WAVE KNOCKED IT SIDEWAYS. David adjusted its course and the boat began to make headway again. Four more shots rang out in a staccato burst, and Kit heard David cry out. She looked one more time at the pursuing boat, and then her heart jumped. "He's leaving! He's leaving!" she said.

David turned, saw the same thing, and straightened their course, heading directly for the Chincoteague Channel. Another large wave broke over their stern and doused them, one last parry from the sea. Kit glanced over her shoulder twice more. The pursuers were definitely giving up. She moved up into the seat next to David. "Are you all right?" she asked, but he didn't respond.

The lighted buoy marking the entrance to the channel appeared. As David swung north, cutting below the tip of Assateague, Kit got out the chart and flashlight and started guiding David through the marker buoys. Once they were well in the channel, David switched on their running lights again. That's when Kit saw the blood.

David stood over the sink in the Main Street house, his hand gripped in a tight fist, blood dripping from a cut on his arm.

The bullet—Kit presumed it was a bullet—had scored his arm and dug a little deeper into the flesh just behind his wrist.

"I think we should go to a hospital," she said.

"No."

"This is a gunshot wound."

"No, it's not."

"It has to be reported."

"No way."

Kit stared at his face, trying to read it. "David . . ."

"There must be some sharp metal on the boat. A burr or something. I just ran into it, that's all."

Yeah, right. Kit didn't buy it. "It could be cut to the bone."

He didn't respond.

"Does it hurt?"

"I just need to wash it."

But his hands were shaking and he seemed frozen, staring at the blood, so Kit took over. She found a minimal first-aid kit and a washcloth in the bathroom, soaped up the cloth, and gently washed the cut. Then she made David sit down on a kitchen chair, and she laid a bead of Neosporin along the entire wound. She used butterfly bandages on the deepest portion to bring the edges closer together, and then covered those with large adhesive bandages. While she worked, she was aware of the feel of his skin, the sound of his breathing, and the smell of Irish Spring soap. At one point he leaned forward to see what she was doing, and his cheek brushed her cheek, and she felt the faint bit of stubble on his face, and she remembered what it was like when she was married, to have that intimacy with a man.

When she finished, he said, "I am really sorry. I never should have taken you out there. I put you at risk."

Kit rolled her eyes. "I'm an FBI agent. I'm supposed to chase criminals. What do you think I do for the Bureau? Knit bulletproof vests?"

That drew the hint of smile.

"And anyway, this is my case, remember? You think I'm going to solve it sitting in an office?" She threw the paper trash away and began rinsing the washcloth out in the sink. David got up. He seemed to catch his balance on the kitchen chair; then he walked into the living room.

Kit plunged her hands under the faucet stream. It was the very sink in which she'd washed dishes when her grandmother lived there. It was so odd, being in this house—so familiar, but different. Same squeaks in the floor, same old hot water heater, same sink . . . but different paint and furniture and carpeting and curtains—and people.

When she finished, she dried her hands and walked into the living room. He sat on the blue couch, his arms resting on his knees, his eyes riveted to a spot on the floor.

"Are you all right?" she asked.

He startled. "Sure. Yeah." He sat up straight.

But Kit saw something in his eyes. Her heart twisted. "What's going on?"

"Nothing. I'm fine."

"You've just been shot for the second time, in how long?"

He looked at her sharply. "I wasn't shot!"

"Maybe not tonight. But I saw the scar on your shoulder. It looks fresh." She saw him take a deep breath. "How did it happen?"

He looked down.

"David?"

The air seemed heavy around them. Finally, the story began to trickle out. "My partner and I were coming back from our sixth homicide in five days in northeast D.C." David's voice sounded low, distant. "We hear the dispatcher put out the call for a pedestrian down, hit-and-run, white Chevy Tahoe. Suddenly, my partner, Russ, sees the Tahoe up ahead. I'm thinking, we should just call it in. But I'm frustrated and I want some action, so instead, I flip up the blue light and chase him. Russ is yelling 'Go! Go!' We follow the guy into an alley. We don't know the other end is blocked by a delivery truck. So now the suspect is trapped. He bails, and I can see he's young, maybe sixteen, if that. Just a punk kid. Russ and I jump out, yell at him to put his hands up, and the kid . . . the kid draws on us."

Kit stayed quiet but her heart pounded.

"Our guns are out, too. So we shout, 'Put the gun down! Put it down!' But he doesn't. I can still see him standing there, his hand shaking so hard. Then somebody fires and all hell breaks loose. The sound in that alley is incredible. His gun, our guns . . . I get tunnel vision: all I can see is the kid. Everything seems like slow motion . . . as though I can almost catch the bullets coming toward me. My gun is roaring in my ears. Then I feel a white heat rip through my shoulder and I realize I can't pull the trigger anymore. So, I switch to my right hand and fire again. It went on for what seemed like a long time. In reality, it's like seventeen seconds. And in the end, the kid is dead, and I am standing there with blood running off my arm."

Just like tonight, Kit thought. Her heart thumped. "And Russ?"

"He's fine."

"How long ago did this happen?"

"March." David sighed.

"Sounds like it wasn't your fault."

"I should have let the uniforms handle it. If I had, the kid would be alive. He was young, that's all, young and scared."

"He'd just committed a hit-and-run!"

"He was an A-student, headed for college. Some dudes had been bullying him; that's why he was carrying a gun. He'd never been in trouble before. Didn't have a record. He was scared and he overreacted. And we killed him," David snapped his fingers, "just like that."

Kit knew that typically after a police shooting the department takes the officer's gun, puts him on administrative leave, and tells him not to talk about the incident. Those actions convey a presumption of guilt, which, more often than not, imprints itself on the officer's conscience. Even a later finding that the shooting was justified sometimes can't erase those feelings. "Did you go through an inquiry board?"

"Sure."

"And?"

He shook his head. "We were cleared."

"How's Russ dealing with it?"

David shrugged. "He doesn't seem to have a problem with it."

"He's still on the force?"

"Yeah."

"When's the last time you spoke with him?"

"I tried calling him a week or so ago. Couldn't get him. Somebody told me he and his wife have been arguing. I think she may have kicked him out."

Kit bit her lip. Didn't David see the connection? "What have you done to try to let go of this? Counseling?" she asked.

"I did the mandatory counseling. It didn't help. So I figured I'd quit. My boss suggested I take a break. Somebody told me about Chincoteague. It seemed like a good idea." He rubbed his hand on his leg. "I don't know why this one bothered me so much. I mean, I've seen a lot of death."

"But you'd never shot anyone?"

"Not a kid." David's eyes seemed focused far off. "You don't treat kids like that."

Kit didn't sleep that night. She kept feeling the ocean tossing them, kept hearing the gunfire, kept seeing the blood dripping from David's arm, kept rolling David's words over and over in her mind. *You don't treat kids like that.* He sounded so . . . lost.

As the clock crawled past five, she sat up in bed. At one time, she would have had half a dozen verses to encourage a person in David's situation. Verses like, "I know the plans I have in mind for you, declares the LORD; they are plans for peace, not disaster, to give you a future filled with hope." And "Trust in the LORD with all your heart; don't rely on your own intelligence."

But somehow those verses were now caught in her throat, tangled in the tight web of her emotions surrounding her divorce. They seemed like platitudes, not promises—wishful thinking, not the word of God.

Moved by her uncomfortable thoughts, Kit slipped through the darkened house and stepped out on the deck. The fingers of dawn were spreading over the marsh, summoning the day. Shafts of pink and blue light emerged from the east. Across the Assateague Channel, the lighthouse still blinked its ancient warning: shoals ahead. A heron took off from the shallows just twenty-five feet from her, his huge wings beating a slow rhythm as he skimmed just above the water. Off in the distance, someone started an outboard motor.

Her thoughts skipped like a stone across the water. It had been easy to cast herself as the victim in the divorce, to place the blame on Eric. Just about everyone who knew them sympathized with her, everyone, that is, except his new friends in the world of academic law. But what had she contributed to the divorce? What was wrong with her?

Forgiveness eluded her. She hadn't let go. She couldn't let go. Eric had rejected her.

And so, apparently, had God. The God she thought she knew, anyway.

❦

At 8:00 a.m. sharp, Kit pulled into the parking lot at the Coast Guard Station, entered the building, and asked to speak to Rick Sellers.

"Why didn't you tell me about IOOS?" she said, piercing him with her eyes.

"IOOS? Oh, gosh, well ... I guess ... I totally didn't connect it with your case."

"It provided just the information I needed."

"You know, we don't use IOOS much ourselves."

She frowned to convey to him that his excuses were gaining no traction. She told him about the gunfire on the ocean.

His brow wrinkled with concern. "That's incredible!" He ran his hand through his hair. "Do you think this has anything to do with the kid you found?"

"I don't know. But the boat was traveling near where he was probably dumped overboard."

"And who were you with?"

"David O'Connor." She explained who he was, leaving out the part about his wound.

Rick nodded. "Look, I'll file a report ..."

"With whom?"

"The commander. Tonight we'll send a boat out there to see what's going on. What time did you say this happened?"

"Between 11 and midnight," Kit said.

"I'm on it." He stepped behind his desk as if action was imminent. "And I'm sorry, Kit, about IOOS. It honestly skipped my mind."

It "skipped his mind" or he "didn't think it would relate" to her case?

⌒━✦━⌒

Brenda Ramsfeld called Kit's cell phone as Kit drove away from the Coast Guard station. "Hey, I'm referring these reporters to you."

"What are you talking about?" Kit gripped her phone and almost missed her turn.

"They're coming around here, asking questions about that dead kid. Wasting a lot of my time. So I told them it was your case, check with you."

"Did you give them my number?" Kit's face felt hot.

"No. I told them you had rented a place on the island. That's all I said."

"Don't give them my information!"

Kit hung up and called Connie. "For crying out loud, don't tell them anything," Kit said.

"Oh, don't worry, honey. I got your back. I already sent one packing. Told 'em our rental information was confidential. Like medical records."

That brought Kit's heart rate down a notch. Then another thought occurred to her. "Connie, is Bob around? Do you think he'd help me with something?" Her best lead so far was the plant material—the acorns and tomato seeds—found in the victim's clothing. She already knew that plants, like animals, had DNA specific to each individual, and that plant DNA had been used in a few cases to link a suspect to a crime. But the FBI lab didn't do DNA testing on plant material. It had to be sent to a contract forensic botanist at the University of North Carolina at Wilmington.

In the meantime, Kit could pursue general knowledge of agriculture on the Delmarva Peninsula—a subject Connie's husband knew as well as anyone.

"You gonna take him off my hands? Well, honey, have at it," Connie joked. "Can't never tell where he is on his days off. Here's his cell number."

Kit pulled over into a deserted parking lot. The fact that the child was a Latino with a load of tomato seeds in his gut pointed to the possibility, at least, that he was the child of migrant workers employed on one of the vast tomato farms on the Delmarva Peninsula. And that determined her next step— find out as much as she could about tomato growing in the area.

That's where Bob came in.

5

A TRUCKER, CONNIE'S HUSBAND BOB RAN DRY GOODS UP FROM NORFOLK, four days on, three days off. Unlike Connie, he didn't come from Chincoteague—he'd grown up in Salisbury, Maryland, about fifty miles north, which is why Connie went by her maiden name. "If you're a Jester, on Chincoteague you are somebody," she had explained. "Ain't no man can come up to that."

Kit dialed his number. "Bob? It's Kit McGovern."

"Well, hey, girl! What's my favorite Fed up to?"

"I want to know about big farm operations on the Peninsula."

"You thinking about changing careers? Or is this about some farm boy?"

She laughed. "Can I just ask you some questions?"

"Sure."

Kit started in, but Bob stopped her. "Whoa, honey. We need to do this in person. Where are you?"

Ten minutes later, Kit walked up to Bob and Connie's front door. The low brick rambler house sat on Chicken City Road, sheltered by tall pines and trimmed by riotous impatiens in full bloom. "Come in, come in!" Bob said, when he opened the door. His bald head, fringed in white, framed his tanned face.

59

He looked healthy, and considering he'd had a heart attack just a few years before, Kit thought that a blessing.

Bob showed her into the kitchen where he had already spread out a map of the Delmarva Peninsula. "Now, how kin I help you?" he asked. She explained what information she wanted. He started pointing out some relevant features. "You've got major poultry operations here, here, and here," he said, making small circles on the map. "There are smaller plants, too, but those are the big ones."

"Do they use migrant workers?"

"Not usually. Their product isn't really seasonal. Some migrants may find work in the plants and decide to stay on."

"What other big agricultural operations are on the peninsula?"

"A whole lot. You've got major growers here, here, here, and here," he said, drawing triangles this time. "There're a lot of truck farms, too . . . low-acreage operations where they grow melons, tomatoes, squash . . ."

"Tomatoes?"

"They get shipped to the big east coast markets—New York, Philly, D.C.—really all over. Now they would use ag workers. From July on, especially. So do the melon farmers. Virginia's the fourth largest tomato grower in the U.S. Lots of acres planted in tomatoes."

"Where do the field workers come from?"

"South of the border."

"And where do they live when they're here?"

"There aren't many farms that have housing for them anymore. You used to see that, you know . . . those little white houses, almost shacks, around the edge of a farm. Nowadays, most of them are housed in those little strip motels all up and down the peninsula. The ag concerns don't want to be responsible for their immigration status, so they contract with a foreman. He supplies the actual workers. If there's an immigration enforcement problem, it's on him." He stood up straight. "Hey, look. What's your schedule? I don't have to be at work until tomorrow afternoon. Why don't I just show you?"

c—✦—ɔ

Kit climbed into Bob's old red Chevy pickup and they left Chincoteague, traversing the causeway to the mainland. Bob turned right on Rt. 13 and headed north. "I'm guessin' you're interested in illegals," Bob proffered.

"I'm interested in tomato growing," Kit responded. "Growing, harvesting, shipping . . . the whole routine."

Bob glanced at her. "Got some criminal tomatoes around, huh?" He laughed at his own joke. "I heard of 'cereal killers' but nothing 'bout criminal 'maters."

Kit rolled her eyes.

"All right, then. Some of the big growers have been turning to corn to supply the poultry houses. And ethanol, of course. That's the biggest dang boondoggle ever . . . ethanol. Why don't we just shoot ourselves in the foot? Puttin' food in the gas tank. How dumb is that?" He turned off onto a side road. "But this is the right time of year for 'maters. You came at peak pickin' time." He accelerated, and Kit noticed in the outside rearview mirror that a cloud of blue smoke had emerged from his exhaust. "Y'know," Bob continued, "a few years ago we had that dang salmonella scare. 'Bout did farmers in. Kept the 'maters off the market for weeks. Finally found out the stuff was in peppers. Jalapeño peppers. Serrano peppers. From Mexico, no less. Go figure."

"Is that right?"

"Tomato growers lost $250 million, nationwide, and all because a few folks got the trots."

"How many is 'a few'?"

"Thirteen hundred's what I read."

Kit smiled. "That's a bit more than 'a few.' Did you lose some work?"

"Naw. I run dry goods, so I was OK. But other truckers lost money. Truckers along with the growers." Bob turned onto a small, two-lane country road with oyster shells on the shoulders. "It was overreaching by the Feds. That's what I think."

Bob pulled the truck over to the side of the road in the shade of some trees on a small hill overlooking a large field full of tomato plants staked up with twine. Even without getting out of the truck, Kit could see the ripe red fruit waiting for the harvesters who were spread out over the field. They wore long-sleeved white shirts and long pants, and some of them, she could see, had gloves on. They were walking down the rows, bending over, picking individual fruits, and putting them in soft bags worn across their bodies.

"That guy there," Bob said, pointing to a man leaning against a pickup truck parked in the shade, "he would be the boss. The crew chief. He's hired all these pickers, and he's responsible for them."

"How long will they be in this area?"

"A month, maybe six weeks, then they'll move on."

"Where does the crew chief find them?"

"Who knows? I figure most of 'em get jobs by word of mouth. They all got the same last names: Rodriguez, Martinez, Hernandez . . . you know. They're all Mexicans."

"All of them?"

"There may be a Guatemalan crew now and then. Salvadoran. But these days, they're mostly from Mexico."

Kit watched as the workers moved through the field, periodically emptying their bags into a large flat bin on wheels parked in the crosscuts between rows. Down near a stand of trees at the edge of the field, she could see some little children playing while their parents worked. Had her beach child been one of them? "Why do the pickers wear gloves?"

"Cuts down on the salmonella and E. coli. They also make 'em wash their hands good. They keep that wash house clean as a kitchen."

"What happens after they pick them?"

"They put them through a sizing line, wash them, inspect them, squirt 'em with a little bleach water, dry 'em off, and pack them. It's tricky, y'know? Tomatoes are fragile, yes indeed. A split on the skin, a blemish, and diseases, bacteria can get in there and ruin 'em."

"Do they have a lot of culls?"

"Sometimes yes, they do. They can't risk a bad tomato in the batch."

"What happens to them? The culls?"

"Well, it depends. If it's a little blemish, the farm workers take 'em, cut out the bad part, and eat them. Serve them to their families. Nothin' much wrong with 'em, they just ain't suitable for the market."

"I'll bet they're sick of tomatoes by the end of the season."

Bob nodded. "Probably so. The field workers, they've gotta be trained how to pick, how to judge if the 'mater is ripe, and then they've gotta be supervised carefully. It's no small thing, growing 'maters. That's why the FDA ..." Bob stopped himself and shook his head. "Well, you heard me say it before. They got to be more careful putting out these warnings. It ain't fair to the growers, you know?"

On the way back to Chincoteague, Kit thought of another question. "You drive a night run, right?"

"Yes, ma'am. I work 11 to 7, pretty much." Bob shifted into low and turned left onto the road that would take them past Wallops Island and onto the causeway.

"Have you seen anything odd lately?"

"On the road?" Bob frowned. "I tell you one thing. The cops've been pulling people over like crazy. Mostly big sedans that look like they're loaded or SUVs with the windows tinted out." He nodded like he was agreeing with himself. "My theory is drugs. Drug traffickers. That's what they been lookin' for."

"So enforcement has been high."

"Yep. I watch my speed, I'll tell ya. Not going to give them any excuse."

The bridge over Mosquito Creek lay ahead. Kit tried to work out a scenario in her head. If police presence had been heavy on Rt. 13, maybe criminals were moving out onto the ocean. There was no other major north-south route on the peninsula.

"One more thing." Bob interrupted her thoughts. "Some folks been beat up lately on the peninsula, shopkeepers at country stores. One of 'em died. 'Course, he was seventy-two years old, but still. I never have heard such a thing. Don't know why it would be happening, not now."

"If the economy's bad . . ."

"This time of year it ain't." Bob drummed his fingers on the steering wheel. "Something ain't right. My daddy would say the devil's afoot."

⚬━✦━⚬

David O'Connor nudged the nose of his kayak through the cordgrass, mosquitoes swarming around his head. The marshes around Chincoteague, as Connie had promised, teemed with wildlife, more kinds of birds than he knew existed. In the shallows, he could see crabs beneath the water, and clams, minnows and larger fish. The cry of an osprey pierced the sky.

He desperately needed to relax. He'd come to Chincoteague to get away from police work. So why was he getting involved with Kit's case? With Kit, even? As attractive as she was.

The sun felt hot, even at nine in the morning, but a light breeze made the day bearable. The current seemed easier to deal with on this, the east side of the island, and there were many canals and fingers of water for him to explore. The kayak moved smoothly over the surface, and David felt his muscles working rhythmically. His shoulder was getting better and he was relieved about that. The weeks of physical therapy after the shooting had been arduous. At first, the docs expressed doubt about how much of his strength he'd regain. But it was coming back. He could feel it.

Now if only his mind were a muscle. He knew how to rehabilitate muscles, how to work them, how to push them, how to be dogged about exercising them. His mind was something else altogether. Past events had cut deep channels through which his thoughts ebbed and flowed, swirled in whirlpools, and raced in strong currents. Sometimes, he thought he would drown in them. Sometimes, he wished he would.

A splash of saltwater stung his wounded arm. His mind returned involuntarily to the boy on the beach, the body they'd found. Who was he? Why was he there? And why hadn't his family reported him missing?

Ten years he'd spent in homicide. It was a hard habit to break.

I've got to stop this, he thought. *I've got to quit thinking about death.* David steered the kayak around a bend and stopped it suddenly, using his paddle as a brake. Ahead of him, in the shallows next to a stand of marsh grass, stood a big white bird. What had Kit called it? A great egret.

David sat motionless, just ten yards away. The bird seemed intent on something in the water. It moved, its long legs hinged at the back, stepping high, like a man in a business suit moving gingerly through puddles, trying to keep his pants' cuffs dry. Then it stopped. David remained still, barely breathing, his eyes focused on the bird.

Suddenly he sensed movement to his right and his eyes flicked over to the marsh grass. A gray-haired woman dressed in waders, a khaki hat and a camouflage shirt stood in the water, mostly hidden. She had a still camera with an enormous lens on a monopod trained on the bird. She held her finger to her lips to caution David to be quiet.

He looked back at the egret. All at once, its sharp head flashed downward. It thrust its pointed beak into the water, and seconds later, it came up with something, something that was wiggling. David squinted into the sun. It was a crab. Then the egret swallowed it in one gulp. He could hear the woman's camera capturing the sight, clicking and whirring.

The bird moved again, those stilt-legs rising and falling, its eyes bright. And then suddenly it hunched its shoulders, extended its wings, and lifted off, beating the air with its great white wings, its black legs folded beneath.

David watched it fly away, low across the water, beautiful in its pure whiteness and strength. And only when it was out of sight did he speak. "That's pretty cool," he said to the woman.

"My, yes. I think it must be nesting right over there." She motioned to the right.

David nodded toward her camera. "You just shoot birds?"

"Mostly. But put a pony near me, or a crab, and I'll get it, too." Her gray eyes sparkled.

"You look like you know what you're doing."

"I should. Been at it long enough. Now those great egrets, they're common this time of year. Yesterday, I got an American Coot. Very rare in the summer. Want to see?"

"Sure." He put the paddle in the water and moved the kayak forward until he was next to the woman. She pressed some buttons and then turned the camera toward him so he could see the screen on the back. David squinted in the bright light, and pulled his head close until he was able to see the picture—it showed an old man sitting on the shore in a lawn chair, sound asleep.

The old woman laughed out loud at her own joke. "That's him, my old American Coot. He's right over there," she motioned her head. "He can't see what I like about wading through these marshes, but he drives me here, nonetheless."

David grinned.

"You're not from around here, are you?"

"No, ma'am. I'm not. David O'Connor," he said, holding out his hand.

"Alice Pendleton," she responded, shaking it. "You here for the summer?"

"For a few months. Taking a break from my job."

"What's that?"

"I'm a police officer."

Alice Pendleton nodded gravely. "This is a good place to get away for a while. And these birds, they'll teach you a lot. There's a plan, you know, a plan for everything. There's even a reason why you're here."

"Yes, ma'am."

"Alice, who you talking to?" A man's voice came from the shore.

"That's him. That's my old American Coot," she said to David, her eyes wrinkling in amusement. "Coming, dear!" And she turned and slowly made her way back through the marsh. Later, David stood in his rental house drinking a glass of ice water and staring at one of the photographs on the north wall of the living room. It was an amazing picture of a gray bird flying low over the blue water. And as he stared at it, the signature on the bottom right of the print came into focus: *Alice Pendleton.* Immediately, the image of the old woman in the marsh came into his head. "Good grief," he said out loud. "She's a pro."

⊷

Kit inserted the key into the lock on the door to her cottage. That's when she noticed the business card stuck in the crack. She pulled it out. Piper Calhoun, Reporter, *The Norfolk Times* the card said. On it in smudged blue ink were the words *Call me*.

Not a chance, Kit thought, and she pushed in the door. The air conditioning hit her like an open refrigerator door, refreshing after the hot, humid outdoors. She'd spent the day gathering statements from the teenagers who had been on the beach and doing some background checking on Joe Rutgers, the Fish & Wildlife officer, about whom she'd discovered nothing remarkable.

She threw her things down on the big oak harvest table and tossed the business card in the trash. The main room of the cottage was painted blue, the trim an antique white. The high ceiling and exposed beams gave the place a light, airy feel. The kitchen, painted blue and white with yellow accents, stood off to one side. This configuration allowed the entire side of the cottage facing east to be open to the water, with windows and French doors leading to an open deck.

Kit poured a glass of water from the container in the fridge. Fatigue swept over her. She booted up her laptop, ready to write up her reports. A knock at her door interrupted her.

The reporter? Kit braced for a confrontation. But instead, Rick Sellers stood on the porch. She opened the door.

"Hey!" he said, a sheepish grin on his face. "I, uh, felt bad about the IOOS thing and I brought these for you." He held a bunch of papers in his hand.

She eyed him. "How'd you know where I'm staying?"

He shrugged. "Word's out."

Great.

"Here." He handed her the papers.

Kit looked down. Copies of the reports he had filed with the Norfolk Coast Guard office. "Thanks. I appreciate this."

"Sure thing. And if there's anything else I can do, just yell." Sellers grinned. "I'll do better next time. I promise." He turned to leave, then looked back. "If you find something I'd appreciate it if you'd , let me know. So I can update those guys." Sellers nodded toward the papers in Kit's hand.

"OK."

"We're going to go out patrolling for a while, about the time you saw that boat. I'll let you know if we catch 'em."

"Thanks," Kit said and she watched as he walked out to his truck and got in. How did word get out about her location? Should she change cottages?

Her cell phone rang. Another interruption.

"Hey," David said. "I'm done for the day. Feel like going to the beach?"

Kit felt a rush of emotion. "The beach?"

"Yeah, you know: water, sun, sand . . ."

She hesitated.

"You swim, right?"

She could hear the teasing in his voice. "I lifeguarded all the way through college," she said.

"Good. I may need a lifeguard," he laughed. "Look," he said, his voice dropping, "I'd like to talk to you."

He wanted to talk? Kit tried to read the intonation in his voice. Maybe needed to talk? Could she spare the time? "OK. Sure. I can be there in half an hour."

Kit threw on her swimsuit, added shorts and a T-shirt, grabbed a towel and her fanny pack, and left for the beach. Driving over the bridge to Assateague, she saw a collection of snowy egrets in the trees near the road. A herd of wild ponies stood a long way down the salt marsh, grazing. How she'd loved watching them when she was a kid! And Pony Penning, when the firemen would round them up, swim them over to Chincoteague, and sell off the colts—that was sheer heaven to her as a young girl. She rolled down her windows, let the soft salt air swirl into the car, and inhaled deeply.

She parked at the south beach lot, away from the surfing area. The absence of commercial buildings on Assateague was part of its charm. There were no boardwalks or hotels or res-taurants or T-shirt shops, no cotton candy or caramel corn. Just a small museum, restrooms and the beach. David had said to meet him in the vicinity of the last lifeguard stand.

Crossing the dunes, she could see the ocean was calm this day, two-foot waves breaking close to shore, the waves slid-ing up over the sand, foamy-moustache edges leading the way. Some of the beachgoers were packing up to head back for din-ner. To her left, some kids flew a kite that looked like a great green dragon. Kit turned right, heading down toward the tip of the island, away from the surfing area, away from the place she'd found the little boy, toward the end of the island set aside as a nesting area for the endangered piping plover.

Every family she passed reminded her of her case. White, black, Hispanic, Asian—who could possibly lose an eight year old and not report it? Not miss him? Maybe his mother couldn't report it because . . . because why? Fear? Kit ran through the possibilities as she locked her fanny pack in the glove box of her car.

Down the beach, she dropped her towel on the sand, put her ID and keys down and threw her T-shirt on top of them.

David hadn't arrived yet, but she felt hot, so she plunged into the waves, diving through the breakers, her eyes smarting from the green, salty water. She swam out beyond the surf line, and then turned on her back and floated, then swam again, sliding through the waves, feeling the tug of the ocean like an embrace. "God," she whispered, "thank you for this. Thank you for the sea and the sky and the sun, for a place that touches me so deeply." The spontaneous prayer surprised even her. Could the familiar beauty of the barrier islands and the embrace of the sea seduce her back into the love for Jesus she once knew?

She swam north, parallel to the shore, then turned south again. She felt the littoral current pressing along the shore and she let it pull her along for a while, thinking of the little boy, and his body's journey. Did he travel along the bottom? In the middle of the current? Did the surf turn his body over and over as it washed in?

Kit treaded water, looking out at the waves coming toward her, thinking about the victim. Suddenly, something grabbed her leg. Panicked, she jerked around. David O'Connor surfaced, grinning, water streaming off of his face.

"David!" she cried. "Oh! That is so middle school!" Kit cupped her hand and sent a sluice of water shooting toward him.

"But I got you, didn't I?" he said laughing.

"Oh, big deal! Big deal! So you can swim underwater!" Smiling, Kit swam over to the beach side of David, talking all the way, capturing his attention so that he didn't see the huge wave coming before it broke over his head. Deftly, she dove through it, and he came up sputtering.

"All right," he said, shaking the water off his head. "We're even."

"No way!" she said, and she shoved him down into the water.

The two played for half an hour, maybe more, bodysurfing in the waves, diving and laughing, swimming against the current, and floating on top. Then they let a strong wave take them in to the beach. "How'd you spot me?" Kit asked as they walked out of the surf.

"You were the only swimmer pretending to be a dead boy," he said, grinning.

Kit bent down and picked up her towel. "Very funny."

"Seriously. I saw what you were doing out there, and I thought, now there's a girl who needs to play."

"Well thank you, Dr. O'Connor." Kit sat down on the sand and David did as well. He had on blue and white boardshorts. The large bandage on his arm was gone; only the butterfly bandages remained. "How's the arm?" she said, nodding toward it.

"It needed a salt water bath," he replied.

The tiny stubble of his beard glinted in the afternoon light. "What have you been doing?" she asked.

"I went kayaking, and I saw this bird," he paused, and squeezed his eyes shut as he reached for the name, "a great egret. Very cool."

Kit laughed softly.

He told her about the woman he'd met, and about the photograph on the wall of the Main Street house.

"I've heard of her, but never met her!" Kit said. "Her art is all over the place. Not just photographs, but incredible oils, too. She's wonderful."

The breakers rolled in, relentlessly pounding the sand. A flock of brown pelicans flew parallel to the shore, their wings beating the air. "Hey, your friend Sellers came by to see me."

Kit arched her eyebrow. "He did?"

"Yep. Asked me all kinds of questions. Why had we gone out on the ocean, how long had I known you, was I helping you with the investigation, what did I do in D.C. . . . he was really nosy."

"That's weird." She blinked. "Did you tell him where I'm staying?"

"No way!" David ran his hand through the sand. "My guess is he is going to file a report and he wanted to cover all of his bases."

That made sense. Rick had shown her the paperwork. Even given her copies. But how did he and that reporter find out where she lived?

The sound of the breakers murmured a refrain. David glanced toward her. "Kit . . ."

She turned.

"How long were you married?"

The question caught her off guard. She hesitated. "Seven years."

"What happened?"

"That's pretty personal."

"So was my shooting incident."

She couldn't argue with that. Kit picked up a small shell, a white, ridged scalloped shell, fingered it, and tossed it into the sand. She gave him the outline. "By the time he got his PhD, Eric didn't want to be married anymore." She hated the fact that tears formed in the edges of her eyes. She stared straight ahead at the sand, hoping he wouldn't notice.

"He left you."

"Yes."

"That stinks."

She let that comment ride for a minute, secretly agreeing with him. Then she pulled out the response she'd memorized: "I believe God will take care of it somehow." Did she even believe that anymore?

The muscles in David's jaw flexed. He threw a little shell off into the sand. "Law enforcement's pretty hard on relationships."

But what had she done wrong? She'd asked herself a million times if she had neglected Eric, put her career ahead of him, failed to be a good wife. Kit felt her neck tightening up. Off to her right, a kid kept trying to get his mother's attention. The mother, apparently lost in her own thoughts, ignored him.

"It seems like you have to choose one or the other; law enforcement or marriage. The two just don't seem to mix."

Kit bristled. "I don't believe that."

David picked up a handful of sand and let it drain through his fist. "It's hard. It's a consuming profession. A lot of times, spouses don't understand."

"I think it could work. I've seen it work, in fact."

"Not sure it's worth the trouble."

"Sounds like you like being alone."

"Pretty much."

So what was he after? Why did he call her?

Out on the ocean, two kayakers paddled in rhythm. David inhaled deeply. He turned to look at Kit. "I, uh, I wanted to tell you that I just can't get involved with your case right now."

He was pulling back.

"I understand."

"That first day, after I helped you move that boy, I didn't stay because I came here to get away from law enforcement, you know?"

"Sure."

"I was intrigued by the boy, and by Jimmy's story, but then," David stroked his arm, "I realized I . . . I can't do this. Not now. And I'm sorry . . ."

Kit's emotions were swirling. "It's OK. Look, you've already helped me a lot, so don't worry about it. Take care of yourself, OK?"

He nodded and squinted as he stared out over the ocean. His feet burrowed down into the sand. "Do you have any new leads?"

Should she tell him what she'd learned about the littoral currents of the ocean? Or the ag industry on the Eastern Shore? She decided not to feed the law enforcement addiction. "A few," she responded vaguely.

He nodded and continued staring out over the ocean. "The important thing is, keep at it. Somebody intentionally killed that little kid, somebody bigger and stronger. He put something—a cord or a rope—around his neck and watched him as he died. That's no way to treat a kid." He gestured with his hands as he spoke. "There's nobody to speak up for that boy now, nobody but you to bring him justice. It's a sacred trust, you know? Don't let anything get in your way."

6

KIT STOOD IN THE GREAT ROOM OF HER COTTAGE, STARING OUT OVER THE
channel. A group of five or six gulls were fighting over some
crab shells someone had thrown out, swooping and diving,
picking up bits of crab and stealing them from one another.

The house was quiet, too quiet, and loneliness had settled
like an ache in her bones. David was right. It was best not to
mix law enforcement and marriage.

But what about children?

The call from the forensic botanist from the University of
North Carolina at Wilmington distracted her. "I did some ini-
tial testing on that material you sent me," the professor said.
"You have time to talk about it?"

"Sure!" Kit slid a pad of paper in front of her on the table
and picked up a pen.

"What is it you were hoping to learn?"

Kit filled him in on the details of the case. "So I'm wondering: is there a way to use the seeds or the acorns to figure out
where the boy was before he died?"

Kit waited during a long pause. The botanist, Dr. Timothy
Hill, was one of a tiny handful of people in his specialty who
applied his science to criminal investigations. "Unfortunately,"

Dr. Hill said, "tomatoes of this kind are ubiquitous. Now if they'd been heirloom tomatoes, those we could do something with. But these are just simple, common tomatoes grown commercially all over Delmarva, and their DNA would not be traceable."

Kit's hope sank. "I thought that we could link DNA to individual plants."

"It's true, we have done that. Actually, we've been doing it since the early '90s. The first case involved a murder in which the body was found near a palo verde tree out in Arizona. The investigating officer picked up some seed pods. Then, they identified a suspect, and found similar seed pods in the back of his truck. A DNA scan showed that all the pods came from the same plant, thus putting him at the place of the crime."

"And that won't work for tomatoes?"

"Not with these tomatoes. Besides, in the Arizona case, there were two samples to compare: one from the crime scene, one from the suspect's truck. You only have one. But here's something else to consider," Dr. Hill said. "That little boy had been eating tomatoes out the wazoo. According to the medical examiner's report of the number of seeds found in his gut, I'd say he'd ingested a dozen or more in the twelve hours before his death. Either this kid's mother had a heck of a kitchen garden, or his parents are ag workers with lots of access to free tomatoes."

"Which still doesn't answer why he'd be out on the ocean in a boat."

"That's a question outside the field of botany," Dr. Hill said, chuckling.

"So you can't trace the tomatoes . . ." Kit said, pensively.

"The acorns now . . . they're more distinctive. We might be able to work with that. We can often trace those to an individual tree."

"What kind of tree are we talking about?"

"*Quercus virginiana.* Southern live oak. Common from Norfolk south, in sandy-soiled coastal areas."

"Norfolk south? What about the Delmarva Peninsula?"

"They're not native to the Eastern Shore. If they're there, someone planted them." Dr. Hill paused. "Then again, that could work to your advantage, assuming, of course, the little boy had been living on the peninsula. If he hadn't, well, you're totally out of luck."

Kit pressed her phone to her ear. "Let's assume he lived on the peninsula. How can the acorns help?"

"Well, think about it: if we were talking about a red oak or a white oak, they're all over the place. We would find it very hard, probably impossible, to find the mother tree. But live oaks don't grow up there naturally. People plant them as ornamentals."

"Ornamentals?"

"Live oaks are the big tree you see in pictures of the old plantations, the ones with the Spanish moss hanging down from them. So people use them to evoke that Old South image. Since they're not native to Delmarva, there won't be nearly as many and they'll be in fairly predictable places, around houses, along lanes, like that. They're evergreens, with leaves that look kind of like thin magnolia leaves. Go to Hampton University. There's a famous live oak there, the Emancipation Oak. That's where the Emancipation Proclamation was read out loud for the first time in the South, in 1863."

Kit opened up her laptop and Googled "Southern live oak" while she continued to hold the phone.

Dr. Hill continued, "They're resistant to salt spray, and if they're growing right alongside a body of water like the ocean, they'll be kind of scrubby and short. But inland, they get real big—80 feet max. The fact that your boy had acorns in his

pocket at this time of year tells me he was keeping them, playing with them. He had a stash of them somewhere . . . in a jar
or something. They don't drop until September, and if they'd
been on the ground since last winter, they would have been
eaten by animals or rotted. So he had to have had them stored
somewhere.

"Here's what I'd do," Dr. Hill continued. "I'd look at the
big tomato fields, and see if I could find a house with live oaks
around it . . . lining the driveway or just in the yard, anywhere
nearby. Then I'd get a sample from them and check the DNA."

"So you could trace the DNA? To an individual tree?"

"We should be able to." The botanist explained what kind
of samples he'd need. Kit hung up the phone. She had just a
little over a week left to prove her case to her boss.

⌖

David pushed his paintbrush into the corner of the window
frame. He was trying to keep his feelings at bay by focusing on
the painting and playing upbeat music in his iPod.

But he missed her. He barely knew her, but he missed her.
And that violated every practical rule he had established for
himself. Every long-standing principle. Every common-sense,
street-smart, logical game plan he'd ever created.

He looked up every time a car passed, hoping he'd see a
green Subaru Forester. Hers. He caught himself daydream-
ing, his brush poised in midair. He wondered a thousand times
over if he should call her. Take a chance, again.

But those chances had never worked out. Why did he think
another one would? And was he drawn to her, or the adrenaline of the chase?

⌖

Armed with a list of growers from the local agricultural extension agent, Kit spent six hours bent over her laptop, zooming in on satellite photographs of tomato farms on Google Earth, looking for live oaks, based just on their shape—the huge crown, broad, spreading branches, and overall size. After identifying sixteen possibilities, she'd spent two days driving around, checking them out in person, and reducing her list to eight farms. Eight locations on the Virginia portion of the Delmarva Peninsula where there were live oaks near tomato fields.

What a long shot. Kit tried to encourage herself by remembering the case of the federal judge killed by a pipe bomb loaded with nails. The FBI case agent went from hardware store to hardware store, looking for a match for the nails. He finally found exactly what he needed on his vacation.

If that agent could be that persistent, she could, too.

Now, she needed to collect acorn samples and oak leaves and have them tested in the hopes that the DNA from some of them would match the DNA of the acorns in the dead child's pocket. But first, she needed to gather supplies.

The only hardware store in town was small and jam-packed with everything from hammers to nails to seine nets and crab traps. Kit edged through the narrow aisles, collecting things she needed in a small blue bucket. Gloves, zippered plastic bags, a small bottle of hand sanitizer, plastic shoe boxes, paper labels, and Sharpie markers. The last thing on her list was duct tape.

"Aisle 5, near the back," a helpful clerk suggested.

Kit headed that direction. As she rounded a corner, she nearly collided with a broad chest wrapped in a blue T-shirt emblazoned "Law Enforcement 10K Torch Run."

David O'Connor.

"Kit!" The surprise on his face mirrored her own. He grabbed her arm and before she could protest, moved her to a quiet corner of the store. "What are you doing? What's all that?" He nodded toward her bucket.

She lifted her chin. "Tools of the trade."

His eyes showed instant recognition. "Tell me!"

Fifteen minutes later, they were sitting in the coffee shop at the corner, the sweet fragrance of a caramel macchiato mingling with the strong scent of a grande bold, black. Kit perched in her chair, her emotions roller-coastering, marveling at the ease with which David O'Connor had pulled her back into his life. Maybe she had misjudged him. Maybe he wasn't rejecting her.

The sun had begun to slide toward the horizon, sending shafts of light through the stained glass windows of the coffee shop. One golden beam fell across David's face, turning the highlights in his brown eyes golden. Fool's gold, perhaps?

Kit explained the findings of the forensic botanist, her own research, and now, her mission. The words tumbled out, falling over her inhibitions like children at play.

"Why don't we go now? Tonight?" David suggested.

"Tonight?"

"Didn't you say you were short on time? We can snag samples and ship them in the morning. Or we can drive them down to this botanist."

"We? I thought you didn't want to be involved?"

He blushed and ducked his head. He stared out of the window momentarily. When he looked back at her, the skin at the corners of his eyes crinkled with humor. "Despite all my resolutions, I think I am involved."

"David, I don't think ..."

"Wait, wait," he said, raising his hand to stop her. "What was your plan?" He leaned forward, intent. "Do it on your own?" The look on his face told her how unwise that would be.

"I do a lot of things on my own," she countered, "just like you."

"I don't care how tough you are, no way should you be going out there at night by yourself, no backup . . ."

He was right. Her boss would have a fit.

"Let's go. I'll drive." David moved his chair back.

Kit remained still. "You're addicted."

"Addicted? To what?"

"To law enforcement."

"No way. I'm just trying to help a friend."

"You said you were backing off!"

"Off the case, yes. But I never said I'd give up acorns! I love acorns." He grinned. Then his voice dropped. "Kit, I want to help you get these samples. Besides, if something happened to you while you were out there by yourself . . . I couldn't live with myself. Please don't do that to me."

She checked his sincerity. Then she checked her watch. "Pick me up at 9:00."

⌒═✦═⌒

"This is nuts," she said, smiling as she piled into his vehicle.

"Nuts? I thought we were going after acorns!"

She laughed.

"Anyway, you Feds plan too much. Cops are all about spontaneity. Gettin' it done."

Spontaneity? Like jumping into a police pursuit? She kept her mouth shut. He was right: cops played things out differently than agents. Cops had to respond to what was happening on the street. Agents tended to plan their interactions with bad guys more carefully. There were advantages and disadvantages to both methodologies.

David had a gun tucked in beside him, next to the center console of the Jeep. "Expecting trouble?" she asked.

"I'm playing Boy Scout. Be prepared." He also had flashlights, batteries, bottled water, and Power Bars.

Kit opened her laptop and outlined the plan. They'd start up near the Maryland line, then work their way down the peninsula. "Trivia question: what famous ship is constructed of live oak?"

David shifted his jaw. "Give me a hint: is it an aircraft carrier?" He grinned at her.

Kit laughed. "Come on. Didn't you tell me you spent four years in the Navy?"

"Yes, but . . . I give up."

"The U.S.S. Constitution—'Old Ironsides.'"

He looked at her. "Really?"

"Yep. They used live oak to construct it because it was so strong it could take cannon fire."

"No kidding."

"And the Navy still owns stands of live oak trees."

"Well, Miss Wikipedia. I'm impressed."

Fifty minutes later, they arrived at their first farm field. The moon was rising in the east as David pulled over. He had extinguished his headlights half a mile down the road. They both sat still just watching for a few minutes. The field was dark and no one was in sight. Kit glanced over at David. His eyes were shining in the dim light. "You want me to do it?" he asked, looking over at her.

"Do you know how many hours I've spent learning to identify live oaks? I've got it." She quietly opened her door, put her laptop down on her seat, slipped on gloves, and slid out into the night. The air felt thick with humidity. She had on black pants, a black T-shirt, and a black jacket, and she was wearing her fanny pack. She waited until her eyes adjusted to the dark, then started into the field. All of her senses remained on high alert. She heard a dog barking in the distance, smelled the pungent tomato plants, felt the soft loam of the field under her feet, brushed away a cloud of mosquitoes hovering around her face.

Dr. Hill had said six acorns from every tree would be enough, along with some leaves, and she moved around the edges with her small flashlight, following the mental map in her head. There were three live oaks near this field, two on the east side, one on the north. She slipped six acorns and some leaves into an individual, pre-marked plastic bag, and then moved on to the next tree. When she got back into David's Jeep, he had created a label with the location of the farm field for one of the plastic boxes. In less than twenty minutes, they had their first samples labeled and stored.

While David drove to the next field Kit entered information into the database in her computer. Who knew what might be important later? She entered the date, time, number of acorns, and the number of the box they'd been placed in as well as the GPS location. Then she prepared labels for the next farm.

David volunteered to take this one, but Kit demurred. "I'll get the acorns. You cover me."

At the third field, eight live oaks lined either side of a driveway leading to an old, abandoned house, a big house, grand at one time, but now in disrepair, sitting at the edge of a twenty-acre field of tomato plants.

"You want me to drive up to it?" David asked.

"No, just wait here. I'll walk up the lane."

7

DAVID SAT IN HIS TRUCK, WATCHING KIT WALK QUICKLY TOWARD THE eight live oaks, studying the confidence in her gait, and the way she carried herself. Lost in thought, he almost didn't hear the gravel crunching under the feet of the big Latino approaching from behind. When he caught sight of him in his outside rear view mirror, he took action.

"Buenos noches, señor," David said stepping out of his SUV while smoothly sliding his pistol into his waistband at the small of his back.

The Hispanic man looked at him, shined a flashlight in his face, and said, in rapid Spanish, *"Que haces?"* What are you doing?

David smiled reassuringly and held up his hands in a gesture of innocence and quickly came up with a story about Kit being a biology grad student looking for a particular kind of tree. *"Este árbol se denomina en español 'encino' y es muy común en el sur de los Estados Unidos y el norte de México."* This tree is called «encino» in Spanish and is very common in the southern United States and northern Mexico.

The man looked at David, then at Kit, then back to David. "I go tell my boss," he said in English. "This is his property, his land. He no like people coming here. You stealing?" he asked, peering over David's shoulder into the truck.

"No, no . . . she just wants acorns, for her study, you know? Just acorns." David glanced over his shoulder. Kit stood next to the farthest tree, about to turn back to the truck. He didn't want the Hispanic man to get a good view of her.

David reached for his wallet. The Hispanic man instantly stepped back two feet and pulled a huge knife from the small of his back. "Hey, hey," David said, showing the man his wallet. He pulled out forty dollars. "This is for the acorns, OK?" He held out the money. The man looked at him, then looked at the bills. He snatched them out of David's hand, backed away, and took off running. When he had gone around a curve, David gave three quick beeps on the horn, and Kit, picking up on his signal, began running toward the SUV.

"What's up?" she asked breathlessly.

"Gotta go!" David started the engine, swung around on the gravel road, and headed back toward the highway. He told her about the confrontation.

"Did he get your tag number?" Kit asked.

"I don't think so. Once he saw those twenties, he had eyes for nothing else."

⁂

Kit and David worked their way slowly down the peninsula. By the time they neared the tip, they'd grabbed samples from all eight fields. Their contact with that one man had been their only challenge. As they pulled away from the last location, David asked, "How far is it to UNC Wilmington?"

"Five hours."

"Let's do it."

She looked at her watch. Nearly 4:00 a.m.

"C'mon," David said. "We'll be there by 9:00."

"And then we'll have to drive seven hours back to Chincoteague."

"So what else do you have to do?" he asked, grinning.

"What else do YOU have to do, that's the question."

"I'm good," he said.

Soon they were skimming over the Chesapeake Bay Bridge-Tunnel, the twenty-mile connection between the Delmarva Peninsula and Norfolk, where the Chesapeake Bay, the Atlantic Ocean, and the James River all come together. Looking out of her window, Kit could see the lights of ships making their way up and down the shipping lanes, and the smaller lights of a few fishing boats.

David started talking about Norfolk, and the shipyards, and the huge Navy presence there, and she found out his father was a Naval officer who had died in a plane crash when David was a young boy. He'd joined the Navy to imitate his father. And yes, he'd been married once, a long time ago, when he was in the Navy. "It just didn't work out," he said with a shrug.

Kit stiffened internally at that. What does "it didn't work out" mean? she wondered.

"What about you, Kit? You seem so together. Perfect family, right?"

She rolled her eyes. She told him about her brother, Justin, who was a lawyer and her father, James J. McGovern, also a lawyer. How could she explain her mother? Better just skip it.

David seemed not to notice. He was comfortable. Easy to talk to. Funny at times. A good listener. And maybe it was the lateness of the night, or the way the light played across his face, or the calm, masculine assurance of his voice . . . maybe it was all of those things put together that made Kit realize that she felt attracted to him. Very attracted. *I don't want this,* she said to herself. *I definitely don't need another man in my life.* But when they both reached for something at the center console at the same time, and his hand brushed hers, she felt an emotional rush.

They remained silent for a while, the dark water slipping past them in a blur as they skimmed across the bridge-tunnel. David shifted in his seat. "So what'd you get in trouble for at the Bureau?"

She nestled down in her seat. "It's a long story. We were looking for a suspect who'd raped and killed three women. The AUSA and my boss both thought they knew who'd done it, a petty thief named Braxton. So they started going after him with everything they had. Trouble was, they had no hard evidence.

"Then a guy gets killed in a shootout up in Pennsylvania. He'd been involved in similar crimes, and I started lobbying to have his DNA tested in our cases." She glanced over at David. "That was not popular."

"You hit a brick wall."

"Exactly."

"Why not test the evidence if you've got it?"

"You know how it goes with these high-profile cases: the bigwigs get invested in a particular suspect. They convince the Director to hold a press conference and say that all of the resources of the Bureau are being devoted to bring the perpetrator to justice. Yada yada yada. Then he announces they have a 'person of interest'—the bigwigs' main man. By this time, they're so far down the road, it would be embarrassing to admit they had the wrong guy . . . so they just keep pounding and pounding at the case until they get a false confession or until something else happens that's big and they can kind of let this old case slide under the public's radar."

"You tried to get this second man's evidence tested and they wouldn't do it?"

"Over and over until I got chewed out, big time, and suddenly found myself out of the loop." Kit grimaced. "Then I got accused of leaking stuff to the press. After being sidelined for three months, I gave it up, and took a transfer to Norfolk." As Kit finished her story she felt a familiar tightness in her gut. She still couldn't get past it.

"That doesn't say much for justice."

"And that's my problem," Kit admitted. "I have a passion for justice. God made me that way, I guess."

David grew quiet for a moment. "You're pretty religious."

She raised her eyebrows.

He picked up her iPod. "I checked out your play list while you were getting acorns."

Kit looked at him. Until recently, she'd have said her faith was the most important thing about her. "What about you? Do you go to church?" she asked.

"I did for a while."

"What happened?"

"Nothing. That's the problem."

"What did you think would happen?"

"I don't know."

The sun was sending shafts of light into the eastern sky.

"I love watching the dawn," Kit said, looking east. "I love the way the colors play across the sky, the pastels: pink, blue, gray . . ."

David took a deep breath. "My stepfather was an alcoholic."

Kit turned and watched him carefully, trying to guess where he was going with this.

"He had so many DUIs, he eventually lost his license. So he used to make me drive him to bars. I was fourteen years old and here I was, driving him around so he could get plastered. I guess he figured if we got caught, the judge would go easy on me. I'd take a flashlight and do my homework in the car. I hated it, but at least it gave my mother some peace while we were gone." David hesitated. "A kid in my class invited me to church and I went with him a few times. One night, when I was driving my stepfather to a bar, I came to a stoplight, and there's my friend, with his dad, across the intersection, looking at me sitting in the driver's seat, staring with their mouths open." He shrugged. "That kid never invited me again."

"You never went back to church as an adult?"

"I did, a few times. I just didn't feel like I fit in."

Kit stared out of her window, a peculiar churning in her stomach. "When I go to church now, I feel odd, too. There are all those families, those couples, and I'm by myself. I've come up with lots of excuses for why I haven't connected with a new church, now that I've moved to Norfolk, but you know, the truth is, I just feel like I don't fit in. Like you."

"Well, you need to find one," David asserted, shifting in his seat.

"Why? Why me? Why not you?"

"Because it means something to you. It's your framework. You can't let your ex take that away from you."

She bit her lips against the stab of pain she felt. "You didn't know your biological father at all?"

David shook his head. "I was three when he died. Sometimes . . . sometimes I think I have a vague memory of him throwing a ball to me or carrying me on his shoulders. But then, it could just be my imagination." He flexed his hand on the steering wheel. "The thing I don't get is how much you can miss someone so much, when you never even knew him." The increasing light of day slid their conversation into a safer zone, lighter topics like politics, and murder trends, and gang violence. By the time David got through Norfolk and turned onto Rt. 58, Kit could no longer keep her eyes open. Fatigue overwhelmed her and his voice grew muffled and the next thing she knew,

David was nudging her awake. "You'd better call that prof," he said. "We're about fifteen minutes away."

<hr />

Dr. Hill's upbeat mood told Kit he was impressed. Her all-night project had produced twenty-six samples, each containing six acorns and some leaves. He approved of her system of cataloging the samples.

"It'll take a while to do all the testing," he said. "I'll have a grad student work on it."

"What's the process?" Kit figured Dr. Hill was in his late thirties. He had dark hair and dark eyes and a flashing smile and she imagined coeds would sign up for his class just for the view. She felt awkward in her now-grubby jeans and muddy boots, her hair all askew, no make-up, and fatigue-darkened eyes.

Dr. Hill leaned back against a lab table, so charming in his white coat. "It's complicated. Basically, we have found that in oaks, the microsatellite loci exhibit enough variability to link the acorns to an individual tree with a high degree of statistical confidence."

"You're speaking in tongues," Kit said.

The professor grinned. "OK—there's stuff in the DNA that lets us differentiate individual trees fairly well. We extract the DNA, store it in deionized H2O, then put it through a process in which we look at the genetic variations. If all goes well, we'll have a match with the acorns your little boy had in his pocket."

"And if not?"

"You get to have another adventure."

<hr />

Kit drove back to Norfolk while David slept. On the way, she called her neighbor and told her she was going to stop by to collect her mail. Ellen was a perpetually cheery brunette given to long skirts and flowers in her hair. Kit thought she would have done well in the '60s. She'd brought Kit brownies when she moved in, invited her to church three times, and volunteered to care for Kit's nonexistent pets. On sunny days, Ellen proclaimed it delightful. If it was dreary, she pronounced it a nice change.

Kit pulled into the parking lot of the apartment complex and touched David's arm. "I'm going in to collect my mail," she said when he opened his eyes. "Back in a few minutes."

Ellen threw open her door when Kit knocked. Today, she wore a patchwork denim skirt and a flowered shirt. She handed Kit her mail, caught her up on the current gossip, and then said, "Some reporter's been around looking for you," Ellen said. "Name's Piper something. I gave her your cell phone number. Hope you don't mind."

Piper Calhoun from the *Norfolk Times*. Kit's heart sank. Actually, she did mind. Very much. "That's a private number, Ellen. Please don't give it out again. These reporters . . ."

Ellen waved her hand. "Oh, I know. They can be a pain. Sorry if I messed you up. I think I got the last two digits reversed, anyway. She said she couldn't get through. You can tell her to lose the number. You may see her. She called me a while ago and I said you were coming by."

"You told her I was coming here?"

Ellen blinked. "My bad."

Kit was still fuming when she returned to the SUV. David was awake, standing outside, leaning against the passenger door, looking toward her building. "Get in!" she commanded.

He responded quickly. "What's up?"

She turned the key in the ignition and started to tell him about Ellen when a young woman pulled into the space next to her and rolled down the passenger-side window of her battered Ford Focus.

"Kit McGovern?" the young woman called out, peering over her sunglasses.

Kit's mouth straightened into a line. She shoved the car into reverse.

David sat straight up. "What's going on?"

"Reporter."

The young woman jumped out of her car and raced to the driver's door. Kit turned around to back up. "Wait!" the woman called, slapping the hood. "Wait."

"Hold on," David said suddenly, grabbing the dash.

Kit slammed on the brakes. She turned to look forward. That gave the young woman time to race to Kit's door and grab on to the handle. Kit shot David a look. "I could have gotten away."

The reporter was wearing khaki pants and a black top, and the tattoo of some kind of vine wound up the left side of her neck. "Miss McGovern, I'm Piper Calhoun."

"I have no comment," Kit said, turning again to back out. She took her foot off the brake.

"But you're investigating that murder on Assateague, right?" The woman had her hand on Kit's door and was following her at a jog.

"No comment."

"But wait, stop."

Kit stepped hard on the brake. "Look, Miss Calhoun. All inquiries need to go through the press office downtown. You're getting nothing from me."

"Nothing?"

"Nothing." Kit began backing out again.

"So I guess . . . I guess you're not interested in the possibility that human trafficking is involved?"

Kit froze. "What?"

"You heard me."

"Check this out," David said.

She glared at him. "I can't! That's how I got in trouble before! Do you want me to lose my job?"

"Then let me."

8

THEY FOLLOWED PIPER CALHOUN TO A DINGY APARTMENT NEAR THE Norfolk Naval Base. "It's all I could afford," she said apologetically as she stood outside Kit's car. "Reporters don't make much, you know."

Kit didn't know. All she knew was that contacts with the media had to be cleared through the press office, a step she decidedly hadn't taken. "I'll wait here," she said.

"Be right back," David replied.

Kit rolled her eyes and laid her head back on the headrest.

⌇⟶⌇

Piper Calhoun led David into her building. "I've been working on a story for three months, maybe more," she said as she inserted a key in the lock. "Some people in the newsroom are ticked. They think I'm not carrying my weight. But hey, they'll see eventually." She pushed the door in. "Come on in."

David stepped into the small living room. It smelled of food—garlic and something else, cilantro maybe? A worn brown couch covered by a colorful blanket was pushed against one wall. Above it hung a movie poster advertising "Twilight." Two worn armchairs and a beat-up coffee table completed the décor. A bead curtain covered one window and newspapers lay piled in the corner.

"Hold on," Piper said, disappearing into the back, where David presumed the bedrooms were. She emerged a few seconds later, followed by a small, thin Hispanic woman dressed in a bright, orange top and a long black skirt.

"This is Patricia, a friend of mine," Piper said. She pronounced the name the Spanish way, *Pa-tree-si-a.*

The young Latina stared at the floor. David asked her something in Spanish, and the woman's eyes lit up. She looked at him, her eyes searching his face, and then she answered him, hesitantly at first, then with more fluency and as her story came out, he grew increasingly focused.

David emerged from the building after fifteen or twenty minutes. He walked over to Kit's driver's door. "You need to speak to this woman, Patricia."

A curious chill ran down Kit's spine. "David, I . . ."

"You need to talk to her." David opened Kit's door.

When Kit walked into her apartment, Piper looked triumphant. "Sit down."

Kit took an armchair, giving the couch to David and the Hispanic woman. How old was she? Twenty-five, maybe? The sorrow around her eyes aged her, Kit thought.

Piper couldn't stay quiet. "I volunteer with a women's shelter, you know?" she said to Kit. "One day, they brought Patricia to me. When I listened to her story, I decided to bring her home."

"What kind of shelter?"

"A shelter for women and children who need to be away from, you know, from abusive partners or . . . or other stuff." Piper glanced at Patricia.

"Like what other stuff?" Kit asked.

Piper took a deep breath. "Like forced labor."

"Here? In Norfolk?" Kit looked quickly toward David to see if he was catching this.

"Yes!" Piper's eyes were an odd light blue and right now they were shining like ice chips. "They bring them in from all over. Some of them end up in massage parlors near the Navy bases, others in private homes, and the rest . . . well, we don't know where they're headed."

Kit blinked. "Go on." She could tell the rescuer in Piper was engaged.

"I've learned a lot. Here's the way it works." Piper sat forward in her seat. "They come here to be domestic workers, or so they've been told. You know . . . maids or nannies. They get here and their 'employer' takes their passports and forces them to work for pennies. It's human trafficking, the new slavery!"

Kit's mind raced. Could some of the ag workers be part of this scheme? She looked at Patricia, who twisted a tissue in her hands.

The Latina had been sitting quietly. She looked quickly at Piper and began speaking in rapid-fire Spanish. Kit heard the word "ice"—ICE—and realized the woman was asking Piper if she, Kit, was an immigration agent. When Piper responded in the negative, the woman visibly relaxed.

David moved forward in his chair, resting his elbows on his knees. He said something in Spanish to Patricia, then turned to Kit. "I've asked her to tell you her story."

The woman began, speaking in broken English, her large brown eyes shifting between Piper and Kit.

"I am from Mexico," Patricia said. "My family very poor. One day I meet a woman at the market. She say she get me work in America. I am nineteen years old then, the oldest of six children, and my mama says 'Go. Make yourself a life. There is nothing here.' So I go.

"This woman, she takes me to a house, very bad smelling. She gives me to a man. He was not nice. He put me in the back of a truck with twelve others, men, women, and two children. We drive for a long time. It is so hot, I think I die. He gives no water, no food, nothing. Finally, the truck stops. We get out. It is night. I ask where we are. 'Hickory,' the man say."

"That's Hickory, North Carolina," Piper explained.

The Latina continued. "Some people go there. Me and one other, we get back in truck. Then we here, in Norfolk." She took a deep breath. "The man, he take me to a house, a big house. Very beautiful. He tell me if I work hard, I could live like that someday. This is America. He tells me if I leave the house, the ICE will get me. Put me in jail forever. He scares me very much.

"The people in that house, the ones I am to work for, they not nice. I work twelve, fourteen hours every day. Hardly no food. At night, they lock me in a tiny room in the basement. No light, no windows. Nothing. I am very afraid.

"I work there a long time, cleaning, cooking. The wife, she beat me. She think her husband like me. I stay there long time . . . two, three years. Then one night, they not lock my door. They are drinking, smoking . . . and they no come down and lock door. I wait . . . and I wait . . . and when all is quiet, I run. Where I go? I hide in the woods. I am very, very hungry. For two days, I walk. Then I see a priest. I run to him . . ."

Piper interrupted. "The priest brings her to our committee meeting, and voila, here we are. Meanwhile, I'm thinking this is a great story. Then I get sent up to Chincoteague to cover the body on the beach. And you know, I'm thinking there's a connection."

"What connection?" Kit said.

The reporter shook her head. "I dunno."

"Just because the boy was Hispanic?"

"Look. I'm willing to bet he wasn't on vacation. Yeah, maybe he was out fishing with his illegal dad, but that doesn't make sense, you know? How many illegals have the money to do that? All I know is, I'm giving you the lead. It's your job to connect the dots."

"How long ago was all this?" Kit asked.

"Patricia's been here a month. At first, she felt terrified all the time. So afraid the people would find her. She's much better already."

"Are there a lot of trafficked workers in Norfolk?" Kit asked.

"I don't know how far the problem goes. We know there are some people here as domestics, like Patricia, who live in virtual slavery. There are others who are in brothels, like I said. But another thing I'm interested in is migrants. You know, we have a lot of migrant workers up on the Delmarva Peninsula, and I'm wondering, are they all there voluntarily?"

Kit's heart was drumming.

"Patricia, have you heard of people being brought into the U.S. by boat?" David asked.

The Latina looked puzzled, so David said it again, in Spanish. "No," Patricia said, shaking her head.

"But remember, she's been locked in a house for over three years," Piper said.

"What were their names?" Kit asked.

"Who?"

"The people who held her. What were their names and where do they live?" Kit pulled out her notebook and pen.

"Patricia only remembers their first names: Robert and Rhonda. And part of a house number: 167. She can't get past that."

David looked skeptical and Kit had to agree with him. Patricia knew more than she was telling. She looked at Piper. "What do you want out of this?"

"A career-changing story. I'm ready to blow this joint. Try CNN or something."

Kit looked at her curiously.

Piper sighed. "All right. A little justice would be nice, too. It blows my mind that people can treat others like that. I feel sorry for her, and I don't know what to do next."

⸺✦⸺

All the way back to Chincoteague, Kit's mind whirled. Human trafficking. What were the odds? And it was a hot-button issue at the Bureau. Could she make the connection? Was her beach child being trafficked? And what about the people hanging off the gunnels of those darkened boats at midnight?

They were driving over the bridge to the island and David was asking about dinner when her cell phone rang. "Excuse me," she said, and she pulled it off of her belt. She looked at the caller ID and felt a twist of pain. She set her jaw. "Hello?"

Kit glanced upward in frustration, tears welling in her eyes at the sound of his voice. "I'm fine." She turned her head to the side so David wouldn't see. He negotiated the turns in the little town, steering the Jeep to the back side of the island while she listened. "Yes," she said. "I understand."

But she didn't understand. She didn't understand at all! A dark fury rose inside her, a fury coupled with panic, edged in despair. David pulled into her driveway. She forced a response. "No, Eric. I won't be able to. I'm busy that weekend. Yeah, OK. Well, good luck!" And as David slid his SUV into "park," Kit snapped the phone shut, threw it onto the floor of the Jeep, opened her door, and raced into the house, tears streaming down her face.

9

Kit left the door ajar. David pushed it open and walked in. Kit stood in the middle of the great room sobbing. She looked at David through a blur of tears and said, "Eric's getting married again!"

The words came out like a convulsion. Her hands balled into fists and her stomach twisted in knots. "He's getting married! He told me he didn't want to be married, that he wanted to concentrate on his career. And now . . . he's getting married again? That fast? What was wrong with me? Why didn't he want me?" She sobbed—great heaving sobs that captured her breath and made her heart shudder.

David put her cell phone and her bag down on the counter and walked over to her. He wrapped his arms around her. "It's not you, Kit. Don't even think that. It's him. He's a jerk."

She pulled away, too angry to be comforted. "He said he wanted to be single. Not be tied down. And now, he's getting married? Oh, God. What is wrong with men? I hate him!" she cried out. "I hate him!" She buried her face in her hands.

She sensed David near, heard his breathing, felt his arms brush hers as he began to embrace her again.

"Shh, shh," he said. "He isn't worth it." His voice sounded gentle and kind.

But Kit flung her arms out, pushing him away.

He took a step backwards, shocked. He ran his hand through his hair.

Kit's face felt hot. "He's marrying a student! She's twenty-two. 'Fresh out of college' is the way he put it. Oh, God!" She pressed her hands to her temples. "I can't believe this! I'm the one who put him through law school! I'm the one who helped him with his dissertation! I'm the one who supported him so he could study, get those stupid degrees, have that stupid career!"

"Kit, this isn't about you . . . it's about him . . ."

"It *is* about me! He does want to be married—just not to me! And he has the gall to invite me! What a jerk!"

"He's a user. A self-centered user. And that twenty-two-year-old girl is too young to see it."

"He betrayed me, broke our vows . . ." she glared at David. "I don't get it! I did everything the way you're supposed to and this is what I get?"

He cocked his head.

Kit felt her face grow hot. "Of course you don't understand! How could you? For one thing, you're a man. For another, . . ." She threw up her hands.

"Come on. Talk to me. I want to help."

"You can't help! You can't! Listen: I don't want to talk any more. Not to you, not to anybody. Can you go, please?"

He hesitated.

"Get out!"

His eyes widened and, for a moment, she thought he was going to retort in anger. She turned her back. She heard him sigh deeply, and say, "I'm sorry, Kit." She pressed her lips together, heard his footsteps as he moved to leave, heard the cottage door shut behind him, heard the sound of his SUV starting, heard the crunch of its tires on the oyster shell driveway . . . and then he was gone. Gone!

And she cried out in anguish, "God, how could you do this to me?"

Kit had originally come to Chincoteague on an emotional retreat, a vacation, and so she had brought with her a box full of things from her marriage: pictures, theater stubs, UVA football tickets, a menu from Milan, the restaurant where Eric had proposed, and, of course, their wedding album.

Exhausted from her anger and grief, she went back into the bedroom and pulled that box out. She sat on the bed going through it, touching each item, fingering it, studying it like an archaeologist at a dig, as if she were looking for clues in a case. She placed each artifact on the white chenille bedspread. Soon, the entire surface looked like a scrapbook project. Where had it gone wrong? Where had she gone wrong? Why had God allowed this to happen?

She'd followed all the rules. Carefully chosen a man who said he was a Christian. Studied all the books. Tried to be a good wife.

Despite all that she'd been betrayed, abandoned, rejected . . . and not just by Eric. By God, too . . . at least, that's what it felt like. How many times in a lifetime should that happen to one person?

First her mother, then Eric. Her mother had left when she was eight—just walked out on her, her brother, her dad.

Her mother had a new family, now Eric would, too. She, Kit, apparently wasn't good enough for either of them.

Not good enough for God either, no matter how hard she'd tried. She couldn't measure up. Now, he'd left, too. She could feel it.

"Oh, God!" she whispered. "Why did you let this happen to me?"

The tears dripped down onto the pages spread before her. Then one by one, she put every artifact on her bed in the trashcan, except for one. Goodbye, she thought, goodbye. And she finally fell asleep, cradling her wedding album in her arms.

⚓

David left his own rented house, crossed Main Street, and walked through the motel parking lot toward the dock. The sky was black, the horizon dotted with the lights of moving cars on the causeway. He couldn't stop thinking about Kit. Two days after her explosion, he still felt confused and, he had to admit, frustrated.

Why had she rejected him so abruptly? What had he done wrong?

Part of him wanted to write her off. Yet another flaky woman.

The other part remained locked in a deep longing for her.

Crossing the motel parking lot, he looked, out of habit, in the window toward the front desk. Maria was not there.

He continued out onto the dock. His boat shoes, which he wore without socks, made soft sloughing noises as he walked. He took a deep breath, inhaling the salt air and the marsh smell.

He found Kit an unusual woman. Strong. Smart. Driven, but in an attractive way. Not beautiful, but pretty. Her tears over her ex-husband's phone call only deepened his attraction to her. She'd shown her vulnerability, and his heart had responded.

It had been a long time, many years, since he'd felt so drawn to a woman. But why had she pushed him away? Was she messed up because of her divorce? Worth bothering with?

On their trip to Wilmington, while she slept, he'd listened to some of the podcasts on her iPod—sermons, mostly. They raised questions in his mind, made him squirm at times, raised up a resistance within him that he didn't realize was there. But some of what they said was interesting, and seemed to plug in some of the holes he'd been wrestling with. He had resolved to ask her about them, to find out if what they were saying was true. He'd wanted to find out what she believed. He'd been looking forward to getting to know her better.

Now, he wasn't sure that was going to happen. It seemed like the door had been slammed shut. Was it worth trying to open it again?

Frustrated, he kicked a shell off the dock and walked back toward the house. Outside the motel office, a man David recognized as the manager stood catching a smoke. "Hey," David said.

"How's it going?" The man was in his forties, dark-haired, and grizzled.

"You taking a shift?" David said, nodding toward the office window.

The manager spit out a small piece of tobacco. "Got to."

"I haven't seen Maria lately."

"That makes two of us." He squinted at David. "You know her?"

"Just from walking out onto your dock." He frowned. "She quit?"

"Didn't even finish her shift. I came in to do some paperwork and the place was empty."

David's law enforcement brain kicked in. "When was that?"

"Five days ago."

"What time of day?"

"Around 8:30. The schedule had her on duty until 11. I came in early. Figured I'd get some work done before I had to take the desk. Came in . . . and she was gone."

"You have contact information, right? Did you call her?"

"Phone number she gave me was bogus. Address, too. Somebody told me she ran off with her boyfriend." The manager spit again. "You can't trust 'em. Not these Mexicans. She's the last one I'll ever hire."

David walked on, mulling over the manager's words over in his mind. Boyfriend? What boyfriend? Maria never mentioned one and to David she definitely seemed like a woman on the hunt. He walked up the front stairs to his house and opened the door. Something wasn't jiving with him.

———

Overnight, a thick layer of gray clouds had filled the sky. Kit could hear a steady rain beginning to fall as she padded to the kitchen in her pajamas. She looked in the cabinet, rejected the only box of cereal she had, opened the fridge and closed it again. Then she went and sat down on the couch, propped her chin on her knee, and reviewed Eric's desertion all over again.

"There's no peace in this," she muttered, frustrated, and she got up, retrieved her Bible. Hadn't she found comfort there before? She turned to Psalms: "Vindicate me, O God, and defend my cause against an ungodly people. From the deceitful and unjust man, deliver me!"

Could she really call Eric "deceitful and unjust"? Or her mother?

" . . . For you are the God in whom I take refuge; why have you rejected me?"

"Yes, why, God?" she said aloud, and fresh tears began to flow.

David called. He asked her if she wanted to go out for breakfast. She said no.

"We need to talk," he said.

But she refused. Later, she wrote in her journal: *How can I continue seeing him? Frankly, he's too attractive. My feelings are taking me down a wrong path. I messed up once with Eric. And David isn't even a believer! I am not getting involved again. No way. I took my best shot before and look what it got me. I've got a case to solve and a life to live by myself, on my own . . . I don't need anybody. I don't want anybody.*

❧

Her boss, Steve Gould, asked her to come in to Norfolk for a meeting and for once, Kit felt glad to be pulled away from Chincoteague. When she entered his office, she saw a dark-haired Latino-looking man in a navy blue suit and a crisp white shirt already there. He was wearing cufflinks . . . cufflinks and Italian leather shoes. His hair was stylishly cut and his jaw strong. If she had to pick a poster boy for the FBI, he would be it. He looked spit-shined, slim, fit, and very, very much in control.

"This is Chris Cruz," Steve Gould said. Steve motioned for her to sit down in a side chair. "Now talk to me."

She did, outlining the direction of the investigation she'd been pursuing.

"Tell me why you think your dead boy was a trafficking victim," Steve said, moving papers around on his desk.

Kit cleared her throat and told him about Patricia.

"How'd you discover her?"

She told a deep breath and identified Piper Calhoun.

"A reporter?" Steve glared at her. "You haven't learned not to talk to the press?"

"Sir, she wasn't trying to get information; she was trying to give it to me. I considered her a source."

He played with a desk pen. She went on and told him about the reporter's suspicions about the presence of trafficking in the Norfolk area.

"Well, Norfolk isn't Chincoteague," Steve responded. "You got the name of the couple who held her?"

"No, sir. Not yet."

"That's pretty elementary, isn't it?"

"I'm working on it, sir."

"What's the link between the boy and Patricia?" Steve asked. "They're both Latino. So what?"

Kit stiffened. "Why else would the boat full of people be out on the water?"

"Latinos can't fish?"

"Why wasn't the boy reported missing?" Kit retorted.

"Look." Steve was obviously past frustrated. "You two talk. Chris has done this kind of thing before." He turned to the Latino agent. "You tell me if she's wasting time."

"Sir . . ." Kit protested.

"I want you to consult! The last thing this office needs is another dead end."

"How about lunch?" Chris said as they left Steve's office. Was he smiling to be friendly or grinning at her discomfort? Kit didn't know.

10

He took her to a Thai place not far away, a cool, dark restaurant with a fountain in the middle. The hostess must have known him, because she smiled and bowed and guided them to a private table near the back and gave him the seat with a view of the cash register. "Set us up with a round of appetizers, would you please?" Chris said, "I'm starving."

So he came here a lot, Kit thought as she opened the menu. "What do you suggest?"

"How spicy do you like your food?"

"I can take anything."

"All right then." He leaned over and pointed to her menu. "The *Num Tok*. I get the beef. Sliced sirloin tossed with ground rice, and some other stuff like mint and cilantro. Very good. A little less spicy is the *Kai Yang Esan*. Chicken marinated in coconut milk. And then, there's always Pad Thai or the salads."

"I think I'll go with the beef," Kit said, closing her menu as a young waitress arrived.

The waitress smiled, filled their glasses with water, and took their orders. "Appetizers come soon," she said, smiling and nodding.

"And Thai iced tea, for both of us," Chris added. He turned his attention to Kit as he carefully unfolded his napkin. "Tell me more about your case."

Kit filled him in on all the details that Steve Gould had been too impatient to listen to.

The waitress came with the tea and appetizers: chicken satay skewers, spring rolls, wonton, and something Kit didn't recognize.

"What's that?" Kit asked, as the waitress left.

"*Tod Mun Pa*, Thai fish cakes. Very spicy."

Kit reached for one and took a bite, aware that Chris was watching her. The heat filled her mouth, reddened her face, and spread down her throat. She forced herself to not react, to casually reach for her Thai iced tea like it was an afterthought, and not the desperate grab it actually was.

A half-smile crossed Chris's face. Gallantly, he kept quiet. He wiped his mouth with his napkin. He had long fingers, like a pianist, and no wedding band. But he wore a college ring on his right hand. She couldn't quite read the name. "So tell me more about the trafficking angle."

She relayed again the Latina's story of being brought to North Carolina, and held as a virtual slave in a home in Norfolk.

"How'd you get her to talk to you?"

She had to credit David. David had spoken to Patricia in her own language and had drawn her out. He's the one who had insisted Kit listen to her story. David. David. Kit's face flushed. This time, it wasn't the spicy Thai food.

She took a big drink of water. The waitress came with their entrees. Kit told Chris about David.

"So, this guy's an off-duty cop?"

"Yes, but he's not involved any more. He just happened to be around at the time." As soon as the words were out of her mouth, Kit realized how ludicrous they were. "Just happened" to be with her when they spent all night collecting acorns? "Just happened" to drive with her to Wilmington? "Just happened" to be present when they met Piper and Patricia?

Graciously, Chris gave her a pass. "As Steve said, I worked a trafficking case up on the peninsula."

"Tell me about it."

"A guy was bringing women down from New York, running a brothel for the migrant workers," Chris said.

"And these weren't normal prostitutes?"

"We found out they had been trafficked in from Central America . . . they were in forced prostitution in the city and then brought down here for the weekends. These were very poor women. The youngest was thirteen."

Thirteen. Kit flinched inwardly at the thought. Here she was feeling angry and betrayed by a husband who'd left her. Forced into sex at thirteen! "How'd he transport them?"

"By van."

"Not by boat?"

"A boat would be too slow. This guy would bring them down on Thursday and take them back Sunday night. Had quite a business going."

"How did you prosecute him?"

"We got him on a RICO charge. Took the house, the van, everything." Chris chewed his steak thoughtfully. "I'll give you copies from the case file so you can see how we did it."

⊙━✦━⊙

Back on Chincoteague, Kit went over the files Chris had given her. She studied the surveillance procedures he'd used, the evidence collection techniques, the warrants and the subpoenas. She felt impressed. If she ever brought her case to the point of prosecution, the same level of detail would be required.

Granted, she wasn't working trafficking for prostitution, not that she knew of anyway, but the idea was the same.

Chris was thorough. Neat. Very professional. She could tell that from his notes. The 302s, the Reports of Contact, were complete, question after question, statement after statement developing the facts of the case.

She found him good-looking, too. And unmarried. So why, in the restaurant, did the first mention of David send her tumbling into a whirlpool of emotion and longing?

"No way are you getting involved," she told herself out loud, "with either of them."

⌒━━✕━━⌒

Chris had loose ends to clean up on some cases in Norfolk, after which he would come up to Chincoteague to further familiarize himself with the case. Steve had given Kit an extension on her two-week deadline, and she promptly made arrangements to keep the cottage at Chincoteague. Connie had gotten her a good deal on it.

Two days later, on a blistering hot afternoon, Chris arrived at her cottage. He looked so out of place in his dark gray suit and white shirt she almost laughed.

"What are you up to?" he asked, nodding to her open laptop on the big harvest table.

Kit wiped her hands on her khaki shorts, feeling slightly silly in her casual attire. She offered Chris a drink. As she poured his iced tea, she updated him. "I called the State Department, and a guy in the Office of Human Trafficking filled me in. They're figuring about 800,000 people worldwide are transported across national borders every year. That doesn't even count the ones trafficked within the country."

"Mostly as prostitutes."

"Yes."

"Most don't start on that road intentionally," Chris reminded her. "They get tricked into it."

Kit nodded. The stories she'd read on the State Department Trafficking in Persons Report had tugged at her heart.

"These are desperate people," Chris continued. "Mostly women and children, although men can be victims, too."

Kit jumped in. "Criminals kidnapped one guy in Cambodia for his organs. And the kids—some of them were forced to work as domestic servants or in textile mills. Sometimes their parents sell them, even though they know they're being used for sex."

"Poor people have to make decisions sometimes that the rest of us have the luxury of not making. That thirteen-year-old girl we found?" Chris said, "She'd been orphaned. Lived with an aunt for a while, until her uncle sold her off."

"What happened to her?"

"We put her in protective custody. She's living with a cop's family now, as a foster child." Chris took a drink of the iced tea she'd poured for him. "Most of these people," he gestured toward the computer, "aren't that lucky."

"It makes me angry," Kit said. She looked at the laptop screen. "UNICEF says there are 27 million slaves in the world today, and 1.6 million new children are trafficked every year. That's a lot of abuse!"

"But here's the deal: even if Patricia was trafficked, we're a long way from showing a link to your case."

"We may have two cases, is that what you're saying?"

"Right. And if we do, I can guess which one Steve's going to want us to concentrate on."

"They both need justice!"

"I agree. But the Bureau has its priorities."

Kit blew out a breath. She knew he was right. "I was naive to think trafficking didn't happen in America."

Chris laughed. "Yes, you were."

"I read about this case in California where Egyptian diplomats brought with them their house maid, a young girl sold by her poor parents to help feed the rest of their family. And I thought, why didn't anyone notice? Why didn't anyone in that suburban neighborhood realize something was wrong? Call the cops?"

"People don't want to get involved. Or they think it only happens somewhere else. We've found Asian women in suburban 'massage' parlors who expected legitimate jobs in the United States, but were forced into prostitution."

"It's crazy! Why didn't they go for help?"

"They usually don't speak the language, the trafficker has their papers, they're scared, isolated . . . to them, going to the authorities means going to jail." Chris bit his lip thoughtfully. "The trafficker holds all the cards."

By 4:00 p.m., they had gone over all the accumulated evidence in her case. Chris had helped her identify some leads to pursue. He questioned basing a case on such a tenuous link as acorns. He thought she was grabbing at straws.

When she got up to fix another pot of coffee, he stood up and stretched. She spooned the grounds into the filter, poured water from the carafe into the reservoir, and flipped the switch. What could she do to convince him her case was worth pursuing? Perhaps even more importantly, what if she was wrong? Could she afford another black mark? Another allegation that she was intractable? Not a team player?

But the image of the beach child's body lying on the sand, and the thoughts of the mother who might be missing him, stirred her heart. She couldn't give up, not yet, anyway.

Chris stood at the French doors looking out over the channel.

Thunder rumbled in the distance. Kit's head had been throbbing all afternoon, and she'd guessed the weather was changing. "Is a storm coming?"

"I think so."

She opened the door, and the two agents stepped out onto her deck.

Indeed, dark clouds were gathering in the west. Looking east, out over the water, she could see two small fishing boats making their way back toward port. A couple of jet skis, water spraying up like rooster tails behind them, sported in the channel. Far across the water, she saw a lone kayaker.

"He'd better get in," she said.

"You sound like you've had experience," Chris said, laughing.

"I got caught in a storm out there once, when I was a teenager. It's not something I want to repeat." The memory came back easily enough. "I'd been over to Tom's Cove, down there," she pointed generally southeast, "looking for shells with an island boy. We saw the clouds building, but he'd thought he could make it back to Chincoteague. Halfway across the channel, the skies opened up." Even now, she could remember her fear. "It was terrifying. I saw flashes of lightning, streaks of lightning, and balls of lightning, in white, pink, and blue—more varieties than I knew existed."

"Wow." Chris turned and looked west.

"I saw lightning strike the water and the land. Then I saw a transformer on the island explode. Here we were, in a metal boat! By the time we reached the dock, I was shaking."

"I guess you never went out on the water with him again!" Chris laughed.

"You are so right!" Kit shook her head.

"Thunderstorms still amaze me. In Southern California, we don't have them, not often anyway," Chris said.

Another rumble of thunder and the first drops of rain drove them inside. They sat down again at the table. "Tell me more about the agricultural workers on the peninsula," Chris said.

"There are the migrants and the permanent workers. The permanent workers generally work in the poultry processing plants, keeping the broilers, fryers, and roasters moving. They're supporting families back home. Housing is their biggest problem: they double or triple up . . . sometimes even sleep in shifts."

"Do any of them bring their families?"

"Some. And people complain, but the kids honestly often turn out to be as hard-working at school as their parents are on the job."

"And migrants?"

"That's a different story. Migrants never stay in one place long enough to impact the schools or most other community services, so there aren't as many complaints about them."

"People are just happy to eat the produce they pick."

"Right."

A sharp crack of thunder made them both look toward the water. Lightning flashed, then the heavens opened up and sheets of water began dropping from the skies. Then the power failed, and the cottage's lights went out. "My battery's low," Kit said, shutting the lid of her laptop.

"Guess it's time for a break." Chris moved toward the French doors. He raised his glass, took a drink, and lowered it. "What's that?"

"What?" Kit joined him. She thought she saw something off in the distance, but the rain pelting down obscured it. The jet skis were gone, and so were the small boats, and all the birds had disappeared as well, taking cover from the deluge.

She heard clicking on the windows and roof of the house.

"Hail!" Chris said. "Look at that!"

Dime-sized hail collected on the deck. Wind whipped the flag on the dock next door. She could hear it snapping even through the glass. The trees and bushes were shaking back and forth in mad fury, their leaves turned upside down.

Then the storm turned the world into a gray, seamless sheet, making it impossible to tell where water ended and sky began. The storm was beating the water out of the marshes, driving toward Assateague, flattening the marsh grass, the rain and the hail and the wind roaring.

A flash of movement caught Kit's eye. As quickly as her mind registered it, the movement disappeared. "Did you see that?"

"Somebody's out there!"

Thunder rumbled. Kit felt it in her chest. She shivered. She retrieved her binoculars from the bookshelves and lifted them to her eyes. "Tell me if you see it again." She alternated looking with her own eyes and through the binoculars, peering into the gray sheet. Then—a flash of yellow. In an instant, she recognized it: "the kayaker!"

"That can't be safe."

The kayaker was out on the channel! Alarm gripped her. All that lightning. And he was working against the wind. "Why doesn't he just let the storm drive him toward Assateague? At least he'd be on land."

"He got caught out there."

"He should have come in sooner!" Kit lifted her binoculars to her eyes again but the person had disappeared into the gray once more. "He must be inexperienced."

"What can we do?"

"I don't know. My neighbor has a small boat . . . I hate the thought of going out right now."

"Should we call 911? Is there a rescue squad on the island?"

"Yes." Kit raised her binoculars again. Just then, she heard a tremendous crack, and a sizzle as lightning struck the marsh not far from where the kayaker emerged from the gray. In the blinding light, she recognized him. Kit took a sharp breath. "David!"

"Who?"

Kit threw the binoculars down, the look on David's face emblazoned in her mind. "I've got to help him." She grabbed her lifejacket and ran out of the door. "Call 911!"

11

THE RAIN AND HAIL FELT LIKE NEEDLES PELTING HER SKIN. THE STORM sounded so loud! She slipped on some hail, righted herself, and ran across the lawn and onto the neighbor's pier. The end of the dock held a horseshoe life preserver on a long rope. Kit grabbed it, and threw it out onto the water. The wind immediately drove the preserver out into the channel, taking it to the end of the length of its rope. "David! David!" Kit screamed, but the wind whipped her voice away.

Out on the channel, the little kayak bobbed and nodded, tossed by the waves. David kept stabbing at the water, first on one side, then on the other. But Kit could see him faltering, missing strokes. Then the thunder rolled again, and a flash of lightning turned the gray world white. She jumped into the small boat. She wiped the rain out of her eyes, pulled the starter cord sharply, and the small outboard engine flared into life.

Just as quickly, the engine sputtered and died out. "C'mon!" Kit said, jerking the cord again and again. The motor refused to start. The rain plastered down her hair and it ran over her face. She wiped her eyes. David was about fifty feet from the bright yellow-orange horseshoe shaped life preserver. She yelled to him again, but thunder drowned out her voice. She saw him paddling furiously. Then, as she watched, a gust of wind jerked the paddle from his hand. He reached for it, the kayak capsized, and he began flailing about in the water.

She had no choice. She grabbed the flotation cushions from the boat and jumped into the water, her years as a lifeguard automatically guiding her actions. The water felt rough and cold and the current wanted to tug her downstream. As she got into her sidestroke, waves kept breaking erratically over her. At times, she turned her head hard to breathe, only to get a face full of water.

Spit, breathe, stroke, stroke, stroke, breathe, stroke, stroke, stroke . . . Kit pulled herself through the water, ignoring the lightning, ignoring the thunder, her mind and heart set on one goal: David.

She reached him just as he rolled onto his back, exhausted. "David!"

His eyes flew open and he turned to look at her.

"Come on!" she said. She handed him a flotation cushion, grabbed his life jacket, and began pulling him toward the life preserver and the rope, her breath coming hard. They reached it just as another bolt of lightning split the sky.

The storm was moving east. Already the rain had begun slowing down. She could see land now. "Pull yourself to shore," Kit yelled. A wave smacked David in the face and he came up sputtering. "Go!"

He reached forward, grabbed the rope, and pulled. Water sluiced off his shoulders. His hair looked shiny and dark, his muscles taut. Kit stayed right behind him. She could see something was wrong. David was using his left hand on the rope just to hold himself in place while he reached forward with his right and pulled himself forward. A couple of times, he almost lost his grip. The scar from his gunshot wound was bright red.

Several times, she wondered if they'd make it. The storm had begun to move past but the rain was still heavy. Then she looked up and saw flashing lights. Chris had called the rescue squad.

"Just hold on, David! They'll pull you in!"

Chris had grabbed the line attached to the horseshoe collar ring. He pulled it. Two rescue squadsmen joined him.

David rolled onto his back, hanging on with his right hand. When he finally reached the dock, hands reached down to grab him. Kit heard him yell when they pulled him up by his arms.

By the time Kit joined him, David was on his knees, throwing up salt water.

"That kid," David said, gasping through heaves, "he was dead . . . before he hit . . . the water, right?"

"Right." She was breathless, her lungs burning from exertion.

He shook his head. "'Cause this . . . this is no way to die."

❦

David refused transport. Kit thanked the rescue squad and they began packing up their gear. The storm was leaving as quickly as it had arrived. David sat on the dock in the diminishing rain, his muscles trembling, trying to recover his strength. Kit sat next to him, while Chris went inside to find an umbrella and beach towels.

"I'm sorry," David said. "I had no intention . . ."

"Why didn't you come in sooner?" Kit's voice sounded sharper than she intended. "You should never be out . . ." David held up his hand, which was shaking, and Kit shut up. He didn't need a lecture. When Chris came back, she introduced them.

"Thank you," David said, "for helping me."

Chris nodded. His suit pants, white dress shirt, and tie were drenched. Kit wondered if the rain had ruined his shoes. "Why don't we go inside?" he suggested, as he held a golf umbrella over them.

"No," David said. "I'm a mess. I've got to go home." He stood up on shaky legs and began walking toward the road.

"What are you doing?" Kit asked.

"I'll get a ride."

"Don't be ridiculous. Come inside."

"No."

"Then I'll take you home. We can get your car later." She turned to Chris. "Will you excuse me?"

"Sure. We were about done. I'll call you."

———

By the time they arrived at David's house, the rain had slowed considerably. David had regained just enough energy to take a shower. Then he put on sweats and collapsed on the couch. Kit had grabbed dry clothes before they left her cottage. She used the shower after him, got redressed, and now was trying to figure out what to do next. She knew she needed to take him to retrieve his car; but right now, he looked too exhausted. "You need to ice your shoulder," she said. "Can I get an ice pack for you?

"Look, thanks," he said. "You've done enough. Go ahead and go."

"How will you get your car?"

"I'll call a cab."

"That's unnecessary. I'll take you."

"No."

"David, look . . ."

"Kit," he said, sitting up abruptly, "I'm sorry to drag you into this. I appreciate you rescuing me. Honest. I would have drowned. So thank you. I guess I did need that lifeguard. That was incredibly courageous of you." He rubbed his left shoulder.

"Why were you out there in that storm?" The aggression in her voice surprised even her.

"I don't know . . ."

"What's wrong with you? Do you have a death wish or something?" The minute she said it, she regretted it.

"Of course not." David stood up and paced away. He turned around. "All right. I've been frustrated."

"About what?"

"At you. At the situation."

"What situation? What are you talking about?"

David ran his hand over his head. "I'd like to see you. Get to know you better. You seemed to shut the door on that."

"I can't get involved with you."

"Why?"

"It violates a promise I made." She felt a rush of emotion.

"What promise?"

"I don't want to marry a non-Christian, so I'm not dating one."

"So, we can't even be friends?"

"No!"

"And you think you can tell in advance how things are going to play out?"

"Well, yes!"

"How well did that work with Eric?" he said, his eyes flashing.

His rejoinder took her aback. Kit stared at him.

"Honestly, Kit, I'd like to be able to talk to you." David dropped down on the couch and put his head in his hands. "I'm trying so hard to sort things out. Today, I went out kayaking just so I could think. I got out in the middle of the channel. The clouds began building, but I kept going.

"When the thunder got loud, I turned around, and began heading west, toward where my car is parked. But the storm came in quicker than I figured it would. I could barely make any headway. I got frustrated. I couldn't make headway with this woman I like and I couldn't make headway in the storm. And then, I got so angry, angry at myself, angry with God. I yelled at him," he said, ducking his head sheepishly, "and I challenged him to show up.

"That was stupid. That was so stupid. The wind was so strong and the waves got choppy. Then the rain came down so hard and I couldn't see the shore. I couldn't tell where I was, and I was getting swept away. I was paddling like mad. My shoulder was killing me and then . . . and then, it gave out."

Kit's anger was draining out of her. David looked up into her eyes. "I have never, ever been so scared. Even when I was being shot at. Never. Then, in a flash of lightning I saw a white cross."

"What white cross? There's no white cross!"

"I saw a white cross, and I headed for it. And then I saw you." He rubbed his hands on his pants legs. "I realized out there in that channel that I am not ready to die. I'm not. God is way bigger than I am. He is . . ." David stopped, and shivered. "Kit, you understand this stuff. I don't."

"How do you know that?"

"I listened to your podcasts while you were asleep in the car."

Kit closed her eyes and turned away, her heart pounding. On the one hand, she had a responsibility to share her faith. *What faith*, a voice inside her head screamed.

On the other hand, she felt so attracted to him! Right this moment she could take him in her arms! And that terrified her. Oh, God, she thought. What am I supposed to do?

"You're afraid, aren't you?"

Her eyes widened in surprise. She turned around.

"I don't blame you, after what Eric did." David's eyes were soft. "Anyone would feel that way."

"It's not that!"

David raised his eyebrows. Clearly, he didn't believe her.

Kit tried to regroup. "What happened to your first marriage?"

She saw the surprise register in his face. "I was twenty, she was eighteen. Too young, too stupid, and too selfish. It didn't last a year."

Kit paced. "If my brother knew you, what would he warn me about?"

"Is he a good brother?"

"Yes. And smart."

"He would tell you I don't drink, smoke, use drugs, or womanize. But he would say I'm impulsive and hyperactive. And, I watch too much football."

"Redskins?"

"Anything." David took a deep breath. "Is that it?"

Kit crossed her arms in front of her chest. "Why haven't you remarried?"

"I was saving myself for you." David grinned.

"Straight answer!"

"Good grief, I'll bet you aced interrogation techniques . . . OK, here's the straight answer. After I became a cop, I dated other women. Most of them were too much bother. They wanted to settle down and I didn't or they came with a boatload of problems from prior relationships, or they had a list of demands I just didn't want to meet. Then I met this beautiful woman on the beach, standing over a dead body . . . now there's a story we could tell our kids."

Kit had to work hard to suppress her smile.

"Am I doing all right?" David asked.

She paced around the living room again, her arms folded. She shook her head, then looked at him. "Who left?"

David's eyes widened.

"Who left the marriage?"

He looked down and shoved his hands in his pockets. "I did."

Kit bristled. "Why?" She knew her face was red. She glared at him.

Eventually, he looked up. "It wasn't working. It just wasn't working, Kit." His voice was quiet.

She calculated his answer. "You didn't love her anymore."

He took a deep breath. "Right."

"Of course. That's exactly what Eric said." Looking around she spotted a scrap of paper. "Here," she said, scrawling a name and phone number on it and shoving it at David. "You say you've got questions about God? Ben Heitzler is an agent in the Washington Field Office. He's a strong Christian. He'll answer any questions you have."

Kit walked out before David could say anything else.

Later she realized she hadn't taken him to get his car. Later she wondered if she'd been too harsh. Later she shed tears on her pillow, wondering if she would ever be able to love again.

12

WHEN DR. HILL, THE BOTANIST, CALLED THE NEXT DAY, KIT IMMEDIATELY latched on to the excitement in his voice and let it lift her up. "You are a lucky young woman," he said.

Lucky. Sure. Kit closed her eyes. "Why is that?"

"I thought you were going to have to go out in the field again. Many times, in fact. You got a match on your first try."

Kit pressed the phone to her ear. "What did you find?"

"Sample number D6 matches the DNA of five of the six acorns in the boy's pockets."

Kit was booting up her computer as he spoke. She wrote down D6 as she waited for the program to load. "How sure are you?"

"I'd say 95 percent."

"And you could testify to that in court?"

"Absolutely."

"Do you have any kind of graph or readings you could print out?"

"Yes. You want me to email them to you?"

"I'd like that."

Kit hung up and checked her notes. Sample number D6 came from a farm near Glebe Hill in Accomack County. She'd found two live oak trees flanking the lane leading to an abandoned old house. In her mind's eye she could see it: a weathered gray, two-story farmhouse with broken-out windows on the edge of a tomato field. There were boxwoods around the place. Someone who cared about plantings had once lived there.

She wanted to call David. Instead she called Chris. Then, throwing a few things, including a digital camera, into a backpack, she got into her car and headed for Glebe Hill, nearly an hour southwest of Chincoteague.

⁂

Parking up in an old churchyard on a hill near the farm, Kit slung on her backpack, threw on a UVA cap, and rehearsed her story: she was a grad student in botany in search of remarkable trees for a project. She'd heard a rumor that a particularly old oak was the area and that's why she was tromping around the woods.

Her backpack held a tree book, binoculars, her camera, and a notepad. She clipped a water bottle on the carabiner that hung from the pack, and fastened on her fanny pack, which carried her gun. On the drive over she had stopped at Walmart and bought a hand-held GPS. They'd used David's when they'd collected the samples. Now, she stared at the device in her hand. She wondered how it worked and wished she had asked him.

"I'm smart. I can figure it out," she told herself, and she plunged ahead. She found the right screen on the GPS, entered the latitude and longitude of the farm field from her notes, faltered with the GPS menu, tried again, and finally found the screen with the arrow indicating the direction she should walk. She pressed a button to mark her current location and she trudged off into the woods, brushing away a spider web as she did.

About half a mile in, she arrived at a spot which overlooked the farm she was interested in. Staying well back in the treeline, she lifted her binoculars to her eyes. Below her stretched the tomato fields, neat green rows crosshatched about one-third of the way from each end. A dozen workers were there, picking the fruit—eight men and four women.

The old house stood across the field from Kit. Two live oaks stood on the lane leading up to it. Assuming her notes were accurate—and she was sure they were—the tree on the left was the mother of the acorns in the little boy's pocket. It stood seventy, maybe eighty feet high by her calculations. It had a huge trunk, and its limbs spread out at least forty feet. She could imagine a little boy playing in the shade of the tree, swinging from its branches . . . and collecting its acorns. But how did he get from here out onto the ocean? Was he being taken back to Mexico?

Dr. Hill had asked her for a picture of the oak. She hoped she could get close enough to do it justice. For now, she had to be content with standing beneath the poplars, oaks, and dogwoods on the hill and observing the field below. She took pictures with her camera, using a long lens, and wrote down everything she saw.

As Kit watched, a beat-up white truck approached the field. Immediately the pickers began streaming toward it, carrying boxes she could see were full of tomatoes. They put the boxes in the truck, which then took off, a cloud of dust streaming behind. The pickers sat down at the edge of the field, and after a while, another vehicle, a van, came and picked them up. Lunchtime? Or were they moving on to another field?

Kit put down her binoculars, made some notes, and made her way back to her Subaru. Then she drove down the road that went past the field. Because the house stood abandoned, there was no mailbox at the end of the lane, no way of knowing a street address to find the farm on the property maps. So she passed the place by, and grabbed the numbers off of the mailbox for the next house down. Then she turned a corner and was nearly hit head-on by a white Mercedes Benz.

No centerline divided this little country road and the driver of the Benz was apparently used to having it to himself. He blasted his horn. Adrenaline coursed through Kit. She swerved to the right. Her tires hit the rough shoulder. "Watch it!" she said angrily.

The Benz sped off and Kit shook her head. "What a jerk."

Down the road she saw a small, private lane leading back through a stand of tall pine trees. On the other side of the road was a large, white, cinderblock building. Outside of it was the battered van Kit had seen before. Was this the tomato processing plant? She grabbed the GPS and marked the location.

She had so many questions. Where did the workers go? Where were they staying? Who was their crew chief? What about their families? And most of all, was her little boy connected with this crew?

Turning around, Kit drove back past the old farmhouse. The field was still empty. Seized by temptation, Kit found a place to pull off, parked the Forester, slung on her backpack, threw her UVA cap on her head, and began walking up the lane.

This far inland, away from the ocean breezes, the air was stifling, thick with humidity. Locusts buzzed in the bushes and far away, a buzzard circled lazily on an updraft of air. A fine glaze of sweat appeared on Kit's brow. She wiped off her upper lip and took a sip from the aluminum water bottle. The lane stretched for about a quarter of a mile, and in retrospect, she wondered if she should have driven down it instead of leaving her car off the property. She'd thought she'd look less like an intruder on foot. Now, she second-guessed herself.

The tomato plants stretched out in neat rows on either side of the lane, staked up on wooden sticks that were about six feet tall. Kit could see fruit in various stages of ripening still hanging on the vines—these fields weren't finished yet, and she guessed that the pickers rotated from field to field, hitting one every two or three days.

In her mind's eye, Kit could imagine kids playing hide-and-seek in the rows, digging in the dirt along the edges, and chasing each other in the woods that surrounded the farm. Approaching the tree, she took multiple pictures. Then she reached the house and glanced around. Seeing no sign of anyone, Kit stepped past the overgrown boxwoods, up onto the front porch, and peered inside. The broken windows gapped like missing teeth. Wide pine board floors stood empty except for leaves and debris blown in from outside. She walked around the old place, noting the old-fashioned cellar, the tin roof, and the small outbuilding that she guessed had served as a smoke-house. A privy still stood in the back.

From the back porch, Kit could look into what had been the kitchen. One end opened into a large pantry. Kit balanced precariously on the half-rotted boards of the porch, aimed her camera through the broken glass of the back door, and took shot after shot, her neck tight with tension.

Moving around the outside of the house, she gazed up at the live oak, the one she identified as the mother tree from which the boy's acorns had come. The tree's elongated oval leaves were green and thick. Kit placed her hand on the massive trunk, and looked up. The leaves were so dense only tiny bits of sky came through.

Kit took more photos, then headed back for her car. She was nine-tenths of the way back down the lane when a white pickup truck suddenly pulled in. Her heart jumping, Kit stepped into the ditch, hoping the man would just drive by.

No such luck.

A muscular man wearing jeans, a T-shirt, and a cowboy hat stepped out. He looked Hispanic, and stood just a couple of inches taller than her, about five foot eight, Kit figured. A scar bisected his right cheek. His eyes were brown, his skin leathery and dark, and when he looked at Kit, she felt like he was undressing her. "*Buenos dias, señorita.* What are you doing?"

Kit tugged at her UVA cap to draw attention to it, smiled, and said, "Looking for a tree. Found what I was looking for right back there." She gestured back toward the live oak.

"What kind of a tree are you talking about?" The man shifted his weight.

"It's an oak, a live oak. *Quercus virginiana.* You see, we're working on a project . . ." Kit lapsed into a speech full of as much technical jargon as she could think of on the fly, a tactic designed to sound intelligent and bore the man as quickly as possible. It worked—she saw his eyes glaze over.

He finally interrupted her. "This is private property, you understand? You stay off of it." The man spat on the ground.

"Who's the owner?" she said eagerly, "because I'd like to . . ."

The man looked around. "You are here by yourself?"

"Oh, no!" Kit replied. "There's a bunch of us."

"Really, *chica?* Where are the others?"

Kit saw a glint in his eye that she didn't like and when he took a step forward, she quickly moved away. Then her cell phone rang. "Hello? Yes? I got the live oak, Steve. I'm almost to the road. I'll meet you there," she said, without taking her eyes off the man. She snapped the phone shut, making a mental note to call her boss later and explain. "I have to go meet my partners," she said to the man, and walked away, aware that the man's eyes were following her, conscious of any sound he might make. And as she walked past his truck, she glanced back, and memorized his tag number.

⊙══╪══⊙

Grateful to be away from the scarred man, Kit turned onto the main north-south road, Rt. 13, and called Connie Jester back on Chincoteague. She told Connie what information she needed. "Grease the skids for me, would you please?" she asked.

She called her boss, left a voicemail message explaining her odd call but minimizing the danger. Steve wouldn't like her taking risks on her own. Then she dialed a member of the support staff at her office in Norfolk. "I need you to run some plates for me," Kit said.

Juanita was good at her job, and the answer came back just a few minutes later. "C&R Enterprises in Accomack County. You need an address?"

"Sure."

Kit wrote down what she gave her.

When Kit got to the courthouse, she found out quickly that Connie had paved the way. The clerk in the county land records office welcomed her, offering plenty of information. "Well, yes," Mary Granger said. "You can see here: I think this is the property you're talkin' about. Only I'm hopin' you're not thinkin' about a big development or anything, 'cause I'd hate to see all that land get et up."

Kit assured her she was not talking about hundreds of homes.

"Well, this here farm is 237 acres. Owner's name is . . . let's see . . . C&R Enterprises. That'd be Curtis and Richards, Sam Curtis and Tom Richards. Tom's married to Sam's daughter. They own five or six pieces of property in the county, not including their own homes. Don't think they'll sell to you, not as long as they're making money in tomatoes and corn."

"The house on the property looks pretty old."

"Sure is. That's an 1870 farmhouse. Why I remember when Grammy Curtis lived there. Her old man got killed, got messed up in a harvester. She stayed on, though, working that farm and raising them kids on her own." Mary shook her head. "Sammy, he was the smartest of the bunch. Hard work got 'im where he is, that's it. Hard work."

Kit bent over the county tax maps. She pointed to a small rectangle. "What's this building?"

"That'd be the tomato plant. See, the growers' pickin' crews, they bring the tomatoes in, wash 'em, grade 'em, and then ship 'em off."

"Does C&R own that, too?"

"Yes, ma'am. I told ya. Sammy's smart."

◦═══✦═══◦

Accomack County had not yet put its land records on computer, so Kit had to be content with copies of plats and copious notes. Leaving the county office building, her hands full of papers, Kit rounded a hedge and stopped short. There, parked next to her Subaru, sat a white pickup truck like the one she'd seen on the live oak farm's lane. She glanced around. She didn't see the scar-faced man who'd been driving it. But as she approached her Subaru, he stepped out from behind a large van parked nearby.

A cold chill raced through Kit. She'd left her gun in her car in case there was a metal detector in the courthouse. She hugged the papers to her chest and laced her keys through her fingers so that one protruded through each gap in her now-clenched fist. Then she met the man's leering gaze straight on.

"Ah, we meet again," the man said. As he smiled, his gold tooth glinted in the bright sun. "I pay my taxes," he said, tapping an envelope in his left hand. He nodded toward the papers in her hand. "You get everything you need?"

He was standing right in front of her driver's side door. "Yes. Now excuse me," she said, moving forward.

But the man didn't move, and Kit found herself just inches from his face. She could smell the alcohol on his breath, and the sweat that permeated his clothes.

"Let me tell you something," he said, his eyes glittering with anger, "it is not safe for a young woman like you to be alone out there, in the country, so far from help. Things could happen, you know? Bad things, that would be in your dreams for the rest of your life."

"Move away from my car," Kit commanded. "Now."

"Oh, you are a strong woman. I see. But really, you know, it would take only one man, just one, to start the nightmares." Then he stepped back, swept his arm grandly toward her car, and said, "Here you go, señorita. *Buenos dias.*"

The confrontation had Kit adrenalized all the way back to Chincoteague. He was trying to scare her. He had clearly followed her. And now he had identified the car she drove and knew that she'd been to the county records office. Her cover might have been blown—in any case, she wouldn't be as free to explore the area around the farm, or question locals, now that she'd been spotted. She was going to need help.

Kit compulsively glanced in her rear-view mirror. Was the man following her now? Not so that she could see. She'd hate for him to find out she lived alone on Chincoteague.

Convinced no white truck was on her tail, she stopped at an Office Depot and bought an all-in-one printer/copier/fax machine. The time had come to cement the deal with Steve, to get him to commit to her ongoing investigation. She would use Google Earth to create satellite views of the farmhouse where the oaks were located, the tomato fields, the tomato processing plant, and the surrounding area. She'd create a PowerPoint show that would include those views plus the botanist's data, the autopsy report and pictures of the body, and the data she'd collected on migrant labor—basically all the information she'd collected so far. And she'd include information about the man with the gold tooth.

One problem: even she thought her case was thin. She had no suspect, no crime scene, no means, motive, or opportunity. Just a suspicious man, some tomato seeds, a handful of acorns, a little dead beach child—and her gut instincts.

A key piece of the puzzle came from an unexpected quarter.

13

Kit, I'm sorry to call you so late, but she's been crying for three hours." Piper's voice sounded frantic.

"Who has?"

"Patricia. Look, she's ready to talk. She needs to talk."

Kit glanced at her watch. Nearly 11:00 p.m. and she was only halfway through preparing the presentation. "I've got a big meeting tomorrow in Norfolk. Why don't we get together then, late in the afternoon, say around 4:00?"

"Not you, Kit. Or Chris. She wants to talk to that guy—David."

"He's not here, Piper. I don't know where he is." That was the truth. The house on Main Street had been dark every time she'd passed it. His car was gone. The painting had not progressed. Where was he?

Kit swallowed hard. She heard Piper say something to the Latina. Then Piper said, "Listen to her, Kit," and she must have passed her phone to Patricia.

In very broken English, the woman began to speak. "My friend, she has trouble. I scared it is that man, the one brought us from Mexico."

"What man? What's his name?" Kit figured if the woman was serious she'd start giving up some worthwhile information.

The Latina hesitated. "Hector."

"What's his last name?"

"That is all I know. We call him 'Hector.' I hear he get trouble when I run. My friend, she run first. Months before me. Then he find her! He take her. I scared what he do. I really scared, missy."

What was she saying? That the trafficker had tracked down one of his escaped victims? Kit needed to know more. Most of all, she needed to know if Patricia was sincere. "I will try to help you, Patricia, but you have to help me. Who were the people you were forced to work for?"

Silence followed.

"I need to know, Patricia, before I can help."

"OK. I tell you. Barnes. Robert and Rhonda Barnes. They live on Seaview Avenue in Norfolk. Big white house. The number is 2317."

"And what's your friend's name, the one who is missing?"

"Consuela Espinoza."

"She lived in Norfolk, with you?"

"Oh, no. She go up . . . up north. Almost to Maryland. She send me a message maybe six, eight months ago. Give to a man I know who comes to Norfolk sometimes with the tomatoes. It says she get away and go now to a place I do not know. But he find her! I know Hector find her . . . and now . . . please, please help her! He is no good, this Hector. No good."

"How do you know he found her?"

"I hear it. From people who come to the market."

"And where does Hector live?"

"I do not know that. He drive truck . . . a big white truck, from Mexico all the way to here. But I do not know where he lives."

When Kit hung up the phone she felt confused by and irritated at the interruption. What was she supposed to do with that information? Why did Piper have to call her at 11 o'clock at night? What could she do then? And how in the world could she identify a person with a name as common as Hector?

Kit tried getting back to her presentation. She printed some more files, created two new PowerPoint slides . . . but she couldn't let go of Patricia's phone call. So she fixed a pot of coffee and stepped out onto her deck as it brewed.

The night was warm and humid. Crickets and night insects clicked and buzzed in the weeds. The marsh and the channel were black, and from somewhere, Kit heard an owl hoot.

Puzzled both by Piper's phone call and her reaction to it, Kit stepped off the porch and walked down to her neighbor's dock. The neighbor's boat bobbed in the gentle waves of the channel. The horseshoe life preserver was hanging again on its hook, just where it had been when Kit had needed it for David.

She touched it. David. Where was he? She'd seen no sign of him at the house on Main Street. Someone from the police department had called her . . . David's kayak had been found, but they didn't know where he was staying. She'd given them directions, then tried to call him, but all she'd gotten was his voicemail.

In fact, she hadn't seen him for what . . . a week? More than a week. Where was he? And why did she want so much to talk to him?

Right now, smelling the salt marsh, looking out over the water, she was nagged by sadness, and tears came to her eyes.

She thought about how he'd helped her gather the acorns for her investigation, about the conversations they'd had all night, driving all that way to Wilmington, about his sense of humor and sheer masculinity. About how he'd talked—in Spanish— to Patricia, gaining her trust and discerning the basis in truth of her story. David was sharp. He had good law enforcement instincts. He seemed compassionate. And he was . . .

. . . and then, she got it—in a flash, she knew the significance of Piper's phone call: what if the man who brought Patricia up from Mexico was also trafficking people into the peninsula? What if he had moved her beach child's mother into this area? Or the boy himself?

Could he have been trafficking people out on the ocean? Could the boy have become a problem? And who was this man, Hector? And why would someone traffic a mother and child in. Unless . . . unless, he'd tricked the mother, told her she could bring the child, then stole the child to be sold, to whom?

Kit stopped there, fresh anger surging within her.

She turned to go back inside and looked up, and there, above her house appeared a white cross. She'd never noticed it before. Moving right to get a different angle on it, she realized what it was: her neighbor across the street had a flagpole shaped like a mast with a yardarm. You could only see the top of it over Kit's cottage, and it looked like a cross. David's cross. She had doubted him. Dismissed him. But there it was. She closed her eyes. Tears began running down her cheeks. "God, I'm so confused. Please help me figure all this out," she whispered, "my presentation, the case, and . . . and David. Everything, God. Just everything. I know I can't do this without you. But I'm so afraid . . . so afraid you'll let me down again. I'm so afraid."

⌒═╬═⌒

Kit smoothed her navy blue suit jacket as she waited for her boss in the conference room at the Norfolk FBI office. She touched the skin underneath her eyes, hoping no puffiness remained, hoping it didn't show the fatigue from staying up until 4:00 a.m. preparing her presentation. And the drive down had been arduous—police activity along Rt. 13 had delayed her for nearly an hour. It was a good thing she had left very early.

She heard a noise and looked up, expecting to see Steve Gould and the Assistant U. S. Attorney, who Steve had invited to sit in on their meeting. But Chris Cruz walked in, spit-shined and polished. "I see you got the memo," Chris said, tugging at the sleeves of his navy blue suit coat.

She smiled. "But you forgot the ruffled collar."

He laughed.

Steve Gould followed seconds later. Behind him strode a short, intense man with small eyes and a pronounced cowlick, wearing a black suit, a white shirt, and a gray-striped tie, the AUSA, Kit presumed. "This is Mark Handley," Steve said, confirming her guess. "Special Agents Kit McGovern and Chris Cruz." His introductions prompted handshaking all around and then rustling as everyone took a seat around the conference table.

Steve gave her the go-ahead and Kit's stomach clenched as she passed out her handouts. Then she stood behind her laptop and started going through her PowerPoint presentation. As she progressively moved through her slides, she began to relax.

She told them about finding the boy's body on the beach, about the quantity of tomato seeds in his belly and the acorns in his pocket. She went through the findings of the botanist, and then presented the pictures of the live oaks and the farmhouse, and told them about the scar-faced man.

The squad secretary interrupted Kit's presentation, entering the room and handing Steve a note. He frowned as he read it. "A state trooper was shot to death early this morning on Rt. 13," he said to the others.

"That must have been the police activity I passed on the way down!" Kit said. The crime scene investigation she'd passed had completely closed southbound Rt. 13. Traffic had been diverted to the other side of the road, causing massive delays.

"Pulled over a white box truck with stolen plates and apparently the driver shot him and destroyed the dashboard camera."

"Do they have the truck?" Chris asked.

Steve nodded. "They're just now taking it to the state police garage." He took a deep breath and looked at Kit. "Continue."

The men were looking at her expectantly. Kit tucked a stray hair behind her ear. She refocused on her own case. She told them about the gunfire from the boat on the open ocean, the scar-faced man and his aggressive behavior, mentioned the crews she'd observed working in the fields, the basics of tomato production on the Eastern Shore, and then finally brought in the information Patricia had provided her the night before: the indication that she and others had been trafficked into Virginia, forced into domestic servitude, and that at least one victim might have been abducted following her escape from her captors.

The AUSA began peppering her with questions. How long had the boy been dead? What did she think was the connection with her beach child? Why would traffickers move people over the water? What made her think that there was enough of a need for domestic servants on the peninsula to warrant trafficking? Why would an eight-year-old boy be part of this scenario, anyway? "I think it's far more likely that he was just an illegal alien and now his grieving parents just don't want to draw the attention of the law," Mark said.

All the while, Chris Cruz sat with his hand touching his chin, as if he were lost in thought. Kit glanced at him from time to time, trying to read his mind. Finally he spoke. Dropping his hand, he looked at Kit. "What kind of vehicle was Patricia transported in?"

"A large box truck," Kit said, and right away she saw where he was going.

Steve Gould tapped his pen on the table. He got it, too. He glanced at the AUSA, then looked at Kit. "You now have the names of the people who held this victim, right?"

"Yes," Kit confirmed.

Steve nodded. "Start there. You agree, Mark? See where that leads?" Seeing the AUSA nod, he turned to Chris. "You give some hours to this. You work with Kit and see what we need—surveillance, subpoenas, whatever—to go after these people, Robert and Rhonda Barnes."

Kit interrupted him, her heart pounding. "Steve, I think they're just the tip of the iceberg. I want to check out this operation on the peninsula. As Chris suggested, whoever was driving that box truck last night didn't want the trooper to see what was in it. It might have been drugs . . . but it could have been people, too."

Her boss's neck reddened. "You haven't made the connection to my satisfaction. For all we know the trucker was carrying dog food."

Kit thought fast. "Let me look into this C&R Enterprises. Let me check out why that guy driving their truck was so aggressive. See if there's a connection with the trooper who was shot. Let me find out who 'Hector' is."

"Sounds like you're not ready to leave the beach."

His comment took Kit aback. Flustered, she groped for words. Surprisingly, Chris stepped in. "I see her point, boss. How about I work on this Norfolk couple, while Kit takes the lead on the peninsula?"

Steve grimaced. "All right. But Kit, if you hit a dead end, you're back here, understand?"

The scar-faced man could identify her green Subaru Forester, so Kit traded it in for her Bureau car, a dark blue Crown Victoria. Then she drove to her apartment, fixed coffee, and while it brewed, leafed through the stack of mail her neighbor Ellen had left on her counter.

Her heart nearly stopped when she saw the familiar handwriting on the pink envelope. Another card. Gee, thanks.

And maybe it was leftover tension from the meeting, or fatigue, or just sheer loneliness, but tears sprang to her eyes, and she bit her lip to keep the feelings at bay. Then she went to her bedroom, jerked open the closet door, and threw the card in the box with the others—many, many others, collected over the course of twenty-four years.

Kit grabbed what she needed from the apartment and left. Halfway across the Chesapeake Bay Bridge tunnel, she remembered the coffee.

⊙━╳━⊙

Over the next two days, Kit visited the marinas in Wachapreague as well as the ones on Chincoteague and in Ocean City to see if they'd observed any unusual activity lately. She spent an hour with an emotionally engaged state police captain, furious at the loss of one of his own men.

"He called it in: he was pulling over a large white box truck for speeding at 2:00 a.m. on U.S. 13," Captain Roy Grizzle stated succinctly. "The next thing we know, dispatch can't raise him. So our dispatcher sent another trooper to check on him. Meanwhile, a citizen calls in on a cell phone. There's a state police car, he says, on the side of the road, lights flashing, with no trooper in sight. Right behind a white box truck.

"The second trooper found Chip in the ditch with two bullets in his head." Grizzle shook his head. "When I find that son of a . . ."

"I'm sorry," Kit said.

"Chip had a wife and two teenage sons. Plus, he's going to be hard to replace." Grizzle threw a wad of paper toward his trashcan, missed, and let it lie on the floor.

His office was cramped and gray: gray desk, gray chairs, gray carpet. White walls. Kit felt like she was in a fog. "When is the funeral?"

Grizzle scratched out the pertinent information on a note pad, tore off the top sheet, and handed it to her. "Look, what can I do for you? What'd you come here for?"

Kit told him about finding the boy's body on the beach, about the link to the farm where the live oaks were, about the trafficking leads they had, and her concerns that all of this information might be connected.

Grizzle listened to her, but Kit could tell by the way his eyes kept shifting to the paperweight on his desk that he wasn't the least bit interested. "All I can say," he responded when she finished, "is keep in touch. If we find whoever killed Chip, we'll let you know. Maybe then we can help you."

❦

She was pumping gas at the gas station on Main Street in Chincoteague when Rick Sellers pulled up right behind her. "I thought that was you!" he said. "How's it going?" He straightened his Coast Guard uniform. Sweat beaded on his forehead.

"All right. How about you?" Kit squinted into the sun.

"Heard about that cop shooting." Rick leaned against her back fender and ran his hand down the edge of her car. "This is a different car, isn't it? Don't you drive a Forester?"

Kit didn't answer that question. "What's the word about the shooting?"

"Nothing. Just that it happened. Weird summer, I'll tell you that." He flashed a smile. "You feel like dinner sometime?"

She quickly calculated a response. "I'm pretty busy right now."

He laughed. "I'll take that as a no." His tone remained neutral. "You got any more on that kid?"

Kit shook her head. "Not really. You?"

"Haven't heard a thing."

Later that afternoon, Connie called, asking if she could come by and retrieve some items the property owner had left in the cottage. Of course, Kit told her. Reflexively, she put on a pot of coffee. Something in Connie's voice told Kit she needed to talk.

14

Connie kept her red hair pulled back in a low ponytail. She had on white Capris and a bright pink shirt, defying any theory of a redhead's "colors." She gave Kit a hug at the door. "Honey, I'm so sorry to bother you."

"You're no bother! Come in." Kit led her into the cottage.

There was one locked closet in the cottage. Connie went immediately to it, used a key to release the lock, and pulled out a file folder thick with papers. "They may be thinking about selling this place," she said, over her shoulder.

"Really?"

"Yep. She wants this bunch of papers mailed priority. Everybody's in a hurry these days."

"Are you?"

"What?"

"Are you in a hurry? Have time for coffee?"

"Of course, honey. Of course."

They sat on either end of the couch, facing each other, and Connie chattered on about the news of the island. Emma Mae's daughter's gettin' married. Henry Wilson's got cancer. Seems a shame. His momma and poppa both died of it . . . All the while, she twisted a napkin in her hands.

"So what's going on with you?" Kit asked. "You seem tense."

Connie snapped up that grounder. "I tell you, I'm scared."

"About . . ."

"All this stuff goin' on."

"Stuff?"

"The murders! First the boy, then that cop went and got himself shot. They've been stopping every truck out there on 13. Even my Bob got questioned!"

"That's routine. They're looking for witnesses."

"They had a checkpoint. Like Russia or something. Everybody had to stop, show ID, answer a bunch of questions . . . delayed him two hours that night. I was sick to death with worry." Connie sat down on the couch. "That man is never late." She hunched her shoulders and huddled over her steaming mug.

"Bob's innocent, so he's got nothing to worry about." Kit smiled to reassure her. "He runs nights, right? So they wanted to know if he saw anything."

"That's exactly what he said. But I tell you, Kit, it's worrisome." Connie fixed her eyes on Kit. "I'm so tired of all this. Why last night, there I saw this big, lighted sign on Rt. 13 saying 'Murder Info: Call State Police. Reward.'" Connie shivered. "It's givin' me the heebie-jeebies. First, we got a boy's body on the beach. Nobody in my family ever heard of nothin' like that. A little boy! At the beach! Then we got a cop shot. My cousin said a third one's on the way."

"A third what?"

"A third death. They come in threes."

Kit laughed. "They come in a lot more than threes, Connie, let me tell you."

Connie very pointedly did not smile. "You may be used to dealin' with this stuff but we ain't. Not here. Not on Chincoteague. I got a premonition, or something. Been wakin' up at night. That's not like me. Bob says I sleep like a horse that's been run all day. Not now."

Kit traced her finger around the edge of her coffee mug. Why did she derive such comfort from a cup of coffee, even on a hot day? Connie clutched hers as if her life depended on it. Her fingernails were white from the force of her grip. "Connie, I understand you're spooked. But I don't see any connection between the little boy we found and the state trooper. It's just coincidental. Bad timing. Don't get superstitious! Besides, what do you always tell me? 'God's in charge.'"

Connie's eyes narrowed. "God's in charge, all right. That don't mean we got to like what he's lettin' happen. I'm tellin' you, there's a third death comin'. And if you don't watch it, it could be you."

"What are you talking about?"

"I heard what you did for David O'Connor."

Kit's face grew hot. "From whom?"

"He told me."

"When?"

"The other day."

The other day? So David was here, on the island? Just the other day? Why hadn't she seen him, Kit wondered. She tried to minimize the rescue. "It was easier than when I was life-guarding on the ocean."

"I remember you doing that," Connie responded. "One of the few women they'd take."

Kit took a sip of coffee. "He shouldn't have been out in that storm, that's all."

"He said you risked your life. Said he would've drowned but for you." Connie rubbed her hand on her Capris. "You cheated the Grim Reaper outta Number Three. He won't let that go by."

Kit laughed. "Connie, that's ridiculous." What did they teach at Connie's little island church?

"You'd best be careful, Kit. I don't want to have to be calling your father and explainin' how you met your demise here on Chincoteague." She shook her head. "It was bad enough, him going through . . ." she hesitated, looking like someone who'd just realized she'd walked into a private room, ". . . what he did."

Kit felt a rush of emotion, like a primal scream, race through her.

Connie watched her over the rim of her cup as she took a sip. "You ever see your momma?"

Her heart pounded. She set her jaw. "No."

"She don't call you?"

"No." Kit put her mug down, stood up, and walked away. "Her idea of motherhood is sending me a card once in a while."

"She tell you how she is?"

"I don't know. I never open them."

Connie's hand rubbed her coffee mug. "It must have hurt your dad bad, her walkin' off like that. Your dad and you kids, too."

Kit shrugged. "Hey, it is what it is. I don't think about it anymore."

"How old were you?"

"Eight."

Connie seemed to chew on that for a bit. She smoothed her Capris. "I saw your momma after she left."

I don't care, Kit thought. *I don't care, I don't care, I don't care.*

"She came over here to talk to your Daddy's mother, Miss Margaret. Right there in that Main Street house. I happened to be there when she showed up."

Kit felt her jaw tighten. Words and images began appearing and disappearing on the walls of her mind, things she hadn't thought about in years, exploding and fading like fireworks in a darkened sky. Please stop.

"I think she wanted to explain, needed to explain . . ."

"There was nothing to explain!" Kit exploded. "She walked away from her family. Quit. Abandoned a husband and two children who loved her to pursue her own life."

"Is that what your daddy told you?"

"My father never said a bad word about her." Kit crossed her arms. "He didn't need to. I saw it myself. Saw the selfishness. Even at age eight." She frowned. "She left . . ."

"Just like Eric."

Kit's eyes widened.

Connie didn't stop. "And you came here to grieve that." She shook her head. "Only next thing I know, you're working again." She stood up and walked to the kitchen sink, poured out what remained of her coffee, rinsed her cup, and filled it with water. She turned around to face Kit again, and leaned against the counter. "Your dad's done good, raisin' you two." She lifted her mug to her lips, took a drink, lowered it again. "He's such a fine lawyer. So smart. I remember when he won that big case in D.C., that Mobley case, everyone was so proud."

Kit lifted her chin. She was only five or six when that case claimed the front page of *The Washington Post* for days and cemented her father's reputation. She'd read the stories much, much later.

"And your brother . . . brilliant. All of you are bright, aggressive people." She pursed her lips, then looked straight at Kit, her eyes soft. "Did you ever think . . . did you ever think it was just too much? Too much for her?"

"Too much? One husband? Two little kids? I was eight. How threatening can an eight-year-old be?" Why did an image of Eric run through her mind?

"Your mother is so creative, so artistic . . ."

Kit shot her a look. "What did my grandmother say to her?"

"I didn't stay for their whole talk. I know Miss Margaret was surprised. I also know she invited her in and made tea. Your mother had the look of a rabbit chased near to death by hounds. I felt sorry for her." Connie took a deep breath.

Kit attacked. "Sorry for her? My dad didn't abuse her, didn't yell at her, didn't do anything but be who he was. I guess that wasn't good enough for her. You know she has a whole new family on the West Coast? She left us and started over. Traded us in." Kit paced away. "I guess we weren't what she wanted. 'Smart' and 'aggressive' weren't good enough for her. So she had to try again. I sure hope those kids measure up, because if they don't," she gestured as if she was cutting her throat. "My mother," Kit said, "is totally unreliable." She lifted her chin. "I'm glad she left."

Connie's eyes reflected shock. She cleared her throat, paused, then spoke in a soft, distant voice. "Y'know, my mother had a hard time lovin' me. Took me 'til my thirties before I began to see what the problem was. My momma saw in me a dim reflection of herself and *that's* who she was rejecting over and over and over. Not me. Her."

What's that got to do with me? Kit wanted to scream.

"I started gettin' over it, when I realized that. But it took forgiving, and that took letting go of something deep inside. I had to let the little girl inside cry, and then ask God to heal her. I had to believe that Scripture that says 'All things work together for good for those who love the Lord and are called according to his purpose.' I had to believe that. Then I could forgive my momma."

Kit's fists clenched but she remained speechless.

Connie shook her head as if dislodging her thoughts. She gave Kit a hug and picked up her keys. "Thanks for the coffee. I'm sorry if I stirred the pot. I guess I'm jus' scared. Bob says the devil's afoot. I laughed at him, but I'm beginning to b'lieve him. Thing is, God's in charge. Thanks for the reminder, honey. I hope I didn't upset you none."

❦

For two restless days and nights, Connie's visit plagued Kit. Images swarmed her like wasps every time she dropped her guard. She saw her father, sitting at the kitchen table with his head in his hands. She saw the empty space in the garage where her mother's car used to be. And she saw the day she came home from school, second-grade papers in hand, to find her older brother eating cereal at the kitchen table.

Where's Mom? she had asked.

She's gone.

Where?

I dunno. Just gone. Gone for good. Justin got up and threw his cereal milk down the drain. *Go look in her room.*

Kit raced up the stairs. She stood staring at her mother's empty closet, the papers in her hand fluttering to the floor. Then she burst into tears.

Shut up! Justin said as she came back into the kitchen. *Don't cry! Dad will be home when he gets out of court. Now shut up. Only girls cry.*

Only girls cry. Thinking about those days left Kit feeling like a little kid. Why? Why now? She'd dealt with the reality of her mother's abandonment for years. Why were these feelings still so potent?

It's true: she'd never really talked out what happened, and the way she felt, with the men in her life. Not her father. Or her brother. They all just soldiered on. And when was the last time she'd had a heart-to-heart talk with a female friend? In college? With her roommates? Before her marriage?

153

She lived in a man's world. Her father. Her brother. Her husband. The men at work. It felt natural to her, but just now, talking to Connie, she realized she'd left her heart behind somewhere. Misplaced it. And she wondered if she'd ever get it back.

⊙━┿━⊙

Several nights later, Kit's cell phone rang. She looked at the caller ID. Her heart jumped. Oh, God, she thought, please help me stay strong. Bracing herself, she resolutely pushed the button.

"Kit," David said. His voice sounded tense.

What was wrong? "Where have you been?"

"I'll tell you about that later. I need your help."

"What now, David? What now? I told you . . ."

"Look," he said, taking a deep breath, "this is not about you. Or me. Honest."

She didn't respond.

"Can you come over here?"

"Why?" she could hear the resistance in her own voice.

"Kit, listen to this."

Another voice came on the phone. "Miss McGovern? Alice Pendleton here."

The famous photographer?

"We need you ASAP."

15

HOW LONG HAD DAVID BEEN BACK ON CHINCOTEAGUE? WHERE HAD he been? What did he want? Why was Alice Pendleton at his house? Kit alternately chastised herself for her rudeness and prayed on the eight-minute drive to David's. What in the world did he want?

An old, battered Ford sedan sat in the driveway. Kit pulled up beside it, jogged to the front porch, and mounted the steps.

"Evenin'," a man's voice said, startling her. An elderly man with a bald head and a big potbelly sat in the wicker rocker on the dark front porch.

"Hi," Kit said, cautiously. "Is David inside?"

"Yep. Alone with my wife."

Just then, David came to the door, and Kit felt a rush of emotion. Her eyes were captured by his arm, held in a sling. "What happened?"

"The doc said to rest it."

"What doc?"

"The guy who put me back together after I got shot. I went back to D.C. for a while." David's eyes were searching her face like a rock climber searching for a handhold. She looked away to break his gaze. "Come in," he said, suddenly. "I'm sorry . . . I . . . uh . . ."

She stepped past him into the familiar room. She could feel his presence. The smell of his aftershave, the brush of his arm against hers, the look in his face all sent emotions surging inside her. She wanted to tell him about the cop. She wanted to tell him about farm and the man with the scar on his face. She wanted to tell him about Connie and her mother and all the stuff that churned inside her. She put her hand to her forehead to calm down.

"Go into the kitchen," David said.

Kit threaded her way through the living room. A gray-haired woman sat at the kitchen table, photographs spread out before her.

"Kit, this is Alice Pendleton," David said. There was a quiet tension in his voice, like a taut wire vibrating. "Ms. Pendleton, Kit McGovern."

"Good evening, young lady." Alice Pendleton had a mass of gray hair caught up in a bun and held in place with a tortoiseshell barrette. Her gray eyes were sharp but the wrinkles around their edges made her look kind. She wore khaki pants and a long-sleeved green L. L. Bean shirt with an egret pin on the collar.

"It's very nice to meet you, Mrs. Pendleton," Kit said. "I've admired your work for a long time."

"Nothing to it," Alice responded, "long as you're willing to tromp through a marsh."

David picked up a photo from the table and handed it to her. "Look at this," he said.

In the photo, Kit saw a dock. On the tops of three pilings sat three seagulls, all looking the same direction. In the background, she could see what looked like the corner of a building and the edges of a parking lot. She looked at David, puzzled.

"Now check these out." He handed her three more photographs. Each was a progressive enlargement of the background of the first shot, which grew fuzzier with each frame. "What do you see?"

"The edge of a building. A car or truck, three people . . . wait, what is this, David?" Kit looked up at him. "Is someone forcing the woman into that truck? Abducting her?"

"That's what I think."

Kit's stomach tightened. She studied the pictures carefully, using light and angle to see every square inch, holding them close and then at arm's length.

"I never did see it the day I got those shots," Mrs. Pendleton said. "I was just taking pictures, like I always do. But when I looked at them on my computer, I couldn't believe my eyes. So I thought, I'll have this nice young man look at them, since he's a police officer."

"Where did you take them?" Kit asked.

"Behind that motel across the street. At their dock. I went out there to get the sunset. But I saw these seagulls and, well, something made me take that shot."

Kit looked at David. "What are you thinking?"

"I'm thinking that's Maria, the desk clerk. I know her. Well, I talked to her sometimes. I recognize the dress."

Kit felt an odd twinge. Of course, he'd be attracted to other women. And they to him. She closed her eyes momentarily, trying to refocus. "When did you last see her?"

"The day before Mrs. Pendleton took those shots."

"And when was that?"

"Thursday, three weeks ago," David and the photographer said in unison.

"Look, Kit," David said, running his hand through his hair, "here's what I want. Can you run those tags for me?" Kit looked at the photographs again. Visible beside the building's edge was the front of a truck, and a partial license plate.

"It's a Ford Super Duty," David said. "I can tell by the grill design. Not too many of those around, compared to the 150. So if we looked up the model and the vehicle color . . ."

"What are these numbers?" Kit became aware of a growing tension in her shoulders and her neck.

"Those last three digits? 5-3-9. That's what I'm seeing, anyway."

A cold chill swept over Kit. "Could they be 5-8-9?"

David squinted at the photographic blow-up. "Well, yes, yes, I think so. Why?"

"Because if those are the numbers, I know that truck." She glanced toward Mrs. Pendleton, then back to David. "It belongs to the company that owns the farm where the live oaks are."

"The oaks? You got an identification?" David asked, raising his eyebrows.

"Yes." Then, because she didn't want to reveal anything else, she said, "Mrs. Pendleton, may we keep these photos?"

"Of course!"

"Thank you so much for bringing this to our attention."

Mrs. Pendleton waved her hand. "Say no more, young lady. I'll be getting on out of here." She rose. "My work is done."

❦

David rubbed his left arm, still in a sling, with his right hand. "What do we have?" he asked Kit, when the Pendletons had left.

We? Kit took a deep breath. "The forensic botanist identified the acorns in the boy's pockets as coming from the same tree as our sample D6."

"Which one was that?"

"Do you remember the farm with the long lane, and the old house with all the windows broken out? The tomato fields were in front of the house, stretching out quite a ways."

"Yeah. I remember." David paced. "So who owns it?"

"C&R Enterprises. Same company that owns the truck." She gestured toward the photo on the table.

"You want to go take a look? In the morning?"

"I've been there."

"With who?"

"By myself."

His frown conveyed his disapproval.

She told him about the farm, then asked, "What's Maria's last name?"

"I don't know."

"All right. That's the first step: I need to check with the motel and get all the info on her I can." She tossed her head. "Thanks, David. I'll take it from here."

"No, I'll go to the motel."

"No."

"Yes." He rubbed his arm. "Kit, I knew this girl. I spoke with her many times. I can't just pretend she's a stranger." The tendons in his jaw were popping. "You have pictures of the farm?"

She nodded.

"I want to see them."

Her resistance lasted two seconds. "OK. Go talk to the motel manager, then . . . then come to my place. I'll fill you in."

Why did I invite him to my house, Kit wondered as she drove back to her place. She hit the steering wheel with her hand. "I hate this!" she said out loud, but a large part of her didn't hate it at all. A large part of her couldn't wait until he showed up.

"The guy's not right," David said half an hour later when he walked into Kit's kitchen.

"What do you mean?"

"Jackson Montgomery. The motel manager. He's hiding something."

"What?"

"Maybe he's part of the abduction. Maybe he was using her. Maybe he smokes dope. I don't know yet."

"Did he give you the information?"

David held out a paper. "He said it was everything he had on her."

Kit took it and read Maria's name, "Maria Allessandro," her Social Security number, address of record, and a phone number.

"I tried the phone number on the way over here. It's not in service. You look up the social and I'll bet you find the same thing."

Indeed, the Social Security number traced back to one Maria Allessandro of Philadelphia, an 85-year-old widow. "False identity," Kit confirmed to David when she hung up the phone. "The 'home address' is an abandoned warehouse in Salisbury."

"All right. So she's illegal ..."

"Not necessarily," Kit said, pacing. "If she's a trafficking victim she might have been brought into the country on a valid six-month visa. Most victims don't even know their visas will expire in that time. The trafficker, who provided them with the visa, keeps the passport, and the victim is then trapped. They don't go to the authorities because they've been told they'll be in trouble. Or the trafficker threatens their family back home. So she could be using a false identity because the trafficker has her legal papers." Kit looked at David. His deep brown eyes were fixed on her and in them she saw the emotion she was trying to resist. She took a deep breath. "You want to see the whole slide show? The presentation I gave my boss and the AUSA?"

"Absolutely."

David sat beside her at the table. Slide by slide, they went through her presentation. She could hear him breathing, feel his leg when he moved, smell the Irish Spring soap he'd showered with. She fought to stay focused on her work.

When they finished, he said, "I'm impressed."

Kit smiled.

"No, really. I'm impressed. Cops don't do stuff like that, not at my level, anyway."

"I had to make the case to get approval to continue. I just kept thinking that I couldn't leave that boy on the beach, all by himself. Remember what you told me? A homicide case is a sacred trust. I owe him a fight for justice in his case. And now ... now I think we may also be fighting for some living people. The boy is pointing us to them, you know what I mean?"

"I know exactly what you mean."

Kit turned back to the photos on the table. "I need to go to Norfolk. I want to look at the financial records of this C&R Enterprises. I want to talk to Immigration. My partner," she saw David's eyes flicker, "my partner needs to see these photos."

"Your partner?"

"Yes. Chris Cruz. You remember him? He helped pull you out of the channel."

"Oh, yeah."

"He worked a prostitution trafficking case up here a couple of years ago so our boss thought he might be helpful to me." Kit reminded him about Patricia's panicked phone call, which Kit had outlined in the presentation. "Chris is checking out that couple. I think we need to compare notes. Plus, I need to recruit some more help. We need to set up surveillance, find out the identity of the guy I saw driving that truck . . ." She looked at David. "We can take it from here, David."

He set his jaw. "I'm going to the farm."

"No, don't."

"I've got to see it."

"Stay out of it, David."

Kit saw something—anger?—ignite in his eyes. "Maria's in trouble, Kit. There's no way I can just sit in Chincoteague like some . . . some cripple waiting for the FBI to fix it."

"It's not your case."

"I may not have jurisdiction, but I can go to a farm in Glebe Hill. As far as I know, common citizens are still allowed there."

"By yourself?"

His face reddened. "If this is the same guy that killed that boy, he didn't kidnap Maria to take her to a baseball game. Somebody's got to find her. Now. Without waiting to put together a PowerPoint show."

She felt a surge of anger. "So go talk to the police!"

"And say what? Some girl whose name probably isn't Maria didn't look happy when she got shoved into a truck? The Chincoteague cops will say they don't have enough to go on. And do you think the state police . . . fired up because they just lost one of their own . . . are gonna care?"

"OK, David. Go where you want. Do whatever!" She waved her hand in the air. "That's always worked for you before, from what I understand."

On the drive down to Norfolk the next day, Kit tried to characterize David's reactions. Bullheaded came to mind. Stubborn. Insistent. Impulsive. When "loyal" and "courageous" tried to sneak in the lineup, she thrust them aside. Likewise the guilt from her own sarcasm, which rose in her throat like bile.

Why were things so complicated?

16

Sliding on jeans and a chambray shirt, David O'Connor put a snub-nosed revolver into the sling he was wearing. Leaving the house, he got into his car and put his automatic pistol under the seat. He had armed himself as well with dozens of pictures of Maria—he'd convinced the motel manager to give him one from her employment files—with his cell phone number written on the back. David had concocted a story—Maria had ripped him off for $1,000 and he swore he'd find her. And although he didn't have a lot in his savings account, David had pulled out $400 in twenties. Information cost money, and he wasn't going to let money keep him from finding Maria. Or whatever her name was.

To cover his bases, before he left the island, David stopped at the Chincoteague Police Station, reported what he knew about the missing woman, and, as he suspected, the officer on duty wrote out a report but didn't offer a lot of encouragement. Leaving the station, he turned his Jeep toward the bridge, and left the island.

Driving over the causeway, David looked out over the marshes and felt a momentary twinge of regret. He saw cattle egrets, a great blue heron, two great egrets, a dozen or more fishing gulls, a few terns, and one osprey. He wished he were kayaking, a human invader quietly slipping through the salt marsh world, smelling the stands of cord grass, fending off mosquitoes, and watching as the natural world unfolded before him. Crabs, minnows, fish, turtles, birds, and insects, living together, dying together. He was a long way from the stress of his D.C. job. But he was walking right back into it. Intentionally. That struck even him as a little crazy.

Still, what could he do? Ignore a woman in trouble?

It took him about an hour to get to Glebe Hill. He had the farm's position marked in his GPS. At 9:00 a.m., the workers were in the field as David drove past, well aware he had one shot at making an initial reconnaissance. He looked for the pickup, but it was nowhere in sight, so he swung back around the loop he'd marked on his map, found a place to stow the Jeep, and walked through the woods to watch the place from a hill nearby. He took notes, standing under the oaks and poplars, counting the workers, watching their progress, noting the other buildings he'd seen while driving.

Then, around noon, he saw a van pull up and the workers get in, and he watched as it left the property and drove west on the small road abutting the farm. He was about to leave himself, when he saw the dust trail of a vehicle approaching. He waited, saw a white truck pull into the lane, and watched as a man got out and walked behind the house, disappearing as he did.

Where was that man going? David ran through the woods to get a different angle so he could see better. He stumbled down a hill, slammed his hurt shoulder into a tree, and, out of breath, stopped at the edge of the forest. He still couldn't quite see. But the corn in a field nearby stood about six-feet tall, and that gave him an idea.

David made his way down to the cornfield, and ran quickly across the twenty-foot grassy border around the field, an action which left him momentarily exposed. He ducked into a row of corn, began moving through the plants. The leaves rustled around him like paper. It felt eerie, not being able to see further than a row or two away—he realized in the middle of the field, surrounded by tall corn, that a churning harvester would never see him, or hear him, for that matter, and he could easily be killed in there. He wondered exactly when the corn would be taken down. Not today, he hoped. Please, not today.

His own words surprised him.

Near the end of the row, David crouched down in the dirt. He was a good twelve feet in from the edge of the cornfield and he hoped that that was enough to hide him. From there he could see that there was an old shed of some sort behind the house, and while he watched, the man he had seen driving the truck emerged, a package in his hand.

He looked Hispanic, about 5'8" or 5'9", cowboy hat . . . as David scribbled notes he saw the man glance over his shoulder, looking straight at the cornfield, and David froze.

But he must not have seen him, because the man turned and walked to his truck and drove off. That's when David noticed his slight limp.

What was in the package? Was the shed a drop zone? Why was the guy limping?

David waited five minutes, by his watch, and then walked quickly from the cornfield to the shed, which stood about twenty yards away.

Built of weathered boards, the shed was about ten by ten, with a roof which had a rudimentary chimney in the middle of it. David knew that on old farms, people smoked their meat, hams in particular, to preserve them. This building would fit that use.

The door was padlocked. David pulled it, but the lock didn't give. He peered through a crack in the boards, but the interior was dark. Walking around the shed, he used his free hand to feel for a loose board that would give him access. Nothing. The second time around he noticed a place on the back of the shed near the top where some boards had rotted just under the roof.

The sweat poured off of him as he paused to consider his next move. Looking through the rotting boards would mean jumping, and pulling himself up with both arms, despite his bad shoulder.

He took a deep breath. Carefully pulling out the revolver hidden in his sling, he removed both it and the sling and put them on the ground. Then he took out his small flashlight, turned it on, and put it between his teeth. He jumped up and reached for the hole created by the rotten boards, missed the first time, and tried again. This time he caught it. Tears came to his eyes and he groaned as his shoulders caught his weight. He used his legs and hoisted himself up, stuck the flashlight into the opening, and looked down.

David could see the beams of the old smokehouse. He could see hooks where the meat had been hung. On the right were shelves, like pantry shelves, filled with jars. But what was in the jars? It was dark, and brown.

Acorns. The jars were full of acorns. Shining his flashlight down to the left, he could see a large metal trunk—just the kind of thing you'd use to keep varmints out of whatever you were storing. The open lid revealed that it was empty.

He couldn't stay up any longer. David dropped to the ground, falling and grabbing his shoulder and crying out. The pain felt like a knife inserted in his shoulder blade. He sat down his back to the building, to catch his breath. "That probably wasn't smart," he said to himself.

But what was kept in that trunk? Then his hand touched something . . . a loose stone in the foundation. He moved it and was able to pull it out, along with several others. A hole opened up, not big enough for a man, but certainly big enough for a boy.

He was starting to put together a scenario involving a boy, some acorns, and a man doing something secretive when he heard the sound of a vehicle approaching. He looked around the side of the smokehouse. The van was coming back down the lane. He looked toward the cornfield. He had twenty yards of open ground to cover. Could he make it?

David scrambled to his feet. He picked up his sling and his gun. Then he looked around the shed again and saw the van had disappeared behind the house. If he could angle it right, he could keep the house and the shed between him and the van full of field workers. It would be a longer run, but it would be safer.

His heart hammering in his chest, David made a run for it, angling back toward the cornfield, glancing over his shoulder twice to make sure he remained on course. He burst into the space between two rows of corn, and moved quickly into the center of the field. Only then did he look back.

⌒━✦━⌒

Kit spent the morning in the Norfolk office typing up search warrants. Then Chris Cruz joined her, sitting down next to her. He began methodically straightening the pens and pencils scattered on the desk near him. Kit watched, curious. When he looked up, she said, "So, tell me about the Barneses."

"They denied keeping Patricia, of course," Chris said. "They said they hired her as a favor, and hoped to help her get her GED and then go to community college. Oddly, they didn't think to pay her Social Security, nor did they withhold taxes. Funny how that works out."

"And how did they find her?"

"Through an online ad." Chris picked a piece of fuzz off of his slacks. His eyes were blue and striking, so clear, and a marked contrast to his dark hair.

"What do they do for a living?"

"He's a lawyer. She has no job that we can tell."

"No kids?"

"No. Just a lot of art, all around the house. What we could see of it anyway." Chris shook his head. "They acted like Patricia had just run away from a wonderful opportunity. They were so surprised, after all they had done for her. When I pressed them for the name of the person who connected them, and mentioned little details like Social Security and taxes and work permits and so on, they lawyered up. Now, we're blocked until we can connect some more dots."

Chris went on, describing their house , the cars they drove, their looks and demeanor. He talked as if he'd been raised in a sophisticated home, and Kit wondered again how the son of two doctors had become an FBI agent. She'd worked with plenty of ex-cops, lawyers, and accountants. But vocations often ran in families and Chris's just didn't seem to fit.

"What about this woman abducted on the island?" Chris asked when he'd finished recounting his efforts.

"The picture just looks like a possible abduction. We're not sure."

"Could she be Patricia's friend?"

Kit shook her head. "Different name. Ages aren't close. Maria worked as a motel clerk. David O'Connor would talk to her sometimes."

"And where is he now?" Chris asked.

"I . . . I don't know. I have a feeling he may be trying to find her." The hollow in the pit of her stomach grew.

"Lone Ranger?"

"I guess." Kit showed Chris the search warrants she'd written up, detailing the Bureau's interest in C&R Enterprises' employee records, its business property filings, and other financial papers. "So what do you think?" she asked him when he'd had time to scan the paperwork.

"I think these will fly, once I tweak them a little. Let's fix them up and then we need to go see the judge."

◦═╪═◦

His sojourn in the cornfield left David grubby, as grubby as a farm worker, and that suited him just fine. Around 5:00 p.m., after checking into a nearby hotel, he drove to the closest bar.

Chico's was built of cinderblocks that, at some time in the past, had been white. Now they were varying shades of brown and gray . . . dirt and smoke-colored. Surrounded by a crushed oyster-shell parking lot, the bar had gang graffiti on one side and a propane tank out back.

The interior was dark and smelled like smoke. The bar, made of glossy, varnished wood, was scarred by knife marks. David slid onto a barstool, and waited. He was the only patron in the place. A few minutes later, a short man who David bet was from Mexico, walked out from the back.

"Buenos dias," David began. In Spanish, he asked him what there was to eat and ordered a round of enchiladas and Coke. When the man emerged a few minutes later, David casually struck up a conversation. How was business? When did most of his clients come in? How long had he been bartending?

When he'd established rapport, David let it slip that he needed a new ID. Then he pulled out a picture of Maria and asked the man if he'd ever seen the girl. He hadn't, and David slipped him a twenty, told him to keep the photo, and asked him to call him if he ever did. She'd stolen his wallet, David said, and he wanted it back.

He knew most men would buy the implication that she had ripped him off after a sexual encounter. He repeated this scenario many more times that night, stopping at bars, convenience stores, and sleazy restaurants. By midnight he was exhausted and dirty, he smelled like stale cigarettes, his stomach was rumbling from Chico's enchiladas, and he was no closer to finding Maria than he had been at the beginning of the day.

This is all seed work, he told himself. Just seed work. He went back to his motel, took a hot shower, and got into bed. After he turned the light out, he realized that, fatigued as he was, he couldn't sleep. Why? What was he feeling?

It was loneliness, he finally decided, and that in itself was odd, because he'd been by himself for a long, long time.

Frustrated, he turned the bedside light on and picked up one of the books Ben Heitzler, Kit's agent-friend in Washington, had given him. Confused by Kit's rejection, David had retreated to D.C. for a couple of weeks. He needed to see his doctor anyway, after his kayaking misadventure. But while in Washington, he decided to look up Ben, as Kit had suggested, and their time together had rocked his world. Ben was indeed a strong Christian. An initial discussion had led to long talks, late into the night, on topics so deep David thought he'd get lost in them—origin, purpose, destiny—things he thought about but rarely discussed with anyone. Ben's perspectives were new to David and he found them stimulating. The two men hit it off, and when David left, Ben had handed him three books: *The Case for Christ, The Reason for God,* and *Why Jesus?* along with a Bible. Now, David was digging into them whenever he had the chance, calling Ben with questions, and rethinking his life.

He opened *Why Jesus?* and began reading, and sometime after 2:00 a.m., his eyes finally shut.

⊙━━━◦

Kit spent two days going over the public tax and other records of C&R Enterprises, but it was a stray piece of information that she picked up from the state police that motivated her boss to move her case forward.

"A pacifier?" Steve Gould had responded when Kit told him about the item found in the white box truck at the scene of the police shooting.

"Right. Whoever shot that cop was smart enough to smash his dashboard camera. That, to me, implies someone trying to evade more than a routine traffic citation. There was something in that truck the driver didn't want the trooper to see. That truck was pretty big for someone carrying drugs. I think people is a more likely scenario. And the pacifier would go along with that."

"So what happened to the people? And why didn't the driver just drive off after he'd shot the trooper?"

"Because he knew the trooper had already called in his tag number. He shoots the cop, and he's Eastern Shore's Most Wanted. Everybody's after him. So he abandons the truck, which he knows is untraceable anyway, and takes off on foot."

"And where'd the people go?" Steve repeated.

Kit shifted in her seat, knowing she had no answer. "Let me go up there and look at the scene. Maybe there are tracks in the dirt."

"They looked."

"Maybe on the shoulder and the brush next to it. I'll look farther."

Gould shook his head. "You find tracks, or any other evidence of human cargo, and I'll authorize an offsite office up there for you."

"And more staff?"

Steve Gould blew out a breath. "And more staff."

⚬═══✦═══⚬

Chris Cruz, dressed in his blue business suit and Italian leather shoes, stepped daintily over the drainage ditch. "Over here," Kit said. She'd pushed her way through some briars on the edge of the road and had emerged on the edge of a soybean field. She watched as Chris worked his way carefully through an opening in the brush. She figured he was in the process of ruining another set of shoes.

"Look," Kit said, pointing down. The field was slightly muddy, and at one point, the dirt was compressed, like a path. The soybean plants beyond it lay crushed and flattened. Kit aimed her camera and took picture after picture.

A state trooper followed Chris. "I'll be darned," he said. "Are you telling me there were people in that truck?"

"That's what I think," Kit said. "I'd like you to consider having your evidence techs go over it again with that in mind. Maybe they'll find hairs with different DNA, or fibers, or something else that will help us out."

Chris looked around. "Where would they go?" He motioned toward what seemed like an endless field of plants.

"Who knows? In the dark, they could have moved a long way without anyone seeing them."

As Steve promised, the new lead resulted in a new offsite office. It stood in the back of an industrial park just off Rt. 13 in Accomack County. "We can put cots in the back and a mini-fridge and microwave," Kit said, as Tayloe Jones, the support staffer who'd found the place, showed them around. "The middle room will be the squad room, and up front will look like a regular small business reception area."

"Something as uninteresting as possible so no one ever comes in. Something like 'Hoover Radio Repair,'" Chris said.

Tayloe replied, "I'll have a sign made."

Kit looked at her watch. "We need to go. We're due to meet with Roger Lee from the state police in thirty minutes."

17

ROGER LEE WAS A FORTY-SOMETHING MAN WITH SALT-AND-PEPPER HAIR. Slim and fit, he wore his gray state police uniform well. His eyes were gray, too, and Kit noticed right away that he was left-handed. Like David. David's left shoulder bore the scar from his shooting incident. He'd been using his strong hand when he and his partner confronted the boy and had been shot in the left shoulder.

David. She needed to tell him about the investigation. She needed to warn him to stay out of it. She needed to make sure he remained out of the way if any arrests or shooting went down. She needed to . . . Kit forced her mind back into the present.

"So how can we help you?" Lee began.

Kit briefed him on the case so far. She told him about the boy, the acorns, the link to the farm, the human trafficking angle, and the possibility the trooper who had been shot had been killed by a trafficker. "You know they found a baby's pacifier in the back the truck?" Kit asked.

Lee nodded. "I guess I just figured that it came from a shipment of household goods."

"I don't think so." Kit shifted in her chair. "We've got warrants for the business records of C&R Enterprises. We want employees' names, a list of vehicles they own, and other data. When we get those, we'll go for IRS data and eventually, wiretaps. We've got to find out if there's a link between the dead boy, the missing woman, the ambushed trooper, and some of the other things going on."

"And what do you want from us?"

Chris Cruz leaned forward, his navy blue suit stretching across his back. "Here's the deal, Roger. You'll be our main link to the state police. We may need help with surveillance, records searches, and, when it comes down to it, arrests. We'd like you to be part of our team, and work with us until we get this case solved. We're setting up an offsite, and we'll give you a key and access to all of our records. We'd also like your help in enlisting the aid of the sheriff's office if we need it."

Lee nodded. "That's what my boss said, and that's fine with me. I'll need to clear some things off my desk first. I'll be ready to go tomorrow."

Immediately after the meeting, the Chincoteague police chief called Kit. "We got somebody here you might want to talk to."

"Who's that?'

"Latino fella. We picked him up with a whole lotta meth. Down at one of the marinas. I thought that was right odd. Thought it might make you prick up your ears."

"What made you suspect him?" Kit asked Chief Daisey later as he walked with her to an interview room.

"Got a tip."

"From . . . ?"

"Anonymous." Daisey put his hand on the door of the room and looked full at Kit. "We don't get too many tips like this."

Miguel Martinez looked almost like a child, sitting at the table. Small, with brown skin, the furtive glances he stole as Kit and the chief entered the room conveyed fear to her. A police officer stood leaning against the wall. Kit guessed he was there to translate.

But it was quickly clear the officer knew very little Spanish, and Martinez knew no English. To every hesitantly phrased question, Martinez shook his head and cast plaintive glances at everyone in the room.

Back in the chief's office, Kit found out that two officers had responded to a small fishing boat marina near the tip of the island. The suspect was standing out in clear view, a backpack in his hand. When the officer asked if he could look inside, using gestures to indicate what he wanted, Martinez readily handed it over. Inside was two hundred grams of crystal meth, enough to book Martinez on possession with intent to distribute.

"We got no use for crystal meth here," Chief Daisey said. "Migrants been bringing it in to the U.S. from Mexico, I hear. That's one import we don't need."

"Did the officers ask him why he was here?"

"They did, but, as you saw, there isn't much communication going on. We got someone coming down from Salisbury to help us out. He kept saying something like 'boy.' That's what made me think of you. Why was he at a marina? Why was he looking for a boy? Could it have to do with your case? I mean," Chief Daisey leaned forward, "what if this guy ran afoul of some drug dealer . . . or user? What if they took his kid to get back at him? Wouldn't that be a possibility?"

Kit nodded. "That would be." She asked for a piece of paper and wrote down some questions she wanted answered. "When you get a fluent translator, see if you can get answers to these."

On his second visit to Chico's, the bartender gave David the number of a man who could help him with the new ID he needed. Two hours and $200 later, David had a Virginia commercial driver's license with his picture and the name "David Castillo" on it, and a new Social Security number. He was dark enough he figured he might pass for Hispanic. At any rate, using his own first name would give him a fighting chance to remember his alias when he had to introduce himself.

He hung out in a couple of bars, drinking Cokes and non-alcoholic beer, and he let it drop that he was looking for work as a trucker. He had two hookers approach him and one guy offer him drugs, and he'd collected more smoke in his lungs than he'd had in years.

But late that second night, while David was sitting back at Chico's, staring at an international soccer game on the TV, a man walked in wearing a cowboy hat and boots. He had a small cigar in his hand. And he limped.

The man stopped at the table right inside the door. A Latino stood up, lit the cigar for the newcomer, and sat back down.

David moved his eyes back on the soccer game. He listened carefully, heard the man approach, and pretended not to notice when the man sat down on the stool next to him. "Yeah, go!" David yelled, pumping his arm up in the air as a player took a shot at the goal. A thin stream of cigar smoke wafted his way. Slowly he turned his head to the right, casually taking a drink as he did.

The man was Latino, probably forty years old, short, brown hair, black eyes, and he had a scar which bisected his right cheek. "You rooting for Mexico?" the man said in Spanish.

"I'm rooting for whoever is strong enough to win, you know?" David replied in Spanish, chewing on a piece of ice.

Was this the guy Kit had seen at the live oak farm? The man who seemed threatening to her? The one with the scar? If so, he might be the same guy David had seen there. David turned back to watch the game.

Moments later, the man spoke again. "You the loser last time, eh?"

David looked. The man grinned and gestured toward David's left arm, which was in a sling. He refused to respond, turning instead back to the game.

But his skin was crawling. He took a long drink of Coke, then casually turned to his right. "You know anyone looking for a truck driver?" he asked in Spanish.

"You know one?" the man said, puffing on his cigar.

"Me."

The Mexican laughed. "With that?" he gestured again.

David took a long drink. "I can do more with one hand than most guys can with two."

"Sí? Let's go!" The Mexican propped his right elbow on the bar.

David eyed him. "What's your name?"

"They call me 'Jefe.'"

Jefe. Boss. David swallowed. "OK." He put his right elbow on the bar and gripped the man's hand. What was this guy's game? In the mirror, he could see others watching them. First one man, then another stood up. A few walked slowly over in their direction.

El Jefe glanced around the room. He made some comment David didn't quite catch and the men laughed. Clearly they knew this guy well. The bartender came over and said "Ready?" Then he slapped his hand on the bar, and said, "Go!" and the two men began.

The man was strong, no doubt about that. His face reddened and veins began popping out on his forehead. David felt his own face grow hot and his muscles swell. He kept up the pressure, but as he stared into El Jefe's eyes his adrenaline flowed. They were small and dark, coal black, cold as sharks' eyes.

A drop of sweat ran down David's face. He blinked, and then he felt it, the slightest wavering in the man's hand, the hint of weakness in his grip, and David pressed harder and harder until El Jefe's hand slammed onto the bar.

A general murmur of surprise filled the room. The man laughed, and slid off the bar stool, and slapped David on the shoulder. Then he took one step more, and David thought he was going to move away. Instead, he grabbed David by the shirt, swung around, and landed a blow on his back. A searing pain ripped through David's shoulder.

David jumped to his feet, fist clenched, but the man just laughed. "Now we are even," he said, and he walked off and left the bar.

David watched him go. A young Latino said, "El Jefe, he doesn't like to lose."

"I'll try to remember that." He blew out a breath. "What's his name, anyway?"

"Lopez. Hector Lopez."

<hr />

David used that incident the next time he saw Lopez. El Jefe was sitting at the bar drinking when David spotted him. He walked over, slid on to the bar stool next to him and said, "You owe me."

Lopez continued chewing his ice.

"I beat you. Now, I want a job."

The man stared straight ahead.

"I heard you need a trucker. I can go short-haul, long-haul, box trucks, eighteen-wheelers . . . I done 'em all. I want the job."

Slowly, Lopez turned his face toward David.

"I owe a man some money. I need to pay him," David explained.

Lopez's jaw moved. His eyes scanned David's face. Then he nodded slightly. "I may have a job. You call me next week." And he wrote a number on a napkin and shoved it toward him.

⊙━✦━⊙

Miguel Martinez proved difficult to nail down. After several tries, a translator determined he was an indigenous Guatemalan, and he spoke a native Indian language. He knew practically no Spanish—or English. Finally, the peninsula's Latino advocacy group found someone at a university in Washington who could help over the phone. The professor, who spoke a similar language, was able to find out that Martinez didn't know what was in the backpack, that a white man had given him money to hold it.

Meanwhile, Martinez was being held without bond.

"Didn't you say Patricia and the others who were trafficked with her were from Mexico?" Chris asked Kit.

"Yes."

"Then that's your answer. Martinez isn't connected. It's not worth your time."

Martinez was not worth her time? Kit frowned. There was something really weird about his case. But unless she could link it to her beach child murder it was, in fact, a dead end.

Late that night, back at the motel, Kit's cell phone rang. She looked at the screen and saw a strange number. Something made her answer it anyway.

18

"Hello?" Kit pressed the cell phone to her ear.

"Hey."

David! Kit's heart thumped. "I didn't recognize your number."

"I need some help."

"Where are you?"

"I'm a guest of the Accomack County sheriff."

The jail? "What happened? What'd you do?" Kit crossed her arm in front of her and paced, fixing her eyes on the ugly brown and orange motel room curtains across the room.

He lowered his voice. "Look, I got caught up in a raid on a bar, and they hit me with a concealed weapons charge."

"Because they don't know who you are."

"Exactly. Any chance you could make a phone call?"

Kit glanced at her watch. 11:00 p.m. "I'll come get you."

"No, don't do that. Your friend is here, too."

"My friend?"

"I don't want you to come!" David reiterated.

"I'll send Chris."

"Yes, that's right. Be sure he knows there are two Ls in my name."

"What?"

"Castillo. C A S T I L L O. David's spelled the usual way."

"Good grief," Kit said, rolling her eyes.

❦

It was almost 1:30 a.m. by the time Chris and David returned to the motel. Kit had rehearsed a speech chastising David for getting too involved in this investigation many times, but when David walked into her room, when she saw how tired and grubby he looked, she held her tongue. His face was swollen and there was a bruise on his right cheek, a cut on his lip, and blood on the front of his shirt. "What happened?" she asked.

"I was in a bar that they busted. I tried to tell the cop I had a gun in my sling, but there was so much noise he couldn't hear me and as soon as his hand touched it, I was on the ground." He grinned. "I thought it best at that point to cooperate with him."

Kit's heart was drumming. "Wait. Why were you in the bar? David, what have you been doing? Didn't I tell you . . ."

Chris raised his hand. "Hold on. Listen to what he's found out."

She felt a chill run up her spine. "Sit down." She motioned toward the second bed in her room.

David shook his head. "I'm not fit to sit anywhere."

"Sit down!"

"You have any coffee?"

Kit brewed a pot of coffee from the in-room coffee-maker, poured two cups and made a second batch. "All right," she said sitting down on the edge of her bed. "What's going on?"

David had chosen a position on the floor, his back to the wall next to the door. Chris sat in a chair. They were a study in contrasts, these two men: David, barrel-chested, almost burly, and Chris, slim and refined, as neat and proper as David was grubby.

"Tell her," Chris said.

David fixed his brown eyes on Kit and she felt her stomach tighten some more. He told her about his trip to the farm, his foray through the cornfield, and then about the smokehouse. "I don't know what's in there besides the acorns," he said, his eyes bright, "but it's something that shouldn't be."

"There are acorns in there?"

"Jars of them. Like some kid had stashed them. His weapons cache, you know? No adult is going to put all those acorns in jars like that."

"Why didn't you tell me you'd done this?"

"I was going to."

"Do you think the little boy found out about the contraband? Was that his death warrant?"

"That's exactly what I think," David replied, and he told her about the loose foundation stones that would allow a child access.

Kit stood up and paced.

"It gets better," Chris said.

She turned around.

"I started hanging out in bars," he said, "and passing Maria's picture around. I said she'd ripped me off and I was determined to find her. I found out how to get a false ID, and now I've got a Virginia commercial driver's license under the name 'David Castillo.'"

"Just like that."

"Just like that. Then, one night, I'm sitting at this bar and in walks the guy."

"The guy? Who are you talking about? The guy with the limp? The one you saw at the farm?"

"Exactly."

"What did he look like?"

"Short. Mexican. One gold front tooth. And a cowboy hat. Oh, and a scar on his right cheek." He motioned with his hand.

Kit felt a chill run through her. "The guy I talked to!" Her mind went back to her visit to the farm, when she'd actually walked up the lane to look at the house, and the man in the white truck who had stopped her and then followed her to the county offices.

"That's what I think. He's dangerous, Kit," David responded. "Dead eyes. Stay away from him."

"Don't tell me, cowboy. I'm not the one hanging out in bars!"

"Stop," Chris said, intervening. "What happened, David? The guy walks into the bar . . ."

David laughed. "That sounds like a joke! Anyway, I've talked to him a couple of times. I told him I heard he needs a trucker, and that I want a job. I think we're headed in that direction."

"A job, from a possible drug runner."

"I promise, I'll stick to tomatoes."

Kit shook her head.

"All right," Chris said, "Let's back up. We have a farm which may be associated with a dead boy, acorns in jars, a cop shot, a white truck which may be being used to transport people, some possible contraband in the shed, a white pickup truck, a possible connection with the abduction of Maria, last name unknown . . ."

Kit turned toward Chris. "We have got to get those employee records. The white pickup was registered to C&R Enterprises." She looked to her right. "David, did you hear what the other men called him?"

"Jefe."

She frowned.

"That means 'boss'."

"So you don't know his real name."

"Hector Lopez."

"Hector! That's the name Patricia gave me!"

"What?"

She reminded David of her conversation with Piper Calhoun. "She said the driver of the truck that brought Patricia to the U.S. was named Hector."

"What'd your bar buddies say when the cop took you down and took your gun?" Chris asked David.

"It definitely raised my status."

"No idea you're a cop?"

"No clue."

Chris looked at Kit. "I think we have an undercover source here."

"No. No way," she replied, her face suddenly hot.

"Why not? He's a cop. He can keep it clean. He speaks Spanish. He's already in."

Kit glared at David. "Have you told him?"

"What?" Chris asked.

Kit launched into David's story, including the shooting incident in D.C., the gunfire on the ocean, and post-traumatic stress. "He shouldn't even have done this much on the case," she asserted, "much less become a source."

Tension ballooned in the room. "I would think that would be his decision," Chris said evenly.

Frustrated, Kit turned to David but the look on his face gave her no reassurance whatsoever.

"What do you say?" Chris said to him.

David didn't think long. "I'm in. You two define what you want, and I'll get it for you."

⊙═╬═⊙

The next morning as Kit showered in her motel room, she tried to imagine her frustration and anger going down the drain with the soap. It didn't work. Those little psychological games never did. She vigorously dried herself off while composing arguments against David's participation in her head, even though she knew it was too late. She was outnumbered and had been overruled. Welcome to the Boys Club, she thought, jerking on her khaki cargo pants.

This morning, Chris would enlist the state police's help in getting David's personal belongings and vehicle back. The four of them would meet to strategize at 2:00 p.m. David had suggested they meet at Kit's rental cottage on Chincoteague, far away from the live oak farm and C&R's produce operations. Kit had insisted on the offsite office. She wasn't even sure why. But she had to reestablish control over this investigation and in her mind, this was a start.

What's more, she'd decided that if David wanted to put himself at risk, she'd let him. She didn't want to care anymore.

The minute that thought jelled in her mind, she knew it was a lie.

❦

When they were all assembled, Kit restated the mission for the benefit of Roger Lee, the state trooper. "We are interested in finding out who killed the child on the beach," Kit said, "and determining what happened to the woman who appears to have been forced into the truck. On a larger scale, we're looking for a criminal enterprise: a human trafficking scheme which could involve an unknown number of victims.

"We have identified one possible victim in Virginia Beach, a woman named Patricia Hernandez. She was brought here from Mexico by a man named Hector who transported her in a white box truck along with fourteen or fifteen others. We think this could be Hector Lopez, the guy David has met. Patricia was told she would be able to work as a nanny. But when she got here, her passport was taken away. Her employers confined her to their house, forced her to work long hours, paid her scant wages, and physically abused her. She was finally able to escape. Now she is concerned that a friend of hers in a similar situation is in trouble."

All the time Kit was speaking she stayed focused on Roger Lee or Chris Cruz. But out of the corner of her eye, she saw David leaning forward, his elbows on his knees, watching her intently. And she fought the feelings that rose like the tide within her.

"As I said, we want to identify the criminal enterprise. Just as in a business, there'll be a CEO, a 'board of directors', a financial manager, an 'enforcer', and then lower-echelon workers. So we will try to discover the framework of this human trafficking organization, assuming that's what we've really got going, and let that lead us to information about the beach child and the woman.

"We've gotten subpoenas for the financial information for C&R Enterprises," Kit said, "and that's where we'll start. You," she said, nodding toward Roger, "will be an invaluable source of local knowledge, so I appreciate you being here. We may need to call on your department for support for surveillance."

Chris interjected, "David already has an in with the group of laborers in this area. He'll be developing information from the inside."

Roger Lee frowned. "What about our trooper? Our primary interest will be finding out who killed him."

"Let's you and me go over that evidence," Chris said. "I'd like to see the truck you found at the scene, and his cruiser. Then I can be looking out for links as well."

Behind the offsite office stood a split rail fence and beyond that, a pond surrounded on three sides by a grove of trees. When Kit walked out following their meeting, David was sitting on the fence, his back to the offsite, his head bowed, almost as if he were praying.

She started toward the parking lot, but he must have heard her, because he turned around, saw her, and climbed down off the fence. As he walked toward her, she braced herself.

David stopped a few feet from her and shoved his hands in the pockets of his jeans. "You're good."

She raised her eyebrows.

"Very professional. Very well put together," he explained, nodding his head toward the offsite office.

"You didn't say much."

"Didn't need to."

Kit took a deep, shaky breath. Chris, using impeccable logic, had pointed out that as the case agent she should be also directing David. That meant staying in close contact with him, something she both wanted and dreaded. "So you're going to meet Lopez at the bar ..."

David nodded. His cheek was still bruised from his arrest. "About that job."

"Do you know the rules about drinking?"

"I don't drink."

"Not at all?"

"Never."

"So how ... ?"

"You order a Coke and put a lot of limes and cherries in it. People think it's a mixed drink. Or you order a longneck bottle of beer and pretend to drink it. Or you order non-alcoholic beer in a glass." He grinned. "I've done it a thousand times."

"Where are you staying?"

He told her the name of a cheap motel not far away.

"The Bureau will pick that up for you, now that you're official."

He nodded. "Many thanks."

The sun brought out the golden highlights in David's eyes. Kit wondered if she had ever seen any that were such a beautiful shade of brown.

"You still at that motel?" he asked.

Kit nodded, her mouth dry.

"I miss Chincoteague, don't you? The peace of it." He looked down and kicked a small stone.

"So go back!"

He shook his head. "I've got to help Maria."

"Why? Why you?"

"Because I know. I've seen the picture. I can't just walk away. I've got to help her. I've got the house through mid-November. I'll get back to it. Finish the painting. And get out on the water again. They say I can surf with a wetsuit until then." He tossed something toward the pond. "It'll give my shoulder time to heal anyway."

Kit looked at the keys in her hand. Her heart was trembling. "Report in frequently," she said, her voice cracking.

"Yes, ma'am."

She nodded, turned, and walked away.

⚬━┿━⚬

Of the twenty-three people on C&R Enterprises' books, ten, Kit eventually discovered, were related. There were the owners, Sam Curtis and his son-in-law, Tom Richards. Tom's wife and two of Sam's other sons were on the rolls, as well as Sam's brothers and some of his cousins. Susan Richards, Tom's wife was the bookkeeper and her sister was in charge of shipping. What's more, the company's tax records showed a healthy profit over the last five years. Tom Richards and his wife had recently bought a new home nearby. Everything pointed to a normal business, normal families, normal lives. With all those family members on the payroll, and with the business doing well, would the owners risk everything to participate in human trafficking?

If C&R was involved, Kit bet it was involuntarily. Maybe someone on their staff, or a supplier, or some peripheral employee was the culprit. She was still working this all out in her mind when Chris called.

"The truck they found at the site of the trooper murder? It was a chop-shop job."

"You've got different VINs?"

"Several. And guess what? One of the axles was from a truck purchased by C&R Enterprises eight years ago."

19

C&R's main office was in Oak Grove, a short drive away from Glebe Hill. Tom Richards was on a deep-sea fishing trip out of Ocean City, but Sam Curtis seemed all too happy to talk to Kit and Chris. "Come right on in!" he said, extending a huge hand toward the two agents. "Have a seat."

Above Curtis's battle-scarred oak desk hung a huge, mounted trophy fish. Chris asked him about it. "White marlin. Caught it right off Ocean City fifteen years ago. Best trip I ever had," Curtis explained. "Now, it ain't every day we have federal agents come to call. What can I do for ya?"

Chris explained about the axle.

"That truck was stolen," Sam Curtis said, "five, maybe six years ago. Hold on." He pressed a button on the phone on his desk. "Helen, get me that file on the stolen truck, hon." A few minutes later, his secretary walked in with it in her hand. "Yessir, let me see," Curtis said, licking his thumb and going through the pages. "We reported it gone December 15, five years ago. Yep. That's right. Five years." He turned the file around so Chris and Kit could read the police report. "Insurance paid us off. So you found the axle?"

"Yes." Kit had been watching the man carefully. She found it hard to believe he was anything other than an agricultural produce businessman. "How's business been lately?" she asked him.

Curtis smiled. "Good. Once't we got over that salmonella scare. You Feds got to be careful about them warnings. Cost us a bundle." He settled back in his chair and propped his folded hands on his ample belly. "We doin' OK, though," he said. "'Nough to keep my grandkids in shoes."

Behind him, on a credenza, were pictures of two little blond-headed kids, one boy and one girl. "Are those your grandchildren?" Kit said, pointing toward the pictures.

"You bet."

"Mr. Curtis . . ."

"Sam. Just call me Sam."

"OK, Sam . . . can you tell me how your operation runs? I mean, I've driven by tomato fields . . . but I've often wondered just how they get to market." Kit hoped her question came across as innocuous as she intended.

"City girl, huh?" he said, laughing. "Tomatoes are an important crop around here. They account for 'bout half of Eastern Shore Virginia's total ag product sales. You got to handle 'em right. The pickers . . ."

"Your employees?"

"Nope. We contract that out. They's mostly migrant workers. All legal, far as I know. Anyway, the pickers got to wear gloves, watch out for cuts in the skin, sort 'em right, wash 'em."

"Then what?"

"We truck 'em north and south, to Salisbury or down to Norfolk. We actually bought that distributor out last year, so we truck 'em now to our own building in Norfolk, and send 'em all over the East Coast. Got to move 'em fast; they're fragile."

"So these truckers," Kit said, tapping her pen against her lip, "they're your employees?"

"Some is, some ain't. Our needs are flexible. So we got a fleet of our own trucks, but then we contract with other guys to take up the slack."

"How many trucks do you own?" Chris asked.

"Let me see now . . . right now, ten. And we contract out with twenty or so more. Keep 'em busy, this time of year."

"What happens in the off season?"

Sam Curtis grinned. "I go to Florida."

"I mean with the trucks."

"We keep 'em 'round the processing plants. That's when that one got stolen, in the off season. Nobody 'round to watch 'em."

Kit looked at Chris, who seemed to read her mind. "Mr. Curtis," he said, "do you have an employee named Hector Lopez?"

Sam looked puzzled. "Lopez . . . Lopez . . . not that I recall." He grinned. "Now if ya said 'Curtis' or 'Richards' I might be able to help you out." He laughed at his own joke. "We contract with Mexicans for field crews. Ain't nobody named Lopez that I recall."

Kit leveled her eyes at him. "He was driving a truck registered to your company."

Sam picked up a pen. "Give me the tag number if you got it. I'll check it out. There been an accident?"

"No," Kit said. She started to write the tag number on a slip of paper. Chris put his hand on hers and stopped her.

"Let it go for now, Mr. Curtis. We'd just as soon not let him know we're looking at him."

Curtis's eyes narrowed. "All right." He set down his pen.

"Could we get a list of those contractors?"

"Absolutely."

When they were done, Kit and Chris exited the one-story building. "You were right," Kit said. "Not tipping off Lopez is the right thing to do."

Chris nodded.

"I don't see any red flags," she said.

"I agree." He started the car. "That means we've got to go deeper."

⌖

"Lopez told me what the job is." David stood in the off-site office, wearing jeans and a white T-shirt. Kit thought he looked fatigued. "I pick up the truck at 8:00 p.m. tonight at the processing plant. Lopez wants me to drive it to Norfolk. So I'll be gone a while."

"You'll be OK driving the truck?" Kit gestured toward his arm, which he still had in a sling.

"It'll have an automatic transmission and power-assisted steering. I'll be fine. I can drive with my knees if I have to!"

Kit rolled her eyes. "Call me when you get back," she said, "even if it's in the middle of the night. And, of course, call me if something goes down bad. Or even if you feel hinky."

"I will."

"What will you be carrying?"

"Tomatoes."

"Anything else?"

"Not that I know of."

Kit paced, her arms crossed over her chest. "How will you protect yourself?"

"Good looks."

Kit rolled her eyes again.

"I'll have my gun." He grinned.

"And you do have my cell phone number in your new phone?" Steve Gould had assigned a technician to help them.

Jason had bought pay-go phones for all of them to keep real FBI cell phone numbers secure.

"Yep."

"Call me then."

"I promise! I will."

⊙━━╪━━⊙

Kit spent the evening in her motel room, going over some of C&R's records and trying not to think about David, trying to get the different parts of her life to line up . . . she'd thought she'd gotten it right with her carefully considered marriage to Eric. The divorce blew that notion to pieces. Now she didn't know what to think. Her cognitive, rational side, the one nurtured and reinforced by her father, was battling with her emotional side. Was she really as flaky as her mother?

She hoped not.

Frustrated, she considered calling her dad, just to talk, then rejected that idea. Her friend Ben, maybe? But when she looked at her watch she realized it was already getting late . . . late for normal people with normal lives, that is. She was stuck. She'd just have to ignore her confusion and focus on work. That seemed to be her favorite coping mechanism anyway.

C&R Enterprise's financial records seemed straightforward. No IRS issues. They had contracts with four crew chiefs to provide workers for the fields. They rented acreage all around the county, paid their bills on time, and made a profit each year.

Kit leafed through page after page of material, studying until the numbers grew blurry and fatigue made her eyelids feel heavy. Finally, David called. Kit jumped when the phone rang at 1:00 a.m. "How did it go?" she asked.

"He sent some young dude with me," David said. "We're about ten miles down the road and the kid pulls out a joint.

195

I told him if he didn't stow that thing I would pull over and throw it and him out of the truck."

"So did he?"

"Yeah. But I had to pull off the road and threaten him again. That's all I need is a dope charge."

"Right. Good move, David." She gripped the phone, her stomach tight. "Nothing else odd?"

"Nope. It was very routine. I found the distribution point, offloaded the tomatoes, and drove back. But I'm going to tell Lopez I'll make future runs by myself. That kid was irritating." David yawned. "Right now though, I'm going to sleep."

Kit hung up the phone, relieved. Still, what was Lopez up to? Did he really need David just to make routine produce runs?

The next day, Kit and Chris drove to the old churchyard, where Chris stowed his FBI SUV in a copse of trees. Together they walked through the woods to the hill overlooking the farm, where the field workers were ending their day. Sure enough, Lopez's pickup truck was parked in the lane.

"So, is he the boss of just this group of workers?" Chris asked.

"We don't know yet. He's at least that," Kit said, staring at the field through her binoculars. "Here comes the van." She put her binoculars down. "I'd like to follow it, but any car, much less a bureau vehicle, is going to stick out on these deserted roads."

"Which is why we need David."

His logic was irrefutable. "Look. Who's this?" she said, gesturing toward the farm.

A shiny blue pickup was driving down the lane. A man got out, walked toward Lopez, and the two of them stood talking. The man looked taller than Hector, and had on jeans and a bright white shirt.

"He's new," Chris said, aiming his camera at the man. "He's too far away to get a great picture, even with this long lens. I'll get what I can."

"I can't quite read the license plate. The angle's . . . " Kit stopped abruptly. "Hold on. There's a woman in the passenger seat. Can you get her?"

"I'll try."

The woman stepped out of the truck. That made it easier.

The sound of Chris's camera seemed an odd counterpoint to their natural surroundings. Kit watched the scene play out before her as if the people were figures on a game board, and once again she felt the pressure to do the right thing. Make the right plays. Her hand was touching the rough bark of a tree. *Dear Jesus,* she prayed silently, *please don't let me fail.*

They showed the pictures to David the next day. "I don't know who the guy is, but that's her," David said, standing in the offsite office. His voice sounded tight, like a spring about to uncoil. "That's Maria. Who's the guy?"

"We don't know yet."

"She's alive, anyway."

"That doesn't mean she wants to be with him."

"Right." The muscles in his jaw were flexing. "Can I keep a copy?"

"Sure."

"I'm going to find out who the dude is."

⚬━◆━⚬

David's plan was simple. He carried the blurry photo of the well-dressed man with Maria folded in his pocket. One night, when no one else was around, he asked a guy he had befriended at the loading dock if he knew the man.

The Mexican's eyes widened and a torrent of Spanish poured out of his mouth. Yes, he knew him. He was the Big

Boss. Lopez's boss. He lived in a big house. Had a beautiful wife. And Lopez acted as his gun, his enforcer.

His name?

"Carlos. That's all I know."

"And how about the woman in this picture?" David asked in Spanish. "You know her?"

No, the man responded. He'd never seen her before.

But David doubted he was telling the truth.

⁘

After David's fourth trip in six days, Kit took half a day to head back to Chincoteague to get clean clothes and handle some errands. She was just about to leave her cottage when the crunch of oyster shells on the driveway announced a visitor. When Kit looked outside, Brenda Ramsfeld, dressed in uniform, was walking up onto her porch.

"I thought you'd like to know," Ramsfeld said when Kit opened the door. "I fired Joe Rutgers."

"Come in," Kit said. She opened the door wider. "Have a seat."

Ramsfeld complied, perching on the couch like a bird ready to fly at a moment's notice. "I found him smoking pot on duty," she said, "just like you said."

Kit nodded.

"He protested of course. Said it was his first time. Said he'd never do it again." Ramsfeld sighed. "We both know that's a lie." Her eyes were fixed on a book holder on the coffee table. "I figured I'd better tell you, since you've had dealings with him. I don't guess he'll get vengeful, but hey, what do I know?"

"I appreciate that."

"First time I ever had to fire anybody. Man, the paperwork!" Ramsfeld looked up.

"Was he arrested?"

"Yes. I had the Chincoteague police do it."

"Where was he buying the stuff?"

"The weed? I don't know. That's for the police to find out, you know?" Ramsfeld stood up to leave. "You got any more on that body?"

Kit hesitated, calculating what she should reveal. "We may have linked him with a farm on the mainland. But we haven't identified him. Haven't even come close."

Brenda nodded. "I figured that might be the case. Kinda glad I didn't waste my time with it." She stood up.

Kit walked her to the door. "Hey, how'd you know where I was staying?"

"I drive by here every day on the way to work. I've seen you coming and going. Saw the car in the driveway just now. Guessed it was you. Your other one's a Subaru, right?" Ramsfeld motioned with her head toward Kit's bureau car in the driveway. "That thing just screams 'cop car'. Anyway, Joe'll be out of the clink in a few hours. That's my guess. Just wanted you to know."

⊶⊷

Brenda Ramsfeld's calculation was right on. But the call Kit got from Chief Daisey as she drove back toward Glebe Hill went even further. "We were booking him," the Chief said, "for simple possession. Doing his fingerprints, when that Guatemalan was being moved. And Martinez goes ballistic, pointing and yelling. Seemed to be saying Joe's the one that paid him to hold that backpack full of meth. We're callin' the translator, but that's what he seemed to be indicatin'."

Curiouser and curiouser, Kit thought. Why would Joe Rutgers want to set Martinez up? When she got to the offsite, she went over the whole thing again with Chris.

"So this guy, Joe, was on patrol the morning you found the body?" Chris asked. Kit confirmed the answer with a nod of her head. "And he lied about how far he'd gone. Do you really think he was involved?"

"With the murder? I doubt it. For one thing, he was on shore. For another he just doesn't seem the type. He strikes me as lazy, a pothead . . . but a killer? I don't get that," Kit said.

"Would be worth another interview. Want me to do it?"

Kit considered that. "Is David making a run tonight?"

"Yes."

"All right. Why don't I monitor that and you go talk to Joe?" Another thought occurred to her. "Are we getting anywhere with these transports?"

Chris stretched out his legs. "These things take time. He's earning Lopez's trust. Something will come of that. Meanwhile, David thinks he's got a handle on that guy with Maria." He paused thoughtfully. "He's making progress, Kit. I'd say we stick with it."

❦

David was driving up Rt. 13 on his fifth trip, making his way back to C&R at 2:00 a.m on a clear, cool night. He was listening to his iPod through the truck's stereo, but he was getting sleepy, so he clicked it off, rolled down the window, and turned his thoughts elsewhere.

After four trips, Lopez hinted he'd have something bigger to transport soon, something that would make him more money, something that would involve an even bigger player. What was he talking about? Drugs? People? David knew if they could just get Lopez talking about something illegal, they'd get authorization to access his financial records, wiretap his phone . . . they'd have all kinds of inroads into his life. And that could lead to rescuing Maria and discovering who killed the beach child.

What would happen after they'd solved the case? He'd go back to Chincoteague and finish painting. And Kit—what about Kit? She'd seemed guarded, cold even, since he'd started working with them. She acted more relaxed . . . even friendly . . . with Chris.

Still, David saw something in her eyes when she looked at him, something that she couldn't mask, something that gave him hope.

He only knew one thing for sure: he'd never felt this way about another woman. He'd never felt so compelled to pursue one, so intrigued by her thinking, so ready to make room in his life for another. No, he thought, correcting himself: give up his life for another. Even with the problems emanating from her divorce, she was attractive to him. Hey, everyone had problems, right?

He took a big drink of cold coffee. As he did, he glimpsed something on the edge of the road. What was it? A red flag went off in his brain. Automatically, his foot pressed down on the brake. He slowed down and then he saw a cut-through.

Why? What had he seen? What had bothered him? Following his instincts, David turned around.

20

FEW VEHICLES TRAVELED THE ROAD AT THAT HOUR, AND DAVID SLOWED as he approached the area again. Wide awake now, straining to see into the dark, he fought to retrieve the image of whatever it was that had alarmed him.

The shoulder of the road fell off to a ditch. Beyond that, a bank rose up to woods. With no streetlights in the area, and no moon that night, all David had to go on were his headlights and his instincts.

But those proved true. As the truck crawled along, half on the shoulder, his headlights picked up what his brain had registered: a hand and an arm emerging from the ditch.

Jerking to a stop, he put on his emergency flashers, grabbed a flashlight, and climbed down from the truck. His heart pounded, hard. He jogged toward the ditch and looked down. There, in the weeds, lay a man dressed in khaki work pants and a short-sleeved white shirt, stained with blood.

David dropped to his knees. He felt the man's neck. He found a thready pulse, grabbed his cell phone off of his belt, and called 911. As he spoke into the phone, the man opened his eyes. "Hang on, partner, help is on the way," David said, clicking his phone off. He used his flashlight to scan the man's body, ripped open his shirt, and found a bloody gunshot wound.

A dark dread swept over him. David shivered. The smell of the blood, the sight of it, washed through him, bringing back memories. He shivered and closed his eyes. In his mind's eye, he saw the man, he saw the kid he shot, he saw a roadside, he saw an alley in the city, he saw life flowing away in a sickening stream.

David forced his eyes open. "Who did this?" he asked as he pressed his hand over the wound.

The man couldn't talk.

"Did you know him?"

The man shook his head. Then he moved his hand, and his gesture sent a deep chill through David. The killer had a scar bisecting his face. Kit's scar-faced man? Hector Lopez?

"Hispanic?" David asked.

The man nodded and then his eyes fluttered.

"Oh, Jesus!" David cried out. The man's eyes opened and he reached out a hand. David gripped it. "You stay with me, man, help's coming," and he held on, pressing one hand on the man's wound and praying out loud, until lights and sirens pierced the darkness and medics appeared at his side.

c——+——o

The phone ringing jarred Kit out of the book she was reading. "David?"

But it wasn't him. "We've got a dead man on the side of 13. Looks like a trucker—shot," Roger Lee said. "Want to go?"

She sat straight up. "Yes!"

He gave her the location and she called Chris. "Meet me at the car when you're ready."

David, where was David? She pulled on clothes while dialing his cell phone number. "C'mon, c'mon . . ." she said. When he didn't answer, her mind began racing with fear.

○══╪══○

The lights from the emergency vehicles created a surreal atmosphere at the crime scene. David shoved his hands into his jeans pockets, fighting to keep from slipping into death's dark despair.

"So you just came upon the victim?" the trooper was asking.

"Yes, sir."

"Mind if we go through your vehicle?"

"Go ahead."

"What were you carrying?"

"Tomatoes. It's empty now." That night, David had forgotten his gun. He'd been mad at himself earlier. Now, he was grateful for that omission.

○══╪══○

Kit pulled up to the scene, her heart in her throat. Chris pulled up right behind her. A white box truck stood parked on the shoulder. Oh, God! It had C&R's logo!

But then she saw him. David was standing on the side of the road, next to a cop, his hands jammed in his pockets, his face drawn. "We don't know him," she cautioned Chris, who nodded his agreement.

Flashing their credentials, they made their way past the cops standing around looking curiously detached, to the body on the ground. "Who's the vic?" Chris asked a trooper.

"We don't know. Wallet's gone. Guy over there spotted him." He gestured toward David.

Kit walked over to the body, which the medics had covered with a sheet. The air felt sticky hot and the crushed weeds smelled sweet, like cut hay. Locusts buzzed all around. Later, she would remember the sound of them, and the smell of the grass, and the oppressive humidity.

Dropping to one knee, Kit gingerly lifted the sheet to look at the victim's face. As she did, her heart stopped. She inhaled sharply. "Oh, God!" she said, "I know this man."

The shock of seeing Connie Jester's husband, Bob, dead on the side of the road, made Kit's head spin. "I know him," she said, standing up. The sound of her own voice seemed strange, distant, like it belonged to someone else. The ground seemed to move under her feet. The trooper put a hand on her elbow to steady her.

"Are you OK? Who is he?"

"He's from Chincoteague. Bob Stewart. He's a trucker. Dear God!" Kit put her hand to her face. Regaining control, she looked at the officer. "Who's in charge?" The man nodded toward the trooper standing near David. That's when she noticed David's eyes were fixed on her.

She walked toward them, fighting to regain composure. "His name is Bob Stewart. He's from Chincoteague. His wife, Connie Jester, is a friend of mine." The words spilled out.

David's eyes widened.

"Wonder where his truck is?" The trooper took a deep breath. "OK. You want to come with us to notify her?"

⌒══╪══⌒

David's chest tightened. Connie's husband! The dead man was Connie's husband?

"So you were just driving and saw him?" Chris questioned David as if he didn't know him.

"Yes, sir. I saw something out of the corner of my eye that struck me as odd. I couldn't just go on. I turned around up there," David motioned up the road, "and came back at it. Then I saw it was a hand. And so I stopped."

"There's nothing in his truck," a trooper said, coming over to them. "He's clean."

"All right," the other trooper replied. "You have any more questions?" he asked Chris.

"Not tonight. Just be sure we can contact him."

The trooper nodded. "Guess that's all, sir. You OK to drive?"

David responded positively, but as he climbed back in his truck, his hands and knees were shaking.

It took David thirty minutes to return the truck to the C&R Enterprises property and pick up his Jeep. Then he didn't know where to go or what to do. But he knew he could not go back to that motel room. He'd feel like a caged animal. He drove by the offsite, and then Kit's motel. Her car wasn't at either place. Didn't the trooper ask her if she'd go with him to notify Connie? Why was everything so blurry in his head?

Lacking a better plan, he drove to Chincoteague. When he got there, he turned his SUV toward Chicken City Road. He knew where Connie lived—he'd picked up paint at her house once. But he'd never met her husband, didn't know what he looked like, until tonight. And tonight, he'd watched him die.

⁂

Kit had seen death before. She'd even been on a notification team one time, when a co-worker had died of a heart attack at the office. She'd gone with the boss to inform the widow.

But this was different.

Connie's house looked dark except for a small lamp in the living room window, no doubt intended to welcome Bob home, and the side porch light.

Kit felt a physical ache in her chest as she and the trooper walked up to the front door. Connie's expression as she opened it indicated instant recognition—and horror.

"What's happened? What's happened?" she said.

The trooper held his hat in his hand. "Ma'am, we have some bad news." The next half hour felt surreal. Connie seemed in shock. She kept crying over and over, "Bob, oh, Bob! Not Bob! Oh, please, not Bob!" Her grief filled the house, a keening wail that plucked the heart like a harp. "He's gone! My Bob is gone!"

Professional or not, Kit cried. She cried for Connie. She cried for Bob. She cried for all the pain and grief that death had caused.

The trooper left. Kit stayed. She held Connie in her arms. Helped her call the children. Phoned Connie's minister and a neighbor. And prayed . . . prayed more than she had in years, because she knew no one but God could touch a grief that raw.

⊂══✦══⊃

There were four or five cars parked outside Connie's house. David scanned the cluster of vehicles. Then he saw it: the Crown Vic Kit had been driving.

He felt foolish, but he wanted to be near her, wanted more than anything to hold her in his arms, as if somehow that would diffuse the feelings that were raging inside. It was impossible, he knew.

At least he could be close. He parked down the street. Turned off his engine and just watched as a few people arrived. As the front door opened and the warmth of the light inside spilled into the night. As the door closed again and the house encircled the mourners inside.

Outside in his car, the dark night enveloped David. He shivered in his aloneness, his stomach a knot of emotion. He looked up through the windshield, into the night. The stars he could see moved across toward the west. He sagged back in his seat, closed his eyes, trying to make sense of it all, trying to understand, trying to let go of what he had seen, and the memories it had stirred.

He couldn't. Finally, he turned to the One who had set the stars on their courses and made the Heavens resound with his thunder. And acknowledging the ache in his chest, he let the tears fall. Hours later, David drove back to the Main Street house, sat on the porch, and watched the dawn arrive. His cell phone rang.

"I didn't wake you, did I?" Kit asked.

His heart jumped at her voice. "No."

"Look, can we meet? You and Chris and I?"

"Where?"

"I'm on Chincoteague."

"Me, too."

"You are? OK, how about your place, in an hour?"

"Fine," he said. His palms were sweaty when he hung up the phone.

❦

Connie's last words haunted Kit: "God's hand is in this, honey, I know it. He's in control. Somehow, he's going to get me through. But honey, life is shorter than you think. Don't give up the fight for joy."

The fight for joy. Right, Kit thought. How could Connie even think about joy in the face of Bob's murder? Where's the justice in that? Much less joy! Good grief. What was Connie thinking?

Oh, God, she breathed as she inserted the key in the ignition of the bureau's Crown Vic, there's so much I don't know. None of this makes sense. I'd like to believe that you're in control. But God! Why Bob? Of all the truckers . . . why Bob?

She drove toward the Main Street house, her stomach churning, questions fluttering like butterflies through her mind. What would Connie do without Bob? Who killed him? How was David? Why did he have to go through this again?

Kit jogged up the front porch steps at her grandmother's old house. David invited her in without meeting her eyes. Her heart grew tender the minute she saw him. She wanted to ask him how he was doing after this latest encounter with death. What was he thinking? What was he feeling?

There was no time for any of that. Chris arrived seconds later, dressed, Kit thought, like a stockbroker—or an undertaker—in his black suit and fresh white shirt. He looked like it was the middle of the day, not 8:00 a.m. after a late night. "I brought breakfast," he said, setting a box of doughnuts and cartons of yogurt down on the coffee table.

David had brewed coffee. Kit and Chris filled their mugs and returned to the living room where David waited. "I know who did it," he said, running his hand through his hair. Energy emanated from him like an electrical field.

"Who?" the others said in unison.

David met Kit's eyes. "The cops asked me if Bob had said anything. I said 'no' and that was true. But when I asked him if he knew who shot him he motioned with his hand, like this." David traced a horizontal line across his right cheek. "I think that means a scar. I think . . . I think Hector Lopez shot him."

Kit's eyes widened. "Why? Why would he?"

"For his truck. I've been thinking about this all night. The cops have the one from the scene of the trooper shooting, you know? Now Lopez needs a replacement. So he follows one, or he pretends to be broken down on the side of the road and signals one to pull over. Bob was goodhearted, right? So he stops, and Lopez shoots him. Now he has the truck he needs."

Kit sagged back on the couch.

"Good theory," Chris said.

"It's more than a theory."

"But C&R has loads of trucks!" Kit protested.

David shook his head. "This is something extracurricular that Hector is doing. Something beyond what he's doing for C&R. Didn't you say the owner seemed straight up?"

"Yes, but . . ."

"But nothing. He needs a truck for his illegal activity . . . we think for trafficking people. Or running drugs. Now he has one. Or at least, the parts for one. He might run it through the chop shop."

"What do we do now?" Kit asked. "We need proof he killed Bob."

"Maybe something will show up on the forensics," Chris suggested.

Kit grimaced.

"I'll get it out of Lopez. You wire me up. I'll get him to implicate himself," David said.

"No, David . . ."

Chris interrupted. "Yes, it's time."

Kit's head felt tight with tension. "What? No!" But the two men kept talking, batting around ideas for a recording device David could wear. Through her mind flashed the look on Connie Jester's face, her devastation at the loss of Bob, and her sobs. She thought about death and grief and loss and the inevitable separation all that caused.

If David wore a wire it would put him at even greater risk than he was in now. Because if Hector Lopez found out . . .

She zoned back in when she heard the word "iPod."

"They've seen me with mine many times," David was saying. "I think that would work."

"All right, I'll take care of it."

"Wait. I think we should see if we can get wiretap authorization without that," Kit said again.

"No. Lopez has been talking with me about making a bigger run," David said. His words jabbed at an invisible foe. "Twice, maybe three times the money. What's he talking about? Drugs? People? Who knows? Now he's got a truck. It's time to move."

Chris interjected. "He's right. I'll go talk to the tech. I may have to get Quantico involved if modifying an iPod is beyond his capability, and that could take some time."

Kit's face flushed. She was losing control of the conversation. "Maybe they can't even do it."

"So let them tell me it can't be done."

"It's an unnecessary risk!"

"It's going to be fine," David said, with finality.

"I'll go get started now," Chris left.

21

Kit turned to David to protest again. Then her cell phone rang. She looked at the caller ID and felt a rush of surprise. She put the phone to her ear. "Ben!" she said, responding to the voice of her friend from D.C. "How are you?" She saw David's eyes shift away from her. Then he left the room, headed for the kitchen.

Kit pressed the phone to her ear. "I'm all right. Yes, it was horrible. What a shock." Kit hesitated. "But how did you know?" She grew silent, listening, and every sentence Ben Heitzler spoke felt like a surgeon's knife cutting deeper and deeper, lancing some deep boil in her soul, releasing the poison. She felt her head grow tight. A strange mixture of fear and . . . and what . . . hope? . . . churned in her. She sat down on the couch, and pressed her hand to her forehead as she concentrated on her friend's words. Questions spilled out of her: when? how?

Then she quietly closed her cell phone.

She walked out to the kitchen. David stood with his two hands braced on the table, his head down. "Why didn't you tell me?" she said, softly.

He straightened up and faced her. "I didn't want you to think I did it for you." He rubbed his hands on his pants like they were sweaty.

"Ben said you spent hours together. Over several days." Her heart was drumming.

"That's what you wanted me to do, right?"

"Will you tell me about it?" When he didn't respond, she repeated herself. "Please?"

"I had a doctor's appointment in D.C. I still had that piece of paper you gave me, the one with Ben's name on it. On impulse I called him. Told him you'd given me his number. Told him I had a lot of questions about God and all. He had tickets to a Redskins preseason game and he invited me to go with him." David looked down and traced an invisible pattern on the kitchen table with his forefinger.

"And?"

"It was a great game. 'Skins won, 21-18."

Kit waited, blood pounding in her temples.

"We talked during the game, after the game, in the car, at his house. We were up most of the night, talking about God. What he said made sense to me, Kit. More than sense. It brought everything into focus for me."

Her heart grew tight. What was he saying? What had happened?

David's eyes were shining. "It's like this: when you're working a homicide, you have bits and pieces of information. Solving it is like putting together a puzzle. That's what Ben did for me. He put together the puzzle."

"What do you mean?"

"I've been pretty churned up inside. Upset that I shot that kid. That seemed to stir up a lot of other stuff: anger toward my stepfather, anger toward my mother.

"Ben's a good guy. I started telling him about all this and he just took it all in, you know? I thought he'd be judgmental, but no. He listened. He understood.

"And then he started talking to me about sin and how we all struggle with it. We hurt other people . . . other people hurt us. I could see how this sin nature he talked about was real, and it had been driving me.

"My stepfather," David tapped his finger on the table, "when he was drunk, he'd beat my mother. The last time he tried to do it, I was seventeen. I nearly killed him." David looked at Kit, as if gauging her reaction. "The judge gave me a choice: the Navy or juvenile detention. I took the Navy."

"I'm so sorry," she said, a tremor in her voice.

"I've been carrying around hatred for that man all these years. I knew it was wrong, but I didn't know what to do about it, you know? There, at his house, Ben explained the cross to me. I'd never understood that before. He told me God could forgive me for that hatred, if I confessed it. But do you know what else he said? He nailed it. He told me that, at some point, I needed to not only let go of my anger, but forgive my step-father. For my own sake, if nothing else.

"He said he'd read a quote somewhere." David closed his eyes, trying to make sure the words came out right. "'Unforgiveness is a poison you drink hoping someone else will die.'"

Kit's stomach tightened.

"My stepfather was an inadequate man desperately try-ing to control his world through violence and alcohol. I knew enough to stay away from booze, but anger was controlling me. Ben told me how to stop that cycle of destruction. We prayed. Asked God to take care of it. Told him I'd trust him. And then, it was . . . it was amazing. It all just fell away."

She paced now, agitation rising within her. "It could come back."

"Ben told me that it might, but that every time I give it to God, it'll have less power over me." David cleared his throat. "I was so tired of being angry! For the first time in my life, I tasted something," he groped for words, "something pure and peaceful. I want more of it, whatever it is. I've talked to Ben at least once a day ever since then. I have a thousand questions. I can keep Ben busy for a long, long time."

"You told him about Bob."

"I called him at six o'clock this morning." He shoved his hands in his pockets and stared out of the window. "I've seen a lot of death. Last night was different."

Kit saw that his eyes were wet with tears.

"Last night, when Bob lay there dying, I prayed for him. Out loud. Everything was slowing down, his breathing, his heart … but when I said the name 'Jesus,' he squeezed my hand, and he got this look … so I kept praying and he squeezed my hand again, and then he was gone."

Kit's heart pounded.

"There was a supernatural peace in his death. I was there. I felt it. I saw it." David faced her. "What happened last night was terrible. But Kit, Jesus showed up on the side of that road. He was there. I knew it, and Bob knew it, too."

<hr />

As she drove back to the offsite office, David's words gripped her. Had he really become a believer? He said he had. What's more he said now, he felt so different. "All these years, it's like I've been numb," he'd said. "Now, it's like someone turned on the lights. I can feel again. It started with you, Kit. Now I know where that was leading."

The thought gained momentum in her mind, like a stone tumbling downstream.

But you know, she argued with herself, as she negotiated the causeway, it's one thing to forgive a parent who's dead. And David's stepfather wasn't a believer. But Eric! Good grief . . . how many Bible studies had they been in together? How many worship services? How many service projects had they worked on? He had betrayed all of his promises. Walked away from her . . . and from God, for all she knew.

The worst of it was, all Eric had to do, she knew, was ask for God's forgiveness and he'd be off the hook. Completely. Where was the justice in that? Didn't God care about her pain? Her abandonment?

She hit the steering wheel in protest. Then, unexpectedly, tears welled in her eyes.

✦

"Quantico's going to FedEx it to me in the next couple of days," Chris told her the next day. "They can modify an iPod. Meanwhile, did you hear? Hector Lopez wants to meet with David."

Kit's stomach tightened. "For what?"

"Not sure yet."

"When?"

"Tonight. David said he'd call you when he knew the details."

"Not tonight! That's when I'm meeting with Sam Curtis!" Kit had made arrangements to interview Curtis again, this time at his house. She wanted to get a different view of the man, and get some more questions answered.

"We can handle it."

But when Kit heard the specifics from David she had her doubts.

"He wants me to meet him at 9:00 tonight at the tomato processing plant." David's voice on the phone was tight.

"Why there?" Kit shifted her weight on her feet.

"I don't know."

"What does he want?"

"He wants me to meet somebody. My guess is, it's his boss."

Kit took a breath. Her knees were shaky. She began to pace. "No good, David. Make it some public place, where we can back you up." She had already cancelled her meeting with Curtis in her mind.

"I don't have a choice."

"He just killed somebody!"

"I know. And I suggested a diner up the road, but Lopez said no. It has to be the plant."

"Then blow it off."

"No. I'm not going to do that."

Kit's mind raced. This felt too risky, too dangerous. She glanced up to see if Chris or the others were around. Maybe he'd listen to Chris, maybe . . .

"Look, Kit, Lopez isn't going to hurt me. I've given him what he wanted. He has no idea I'm law enforcement. Now, the timing is right. He has a new truck. I think he's going to ask me to move something illegal. People, maybe. It's great—a chance to find out who he's working for. Lopez isn't the main man."

"Then who is he?"

"The enforcer. He's a psychopath, Kit. I can see it in his eyes. He likes it when people get hurt."

"Great! So you're going with a psychopath to meet someone else in a place we can't get to!"

"Yeah, well, our clients aren't Boy Scouts, Kit. I'll be all right. Trust me. I'm betting that tonight I'll meet Carlos—and I'll be one step closer to finding Maria and nailing Lopez on Bob's murder." He hesitated. "Who knows? We may find out who killed your little boy."

The other team members were talking to Jason, the tech guy, when Kit walked back into the main room. She outlined David's plan and used the graphics on her computer to show them the tomato processing plant.

"We can't back him up there," Chris said.

"I know. I told him. He says it has to be there."

Roger spoke up. "We can be in the woods. We'll have to walk in a ways, but the three of us can get within twenty yards or so of the building."

"Two. Kit's going to be with Sam Curtis," Chris said.

"I'll cancel that," Kit said.

"No need to. I can get a couple of guys to help out," Roger suggested.

Chris stretched. "Curtis is leaving for a convention tomorrow morning, Kit. If you don't go tonight, you won't have another chance for three or four days."

"If David has his cell phone in his pocket, he can have a number programmed in. Then all he has to do is push one button if he's in trouble," Jason added. "As a backup, he can bust out a window. We hear glass breaking, we move.

Everybody else thought that was good enough. Kit had her doubts.

Kit called David later in the day. "Jason wants to program in a number on your cell so you just have to hit one button if you get in trouble."

"Right. I talked to him."

"Did you get some sleep?"

"Not much. You?"

Kit shivered. "No." She outlined the back-up plan she and the others had concocted and told him she would be at Sam Curtis's home at the same time he was meeting Lopez.

"He may not know Lopez, but he will know Lopez's boss."

Kit chewed her lip. "David, if something looks wrong, get out, OK?"

She heard him take a deep breath. "It'll be all right, Kit."

The hours seemed to stretch out as the sun crawled toward the horizon. The rumble of thunder in the west announced that the predicted thunderstorms were going to materialize eventually. Kit hadn't eaten all day. Her stomach felt knotted. She thought maybe she should eat some yogurt, at least. But even that wouldn't go down.

Sam Curtis's house wasn't far from the tomato processing plant. She'd told Chris to call or text her if anything went wrong. She could leave and be at his location in ten, maybe twelve minutes.

The heavens broke loose at 5:40 p.m. Torrential rains poured down on the thirsty ground as lightning split the sky. Kit stood in the back doorway of the offsite office and watched as rain pelted the little pond in the back, tore leaves from the trees, and sent muddy rivulets racing toward low ground. "God," she whispered, "you are so powerful. Please help us get through tonight."

Lately, she'd been talking to him more. What was changing?

David dressed as if he'd been working, in a grubby T-shirt, jeans, and workboots. He hadn't shaved in a couple of days, and his eyes were bloodshot from lack of sleep. As he looked in the mirror, he saw fatigue and boredom, which was the look he was going for. Low threat.

Carefully putting his real cell phone in a drawer in his room, he clipped the pay-as-you-go phone on his belt and slid his wallet in his back pocket. Then he put a knife in his boot, and picked up a small revolver, and stuck it in his jacket pocket.

The air was still steamy as he stepped out of his room, closing the door behind him and slipping the key in his pocket. The sky was dark. Water from the late afternoon thunderstorm dripped off of the roof. The asphalt in the parking lot remained studded with puddles.

David got into his SUV. The drive to the tomato processing plant was short, just fifteen minutes or so. In his mind's eye, he could imagine Chris and the others skirting through the woods, headed for the area near the tomato processing plant, having hidden their vehicles some distance away. They'd been waiting. He hoped he didn't have to call on them. But he had all of his options in mind.

He felt just as glad Kit would be out of the area. His instincts would be to protect her. Now, he could concentrate on his primary goals: meeting Lopez's boss and not getting killed himself.

22

K IT COULDN'T EAT, SHE COULDN'T SLEEP, AND HER HANDS FELT COLD AS she got into her car and headed for Curtis's house. Calm down, she told herself, but she was spitting into the wind.

The country roads she had to travel were dark and empty, and still wet from the thunderstorm. She watched her speed, and took the curves carefully, aware that an accident was the last thing she needed tonight. Periodically, her headlights would catch the light of some animal's eyes, a cat, perhaps, or a possum, crouching on the edge of the road.

Curtis and his wife Anne lived in a modern brick rambler at the end of a long lane. Surrounded by tomato and cornfields, the house had a wheelchair ramp leading to the side door and a circular driveway made of crushed oyster shells. The lights were on as Kit drove up. She parked in the driveway, and heard dogs barking as she approached the front door and rang the bell.

"Come in, come in!" Curtis said, opening the door wide.

Kit stepped in to the modest home and a black Labrador retriever and a Jack Russell terrier came up to her barking, tails wagging.

"They won't hurt you none. Come on in!"

She walked past the dogs, into the living room, painted blue and carpeted in beige. A high-backed couch sat near the wall to the left. Two wing-backed chairs were arranged in a conversational grouping, near a fireplace with an enormous, natural wood mantle. Over it was the mounted head of a ten-point buck.

"Sit down!" Curtis said. "Can I git ya something to drink?"

"No, thanks. Is anyone else in the house?" Kit stood with her back to the front wall, facing all of the entrances to the room.

"My wife Anne will be out shortly. She's back with Mawmaw. That's her mother. Ninety-six years old. Pretty much bedridden though."

As if on cue, a gray-haired, attractive, sixty-something woman came into the room. "Ms. McGovern? Welcome to our home," she said extending her hand.

Kit rose to meet her. "I'm sorry I had to make it so late."

"Not a problem, dear, we've got a good hour before we go to bed." She pronounced the word "ow-wah." Kit caught the "old Virginia" in her voice. She glanced at her watch. It was 9:05 p.m.

⚬━✦━⚬

David intentionally arrived early at the tomato processing plant. He laid his head back, his iPod earbuds in his ears. He wanted Lopez to see him using the device again. And if his boss saw it, too, all the better. He heard someone drive up, but stayed still, as if he were asleep. He heard footsteps approaching his car, and then slam! Someone hit the side of his Jeep.

"What!" David said, as if he'd been startled awake.

"Wake up, cowboy!" Lopez said, grinning. "Let's go."

David pulled the earbuds out of his ears, stuffed them in his jeans pocket, making sure to leave a little of the white wires showing, and got out of his SUV. "Just catching some sleep," he said to Lopez.

"Give me the gun," Lopez said holding out his hand.

David hesitated, then drew the revolver out of his pocket and slapped it into Lopez's hand. The man jerked David's cell phone off of his belt, and threw it and the gun into David's SUV. Then he turned and patted him down. He didn't find the knife in David's boot.

"All right, let's go, let's go." They began walking toward the main building at the processing plant, then Lopez suddenly stopped. "Oh, I forget. We change the meeting place."

David stopped. A warning flashed through him. "What are you talking about, man?"

"My boss, he say he can't meet here. We go to him. Get in." Lopez motioned with his head toward his truck.

For a split-second, David thought about opting out. Refusing to go. But then, they were so close, so close. He wiped his sweaty hands on his jeans. "I'll follow you in my car."

"Get in, man!" Lopez said.

Heart drumming, David put his hand on the truck door and pulled it open.

⚬══╪══⚬

"What are they doing?" Chris exclaimed. His voice was transmitted to Roger and four other officers scattered in the woods near the tomato processing plant building.

"Looks like they're leaving."

"That wasn't the plan!"

"How can we follow him?"

Chris quickly calculated their options. It would take them ten to fifteen minutes to get back to their cars. By that time, Lopez's truck would be out of sight. "Roger, call your dispatch. See if you've got a car in the area."

He did and they didn't.

Chris called Jason to see if he could track the truck using the GPS bug David had put on it. "It's sitting still, man. He must be in a different vehicle," Jason replied.

"Cell phone?"

"I saw Lopez grab David's off of his belt."

And the realization that David was completely on his own left Chris's mouth dry.

⌘

Kit had her Bureau cell phone on vibrate. Ten minutes into her interview with Curtis and his wife, she felt it go off. Removing it, she glanced down at the screen. A text message from Chris read: "Changed location. Will try to follow." Try? Her heart seized up.

⌘

Lopez was driving a white Ford. David didn't buckle up, preferring to leave his options open. Lopez took the twisty, dark country roads at a breakneck speed, accelerating to sixty-five at one point, and David hung on. The man looked relaxed, but David knew psychopaths were never more at ease than when they were hurting someone.

Twelve minutes later, Lopez pulled off the road and into a driveway. He stopped the truck in front of a low, white cinderblock building. "Here we are, my friend," he said, smiling at David.

Wordlessly, David got out of the truck. He looked up to the sky to try to orient himself, but a blanket of clouds lay over the moon and the stars. There would be no help from the heavens tonight. His heart pounding, he followed Lopez to the rear of the building. He could smell the pines, feel the sweet humidity in the air, hear the crickets chirping innocently in the woods. But he could also sense the presence of evil, dark and foreboding. The hair on the back of his neck stood up.

⊙━━╋━━⊙

Chris was out of breath by the time he got back to his Bureau car. They'd divided up the five roads in the vicinity of the plant and were scattering to see if they could find a trace of Lopez and David.

Thirty minutes later, they all agreed they'd have to give it up.

⊙━━╋━━⊙

Lopez unlocked the door with a key. The building was dark. He motioned David in. "You first," David said, standing his ground. So Lopez entered. He flipped a switch and a single bulb suspended from a fixture in the ceiling came on. David followed, keeping his back to the wall to the left of the door, glancing quickly around as he closed the door behind him.

The room was empty. Lopez walked through it to a second door. David followed. But then Lopez dropped his keys, blocking his path and forcing David to step quickly to the right. In one split second, David knew he'd made a mistake.

Suddenly a strong arm gripped his neck and he felt the blade of a knife pressed against his throat. Instinctively, David reacted, driving his elbow into the gut of the man behind him, jamming his foot down on his instep, and throwing his head back into his assailant's face. He knocked the knife arm away as the man reacted. Then David flexed his knees, twisted, and was free.

He turned. He was face-to-face with the man he'd seen in the surveillance photo with Maria.

Lopez was laughing. "You see, Jefe, I told you. He is a bull-fighter, no?"

The man Lopez called 'jefe' had slicked-back black hair and black eyes. He was taller than David, and not as burly. His black Western shirt had pearlized buttons and he was wearing black jeans and pointed Western boots. A trickle of blood emerged from his nose, and he put down his knife and removed a white handkerchief from his back pocket, wiped his nose, looked at the blood, and said, "You are good."

David's heart was pounding and his mind flashing like someone had lit off a firecracker inside his skull. He exploded, barreling toward the man, slamming him into the wall behind. He backed up, drove his fist into the man's gut, and then his mind registered the click of a gun. He turned. Lopez had a .45 aimed straight at him, four inches from his head.

David's breath came hard. He straightened up, unclenched his hands, and with a sweep of his arm, moved Lopez's gun away and walked across the room. He backed up to a wall, put his hands on his knees, and fought to calm down. He could feel blood trickling down his neck from where the knife had cut him. A white-hot anger coursed through his veins. "Who are you?" he said.

"Carlos Cienfuegos," the man said, extending his hand. "Very pleased to meet you. Hector here says you are the one we have been waiting for."

The guy came across smooth, oily, and David was still trying to figure him out when he shook his hand.

"Please forgive our fun here. We always like to test those we want to do business with, no?"

"Next time, ask for a résumé," David muttered.

"Ah, but ours is physical work, no?"

"What do you want?"

"Hector says you are looking for more work."

"Maybe."

"He says you have good references."

David blanked on that for a minute, then remembered using the name of an MS-13 gang leader with Hector. "So what?"

"So, Señor Castillo, we have more jobs for you. More for you to do. And after that, more again."

"Why would I want to work with you?"

"The best reason. Money. No one pay you more than me."

David shifted his gaze from one man to the other. He was operating on instincts now, instincts developed over a decade of dealing with criminals. The building they were in smelled of mildew and dust. There were hard concrete floors, cinderblock walls, and windows too small and too high to be an escape route. Lopez stood between him and the only door. Behind him, a leak in the roof allowed rainwater from the thunderstorm to drip on the floor.

David forced himself to relax. He unclenched his fists and leaned against the wall, propping one foot behind him and crossing his arms. He looked at Carlos. "I owe a guy. He's holding something that belongs to me. A woman ripped me off. Now I'm short. What do you want me to do?"

Carlos smiled. Lopez moved away from the door. "It's just a delivery, you know? A load of tomatoes. Except maybe there is also something extra under the floor when you come back, you know?"

David shifted his weight. "I don't want to see it."

"You don't have to. But you get stopped . . . it's on you."

"The dogs would find it . . ." David suggested.

"And I would find you before you have time to talk to the cops."

"What do you mean?"

"You get stopped, I kill you."

"You'll be following me."

"That's right."

"How much?"

"1K. One trip, from here to Norfolk and back. 1K."

"Make it three."

The man grinned. "Two. 2K, my friend. That is it."

"When?"

"Tomorrow. You pick up the truck at 8:00 p.m."

"Where?"

"C&R, where else?"

———

Kit felt like her brain would burst from tension. She tried to focus. Curtis was explaining his relationship to the workers who picked his crops. "They're all contract crews. Every one of 'em. Sometimes I've seen them before and sometimes I haven't. Handle everything through the crew chiefs."

"And these three men," Kit handed him a sheet with the names of the three men named Carlos on C&R's employee rolls, "do you know them?"

"Yes, they're my men. These two," Curtis pointed to the first two names, "are maintenance workers. The other one handles my ordering: fertilizer, seeds, equipment, the works."

"He's been with us for ten years, maybe more," Anne broke in.

Kit took a deep breath. "Mr. and Mrs. Curtis, let me tell you what we're concerned about."

23

THE DRIP, DRIP, DRIP OF THE ROOF LEAK SEEMED LIKE A CLOCK TICKING away David's life. Squared off with Carlos Cienfuegos, he asked a few more questions. He got the answers he expected, and then he said, "OK. I'll do it. But don't mess with me anymore, eh?"

Carlos held out his hand. David moved forward to shake it. As he did, he saw the tiniest flicker of Carlos's eyes up and to the right. Before he could react, Lopez was behind him. He grabbed David's left arm and twisted it behind him, sending a bolt of pain screaming through David's body. Tears came to his eyes, and his knees collapsed and then Carlos moved forward and drove his fist into David's nose. A flash of light exploded in his head and he hit the concrete floor. Carlos kicked his boot into David's ribs, doubling him on the ground.

"Now," the man growled, "don't you ever touch me again. *Comprende?*"

⟨──⟩

Kit left the Curtises' house when the text came in at 9:53 p.m.: "Lost him."

Lost him? How could they have?

As soon as she got to her vehicle, Kit called Chris.

"There was nothing we could do!" he said, clearly frustrated.

"Where are you now?"

"At the offsite."

"You haven't heard from David?"

"No. And we can't track him either. Lopez took his phone."

Kit's brain whirred frantically. What could she do?

Pray. That's all. *God, you know where he is. Protect him, because I can't.*

In the darkness, images flashed through her mind. Emergency lights. A body. Blood. Bob. Had Connie prayed for God to protect her husband on that last night? To what end?

She refocused on the roads. Suddenly nothing looked familiar. Had she taken a wrong turn? In the short range of her headlights, what could she see? Trees. Fields. Little gleaming eyes. And not much else.

She wished she'd brought her GPS. That would have been smart. She thought about calling Chris for directions, but where was she? She peered into the darkness ahead, searching for something, anything that would orient her.

A sign indicated a sharp curve and a one-lane bridge ahead. This was bad. She knew she hadn't crossed any small bridges on the drive out. Kit slowed down, preparing for the curve and just as she was about to pull right, a Mercedes came racing from the other direction, taking his half of the road out of the middle.

Kit yelled. She pulled her Bureau sedan as far right as possible. The Mercedes roared past.

Was it the same guy she'd seen before? Kit was half-tempted to follow him. But ahead she could see a green road sign and she wanted to see what it said, so she kept on.

"Bodine Road." Kit read the sign out loud. "Where does that go?" She turned right, accelerated up a hill, and crested it. Below her, she could see the road emerge from the woods and run through a large field. One sharp, right-angle turn lay between here and there.

Kit pulled out her cell phone and glanced down. She had no cell signal. Nothing. Not one bar. And with a sinking feeling, she realized she couldn't call for help even if she wanted to. Maybe David couldn't either. "Oh, God!" she whispered. A sense of total helplessness washed over her.

She negotiated the turn, and was straightening out when she saw headlights coming toward her. With no centerline on the road, and no white sidelines, staying in the lane was difficult. She stayed as far right as she could, but whatever was coming toward her was big and not shy about taking more than his share of the road. She flicked her lights as the vehicle approached, and felt her tires touch the gravel shoulder at the same instant that her headlights caught the faces of the men in the truck.

David sat in the passenger seat. His face was rigid. And his shirt was bloody.

There was no place to turn around. Kit sped up until she saw the graveled entrance to the field. She slammed on her brakes, did a quick U-turn, and floored it. The truck had already disappeared into the wooded area. Kit raced after him, checking her cell phone as she drove, and again seeing no bars.

Where Bodine Road crossed the road she'd been on originally, she had to make a decision. Left, right, or straight?

She decided to retrace her steps. Maybe the Mercedes she'd seen was connected to the truck. She took the road as fast as she dared, her heart racing.

Three turns later, she saw David's Jeep pulling out of the tomato processing plant. Well ahead of him, Hector's white truck continued on. She dropped back, in case Hector was watching. Fumbling for her cell phone, she tried dialing David's number, realized she was using her Bureau phone, hung up, and watched as David made a turn, drove up a hill, and pulled into the parking lot of the abandoned church, the one they'd used before.

Turning off her lights, Kit pulled in next to him, jumped out of the car, and raced toward him. "What happened?" she said.

David sat in the driver's seat, his door open, one leg out of the car. Blood flowed from his nose and he had his arms crossed in front of him, holding his ribs. He looked at her, closed his eyes, and said, "It's all right. I just can't drive anymore."

◦━✦━◦

Kit helped David into her car and drove to the offsite. She pulled around back and Chris and Roger came out to help her get David in the building. "Get me some ice," he mumbled as he sat down on a cot.

"Some water, too," Kit called out. "Where is there a doctor around here?"

"I don't need one." David shook his head firmly. "The guy's name is Carlos Cienfuegos."

"That fits," Kit said, turning to Chris. "That's one of Curtis's contractors."

"He was the dude in that picture with Maria in the truck," David said. He began coughing. He grabbed his ribs, grimacing in pain. "He wants me to do a transport for him tomorrow night. Drugs, I think."

Kit suddenly felt hot.

"Think he needs a medic?" Roger asked.

"No, he doesn't," David said.

Kit rolled her eyes. She looked at Chris. "We can't let this happen again."

"No," he agreed.

"Would you contact the night duty agent in Norfolk? Get him on Carlos Cienfuegos. Everything we can get on him."

"Right," Chris responded. "But let me check David first. My parents were doctors, remember? I learned some stuff. Plus, I was certified as an EMT."

Kit stood by while Chris palpated David's ribs, checked his cheekbones and nose, and looked into his eyes with a flashlight. "He's just roughed up. I think he'll be all right."

"We should have him checked in an ER," Kit said.

"No," David insisted.

Kit rolled her eyes.

"I don't see signs of a concussion and I don't think the ribs are broken," Chris said. "I think if we just watch him he'll be OK."

"I agree," David said.

So Kit got David some ibuprofen, then she sent a couple of troopers to get David's car. "The key is on the top of the back tire on the passenger side," Kit said. "Take it to his motel room and leave the car there. Then come back here with the key. Make sure no one sees you."

David stretched out on the cot. He looked asleep, so Kit joined Chris, Jason, and Roger in the other room.

"These guys are smart," Chris said. "Moving to a different location was designed to thwart any law enforcement that was watching, as well as put David off balance. Taking his cell phone was the topper."

"The thing is," Kit said, "some of those areas out in the country don't have decent cell phone coverage. So our plan might not have helped him anyway."

Chris nodded. "Look, somebody needs to be with him. I'll stay here . . ."

"No, I'll stay." Kit couldn't catch the words before they emerged from her mouth. "You make that call to the night duty agent, OK? See what we can find out about Carlos Cienfuegos."

Her words were forceful enough that Chris complied.

Kit curled up on the couch in the offsite. In the background she could hear Chris talking to Norfolk. She set her watch for an hour so she could check on David. But her thoughts wouldn't let her rest anyway. There were only eighteen hours before his next encounter with Carlos Cienfuegos and Hector Lopez. How could they protect him?

⚬━━◆━━⚬

Kit slept fitfully, her rest interrupted by dreams filled with sound and light and frustration and a stark, black fear. She woke up to the smell of coffee just before 7:00 a.m. Alarmed, then curious, she walked back toward the small kitchen area they'd set up. David was standing in front of a mirror with his shirt up, looking at the bruises on his ribs.

When he saw Kit behind him, David dropped his shirt and turned around. The black and blue bruise on his face ran from the bridge of his nose, down across his right cheek. "This is nothing," he said. "I got beat up a lot worse than this when I played football. Of course, I was sixteen then."

Kit was used to physicality. And aggressive men. They came with the job. Still, something in her trembled at the sight of him. Without responding, she turned, walked over to the coffee, and poured a cup. "You want some?" she called out.

"Sure."

"Thanks for making it." Her voice caught.

"No problem." David sat down at the table. "What's wrong?"

Kit put the coffee in front of him and sat down. "We need to debrief," she said, without looking at him.

"Something else."

She shook her head. "It's nothing."

"Don't give me that." He grinned and put his mug of coffee to his mouth. "Let me guess," he said, wiping his mouth with the back of his hand. "You are upset because I got hurt last night."

"Our job was to protect you."

"I was in danger, and that has you shook up."

"Our backup failed."

"You weren't in control."

"I'm responsible for you!"

"It's more than that."

Kit stood up, her face hot. What was he thinking? "You are so arrogant!"

David laughed. "And I am so right!"

She stared at him incredulously. Her heart was pounding.

David stood up. His smile faded. "Look, Kit. I'm sorry for playing with you." He took two steps away and turned back toward her. "Last night, I knew I was in trouble. And all I could think about was . . . was never getting the chance to really know you." David ran his hand through his hair. "Life is short. I don't want to miss something that could be really good. And I'm hoping, and praying, that one day, when this is done, you'll agree with me, and we'll get to find out what that's all about."

A thousand sparks raced through Kit's body. Her eyes took in his face, from his brown eyes, to the bruise, down to his strong jaw. She thought about their conversation about for-giveness and grace. He seemed to be for real. Ben thought so. And cracks were beginning to appear in the wall she had so carefully built around her heart.

"I know, after Eric," he said, continuing, "it must be hard for you to think about . . ."

"No. It's not," Kit insisted.

". . . it must be hard to think of being in another relationship. I just hope you'll take the risk."

She opened her mouth to respond, then heard someone
coming in the door. Chris. She hesitated.

David's eyes were steady. "If you decide to go for it, Kit, I'll
be there. And if things work out, I promise you, I will never,
ever leave you. Ever."

24

Chris had brought breakfast, but Kit excused herself and drove to her motel, fighting the emotions swirling within her, her heart convulsing in fear and sorrow . . . sorrow over Bob, over Eric, and yes, over her mother. Sorrow, then fear. Fear for David. Fear for herself. What if? Could she? Her excuses were gone, the way forward cleared. Still, she felt afraid. She showered, tears streaming down her face, sobs echoing off the tile, her vision blurred. And when she had finished, when she had exhausted herself and spent her emotion, she curled up in her bed, hugged her Bible to her chest, and prayed.

She arrived back at the offsite at 11:00 a.m. The others were already gathering to strategize.

"Carlos Cienfuegos," she said, reading from a long fax from Norfolk, "is a Mexican citizen with permanent resident status. He makes $40,000 a year as a crew chief for agricultural workers, according to the IRS." She looked up. "$40,000. That doesn't seem right for a guy who wears fancy Western clothes and drives a Mercedes."

"Where does he live?" Chris asked.

Kit repeated the address out loud. He typed it into Google maps and soon they were looking at a satellite view of a large, two-story white house surrounded by trees. A three-car garage sat behind the house to the right, and to the left stood a stable with room for three stalls, at least. "Forty thousand," Kit repeated. "Yeah, right."

"Let's get property tax records," Chris said.

"Good. Do that," Kit said. "We've got a copy of his driver's license but the only vehicle registered in his name is an old pickup . . . a 1996 Ford. You don't need a three-car garage for a Ford pickup."

"What's his wife's name?"

"It looks like 'Carlotta'."

"What about criminal records?" Roger asked.

"Nothing." Kit looked around. "This guy's dirty, but his record is clean."

"What about the shed?" Chris asked.

"At the live oak farm?"

"We should be watching it. Maybe he's loading whatever is in there into the truck David will be driving."

"I'll go," Roger said.

"Wait. I think it's going to be the other way around. I think whatever David is going to be transporting is coming *up* from Norfolk. Cienfuegos told him to call him when he started back across the bridge tunnel." Kit explained about the warning Cienfuegos had given David. "So I need you, Roger, to put the state police on alert, once we know what David's driving. And the same goes for both counties' sheriff's offices. He cannot be pulled over by a cop. But I don't want too much information getting out. Just give them the bare bones."

"Got it," he said.

"How are we going to track him?" Kit asked. "What happened last night cannot be repeated. Can we put a GPS tracer on his body somehow?"

Jason looked up. His brown hair hung down over his eyes and curled around his ears.

"You have something that will fit inside his cell phone?"

"They took away his cell phone before."

"Yes, you're right. Will it fit in his iPod?"

"That might interfere with the transmitter."

"Well, you call him and see what you can arrange. He's supposed to pick up the truck at 8:00, at C&R's. My guess is, he'll be available most of the day."

"OK."

"Can I leave that to you?" Kit fixed her eyes on him, her jaw set.

"Yes, ma'am. I'll take care of it."

"I'll count on that." She looked around. "What else can we find out about this Carlos Cienfuegos? Who does he hang out with? Where does he shop? Where does he go to drink? What does he do for fun? What other growers does he work for? And why was Maria in his truck? We need everything we can uncover."

⊙━━✦━━⊙

They spent the rest of the day in a blur of nervous energy. Steve called from Norfolk to get an update on the case, and said he'd assigned more agents to help out. That, to her, seemed a good sign, a sign of confidence.

Roger reported in, saying that the house was appraised at $529,000, well above the county average, and that it was in his wife's name. Carlotta also owned a white Mercedes, a blue Toyota Sequoia, and a four-wheel drive GMC pickup truck, according to personal property tax records. "He used to keep a large fishing boat in Wachapreague," he said. "Someone in the tax office told me he got tired of paying the county taxes on it."

That triggered a reaction from Kit. "Contact the Maryland Department of Natural Resources and find out if that boat's registered with them, and where it is. He may have just moved it out of state." Maryland didn't assess a personal property tax. Was the boat involved in the ocean shooting, Kit wondered? The beach child's death? Her mind raced through the possibilities.

Roger had also gotten the details on all the cars, driving records on the two Cienfuegoses, and one more juicy tidbit: Carlotta had a lawsuit pending against her. "She apparently has a commercial cleaning business. Someone thinks she didn't provide the services promised."

"So she provides cleaning services and her husband ag workers. Sounds like they would need a lot of laborers," Kit said. "I think it's time to set up some surveillance on these folks." Kit looked at Roger. "Any chance we could get some additional manpower from your agency?"

Roger shook his head. "I'll ask, but everyone's tied up with the trooper shooting."

"Steve's sending agents from Norfolk. I'll see if we can round up some more from Salisbury."

"Carlotta has contracts with some medical and law offices and a county office building," Chris reported.

"Wait: Patricia said that Robert Barnes is a big-deal lawyer. Is that a connection?" Kit asked.

Chris shrugged. "Not sure yet. The lawsuit is over a thirty thousand dollar contract to clean a dental office. Apparently, she didn't provide the level of service the contract required and the dentist is suing her."

"Let's go talk to her lawyer."

"I've set up the appointment for tomorrow."

By the time Kit had contacted and made appointments with the three companies she was going to cover, Roger called back with news that Carlos Cienfuegos did indeed have a boat registered with the Maryland DNR, and he kept it in Ocean City. "Let's bring in Maryland State Police. Ask them to go take a picture of it," Kit said.

Roger agreed, and then said he had contacted the sheriff's offices to alert the deputies coming on to work the three-to-eleven shift about the special instructions they'd be getting. "Basically, I asked them to stay away from Rt. 13 tonight. Just leave traffic enforcement there alone."

"Great. As soon as my agents get here, we'll start surveillance," Kit said.

⟨⸺✦⸺⟩

The offsite would serve as their command center for the duration of David's trip. Kit had bought sub sandwiches and bottled water, a tray of vegetables and some cookies, and as she stowed them in the refrigerator in the kitchen, her mind went over the instructions they'd given David. He would call her when he picked up the truck.

But at 8:05 p.m, he text-messaged Kit with the license plate number of the truck he was driving. Why hadn't he called? She had to presume it was a white box truck loaded with tomatoes. But why had he texted her?

She gave the number to Roger, who immediately contacted dispatch supervisors to make sure state police knew not to pull David over.

"I figure it's going to take him about two hours to get to Norfolk and an hour to offload, then an hour to get back on this side of the bridge. So just after midnight, the fun begins," Chris said. "You want to go get some sleep?"

As if she could. "No. I'll make coffee."

Jason sat hunched over an array of computer equipment. "I gave him two transponders," he said. "One is in his iPod, the other he was supposed to put on the truck. So far, both seem to be working."

"Good." Kit turned toward the kitchen, fear gripping her. Resolutely spooning coffee into the filter, she lectured herself. Be professional. Trust God. Trust David. It's going to be all right.

o—✦—o

The plan they'd devised worked perfectly. Both GPS transponders tracked David down the Delmarva Peninsula, to the bridge tunnel, through Norfolk, to the produce distribution center where the tomatoes were offloaded, then back. Roger called the dispatchers back to reiterate the message when David crossed back over the bridge. One state trooper reported seeing him, but left him alone. David made the return trip, dropped the truck back at C&R, and called Kit.

"Did you get any indication what was in the truck?"

"No. On the way down, the load looked like tomatoes, right? In standard shipping crates. I was empty coming back. I think they've installed a compartment under the floor in the back. That's where they're hiding the stuff. My guess is, it's cocaine. Maybe meth."

Meth? Like Miguel Martinez was holding?

"What about the truck?"

"Same as before." David paused. "They want me to make the same run tonight," he said. "Can we do it again?"

"I guess so," Kit responded. "No sign of Maria?"

"None."

"Everything OK?" Chris asked as she hung up the phone.

"They want him to do it again tonight."

The others began packing up their gear.

Chris nodded. "I had a couple of agents watching the shed. A pickup pulled in there at 4:00 a.m. and a man with a flashlight moved into the shed."

Kit looked at him. "So, do we get a search warrant?" She felt anxious. This had to end soon.

"Not yet. Let's wait."

"OK." A bit of a sigh edged into her voice. "Don't forget, we're working the funeral tomorrow."

◦━━◆━━◦

Murderers sometimes attend their victims' funerals to relive their crimes, so a law enforcement presence at Bob Stewart's funeral would be essential. The Chincoteague police would attend, in uniform. Many of them had been friends with Bob for years, or they'd grown up with Connie, or they just knew the couple—the island was a small community.

The FBI task force planned to be there, too, but would be keeping a lower profile. One of them would watch the parking lot at the small clapboard church and collect the license plate numbers of the people attending. Dressed in civilian clothes, Roger would sit near the back of the church, cataloging the congregation. Kit and Chris would be in the pews as well. Meanwhile, Jason would stage himself in a nearby building, photographing the grieving attendees with a long lens.

The air felt hot inside the sanctuary, heavy with the perfume of the flowers that filled the chancel area. Kit watched as Connie and her children took their places in the front row. Connie looked drawn, somber in her black dress. She wore a pillbox hat with a black net veil, as if to tone down the brightness of her red hair. The kids, in their early 20s, were still gawky as colts, too young, Kit thought, to be losing their father.

She smoothed her black and white dress. Several rows behind her and to the left sat Chris. The high, arching ceiling of the sanctuary was constructed of light wood that matched the packed pews. Organ music filled the room. Kit recognized the hymn, "Blessed Assurance," tucked into the middle of the medley. Somewhere, someone was crying softly. Ahead, Connie sat shoulder-to-shoulder with her daughter and stared at the coffin.

Death, Kit thought, was such a thief. It had stolen good years from Connie and Bob, the satisfaction of seeing their children grown and settled, the joy of grandchildren, the pleasures of old age. Now, Connie would have only memories to comfort her. Connie would be alone. How fair was that? How just?

Kit looked at the bulletin. Her eyes caught the date. Why did it seem familiar?

As the congregation rose to sing the opening hymn, she stood up and that's when it hit her. Today, Eric was getting married again.

25

SHE BIT HER LIP TO KEEP THE TEARS AWAY, ANGRY AT HER OWN SELF-PITY. *"Amazing Grace . . ."* the old hymn proclaimed. But even in light of salvation and a joyous Eternity, the present seemed sad and empty to Kit. Connie and Bob had had a good marriage. What had they done to deserve this? And what had she done to deserve divorce?

These were foolish questions, as Kit well knew. She was well-acquainted with sin. It was the engine driving her profession. She saw it every day, saw its effects, and she was intimately aware of the tears of its victims. So why should she be surprised at its intrusion into her life?

The congregation sat down again. And as Kit took her place again in the pew, her heart felt heavy. Something was bothering her, something just out of reach of her conscious mind. She tried concentrating on the funeral service, tried praying silently, but the shadow wouldn't go away.

The minister began speaking. Kit's eyes were supposed to be watching the congregation, but they kept gravitating toward the cross on the wall behind the altar. The minister's words seemed to swirl in the close, hot air. He turned to the Gospel of John and began to read. "For God so loved the world . . ."

A latecomer appeared next to her, in the outside aisle. People to her left shifted toward the center to make room. Kit glanced up as she moved. Chief Petty Officer Rick Sellers smiled down at her.

"Hi," he whispered, as he slid into the seat.

"Hello." What was he doing here? She wished he'd picked somewhere else to sit. Why next to her?

They settled back in the pew. Was it her imagination, or was he leaning so that his upper arm touched hers? Kit shifted, intentionally increasing the space between them. The air seemed close. The minister continued reading from John: "In my father's house, there are many mansions . . ."

The woman in front of Kit bent down to retrieve a tissue from her purse. In that moment, Kit saw a familiar head four or five rows in front of her and on the other side of the church. David! She had no idea he'd be there. He turned, and their eyes locked and Kit felt a deep rush of emotion.

The woman straightened and blocked Kit's view again. Connie's son stood up and spoke about how much his father had meant to him. Another hymn followed, and then a prayer. A eulogy from Bob's brother. Another one from Connie's. A short sermon.

Kit tried not to focus on the minister's words, tried to stay in her professional law enforcement mode, but she could not escape them. Forgiveness. Grace. The great message of the Gospel weaving through the church on Holy Spirit wings, landing on hearts, bringing healing and hope. Yes, hope.

By the time he finished, Kit was fighting tears. The minister ended with prayer, they sang another hymn, and finally it was over. The minister asked the congregation to stand while the funeral directors moved to the front and began wheeling the coffin down the center aisle and out of the church. Connie and her children followed, holding onto each other, their faces streaked with tears.

"Any idea who did it?" Rick asked Kit quietly as people began to file out behind the coffin.

"I don't know," Kit said, wishing he would get lost.

"Are you going to the burial?"

"No."

Sellers stayed with her. When they stepped out of the narthex, into the bright sunshine, he touched her elbow. "Come here," he said, "I want you to meet somebody."

She didn't want to. She was busy, scanning the crowd. Then she saw David nearby. He had taken a risk, coming to the funeral. Why had he come? It would be better if Rick didn't see him. "All right," she said, taking Rick's arm and turning him away from David. She glanced back and met David's eyes again, and in that brief moment, the thing she'd been avoiding fell into place, the puzzle came together, and she knew the decision she had to make.

Her face grew hot and tears came to her eyes, and she ducked her head and quickly walked with Rick away from the church.

"So what's the connection between this murder and the kid on the beach?" Rick asked.

Kit blinked. "What makes you think there is one?"

"You're here."

"I'm friends with Connie."

"You're close to her?"

Kit raised her eyebrows.

"Your tears," he explained.

"Well, yes. Yes, I am." She wiped a tear away. "Did you think I came here on business?"

He shrugged. "I assumed so."

Curious. Why would he assume that? Safely away from David, she looked for a chance to escape. "Look, Rick," she said, "I'm sorry. I'm not feeling very social right now."

"It'll just take . . ."

"Sorry," she said, "I need to go." Before he could protest, she walked away.

"I'll call you!" Rick shouted as she hurried off.

As soon as she was out of sight, she called David on his cell phone. "I need to talk to you."

"Where?"

Kit got to her car and started her engine. "You know that place at the north end of the island where you told me you met Alice the first time?"

"Tucker Road. On the Assateague side."

"Right."

"I'll be there in five minutes."

◦━◆━◦

He stepped out of his Jeep when Kit pulled up behind him, his white shirt gleaming in the sun.

"Would you walk with me?" she asked.

The humidity was thick, the sun hot as they began down the path which skirted the marsh and led to the grassy area overlooking the channel. "What was Sellers doing there?" David asked.

"I don't know. I was shocked when he sat down next to me." She turned to look at him. "But then, I was equally shocked to see you."

He didn't respond.

"Does anyone from Chincoteague know you were the one who found Bob?"

"No. Not even Connie."

"Weren't you concerned . . ."

"I had to be there," he said, cutting her off. "I just . . . had to be there. And someday I need to tell her what happened that night. But I'll wait. For the sake of the case, I'll wait."

The channel was flowing peacefully this day, with very little breeze to stir up waves. A picnic table stood in the grassy area. "Want to sit down?" David said, gesturing toward it.

"I can't," Kit responded, folding her arms across her chest. "I'm too hyper."

"OK." David climbed up and sat on the table with his feet on the bench, and he rolled up his sleeves. He looked like a businessman on his lunch hour. A rugged, very good-looking businessman.

Kit began to pace. "I was sitting at the funeral, and I realized something."

He cocked his head.

Kit glanced at him out of the corner of her eye. In the shallows, a heron stalked fish, his long legs bending improbably. Kit's throat felt tight. She was trying so hard not to cry.

"Tell me," David said, softly.

———

The white truck moved slowly down Tucker Road until it came to a vacation rental that looked unoccupied. Sellers pulled into the driveway, parked, and walked past the house and down the yard to the water. Easing through some brush, he found a good view of the shoreline. Then he lifted his binoculars. What were they doing?

It irritated him that she'd walked away like that. Women didn't do that to him! He had no chance to find out what she knew.

If he'd known telling Lopez where Maria was would have entangled him in all this, he never would have done it. Not even for the measly meth bonus he got. What a mistake!

Still, he figured he'd be able to get out of it. After all, nothing connected him to Lopez, no paperwork anyway, and he hadn't even given Lopez his real name. Sellers figured he was safe. Still, he needed to keep an eye on this woman.

⊶✦⊷

Kit looked at David. Her vision grew blurry. "Connie and Bob were married for almost thirty years. Now, she's going to have to live alone, without him. She'll have to completely rethink her life. I was sitting there, in the funeral, feeling so sad for her, and I was staring at the bulletin, when the date jumped out at me. Eric's getting married today!"

David waited for her to go on.

"And it occurred to me: Connie lost her husband to death. I lost mine to divorce. Both of us have a choice: move on or get stuck. Believe God is in control, or not." The heron took off, flew about twenty yards away, and set down again near the edge of the marsh.

David nodded. "Right."

"Connie talked to me the night Bob died about joy. Joy! I couldn't believe she would even say that. But she told me not to give up the fight for joy. I've been thinking about that ever since.

"There, in the church, a verse of Scripture jumped into my head: 'Be kind, tenderhearted, forgiving one another as God in Christ has forgiven you.'" Her words emerged like a sob. "I think I've been wrong to hang on to anger toward Eric. I think that's been killing my joy." She felt a rush of emotion, like some large rock outcropping in her soul was breaking apart and tumbling downhill.

David pulled a handkerchief from his pocket and handed it to her.

She blew her nose. "He hurt me, but my anger is wrong, too. Toward him and . . . and toward my mother." She hadn't told David about her mother. She braced herself for a question and was thankful that he was wise enough to let her talk and not ask for details.

Instead, he gently said, "We're all wrong. Isn't that what grace is for?"

She shivered. "It's hard! By day, I function as this in-control FBI agent, but at night . . . at night I am so alone. And so sad."

"You've been abandoned."

"Yes!"

"And that's not fair."

The truth of his words stabbed her heart. Kit closed her eyes and shook her head. She hugged her arms close to her chest. "I wanted so much to have children!"

"It's not too late for that," he said softly.

"It feels like it." She sobbed.

David shook his head. "It's not."

Kit stared at him.

David's jaw shifted. The sun glinted off of his hair. "I don't understand why you got hurt. Or why Bob died. Or why God allows bad things. But Kit, I figure I've got a choice . . ."

Her face grew hot.

"Trust God or walk away from him." He looked up at her. "And I'm not walking away again."

She swallowed. She had a huge lump in her throat. "I'm afraid."

"Of what?"

"Afraid that . . . that Eric will be off the hook. That all the pain I went through will mean nothing."

"You think God was OK with you getting hurt?"

"I don't know!"

"Well, can you trust him on that?"

A deep chill ran through her. She dropped her head into her hands.

"Let it go," he said softly. "Just let it go. Connie's right. Let it go, and fight for joy." He approached her, gently put his finger on her chin, and lifted her head. David must have seen something in her face, some change, because his jaw relaxed, and his lips parted, and he leaned down and kissed her, and their kiss was a sweet, sweet moment of surrender, like a leap into a rushing waterfall, or a ride on a cresting wave. He wrapped his arms around her, and as Kit relaxed into his embrace, she let go of the double weight that had threatened to drown her.

⊙══◆══⊙

Rick Sellers watched the couple through his binoculars. "I wonder how long that's been going on?" he muttered to himself. Bringing the binoculars down, he turned and walked back to his truck. He started the engine and pulled slowly down the road, rolling over and over in his mind the implications of what he'd just seen. How could he use it?

⊙══◆══⊙

The next week seemed like a blur. David made three more runs for Lopez without incident, unless you counted the toll it took on the nerves of all the people involved. Particularly Kit.

The team had gone over the photographs from the funeral, the license plate numbers Roger had collected, and photos taken by Jason. They found nothing out of the ordinary. Those present at the funeral seemed like normal island folk.

Kit consulted with Chris. "Maybe we'd better set up surveillance on Cienfuegos's house," she suggested.

Chris shook his head. "Hard to do, as isolated as it is. Too labor intensive. We'll need more people than Steve can spare right now."

Kit frowned. "Something going on?"

"The president is going to be in Norfolk tomorrow, christening a new aircraft carrier. So Steve has his hands full."

"When did you talk to him?"

"We talk nearly every day," Chris said.

What was the deal with that? Kit wondered. Was Chris reporting on her? She avoided talking to Steve as much as she could!

She swallowed her paranoia. "So, how do we move ahead?" she asked.

Later, David provided the answer. "Lopez told me Cienfuegos has a longer job for me. 'No more tomatoes.' That's what he said," he told her.

"What's he talking about?" Kit asked.

"I have no idea. I just know he asked me if I could drive to North Carolina. I asked him what part. He asked why, so I told him I have reasons not to go in parts of that state. That shut him up." David shoved his hands in his pockets. "He said 'Western.' That's where Hickory is. So, I think we're getting our break. I think this is it, Kit. I think we've got him."

26

THE REST OF THE TEAM SEEMED THRILLED. THEY CHEERED, EVEN, WHEN KIT told them. Kit felt her anxiety sinking deeper into her soul.

David showed up at the offsite later to brief everyone. "He wants me to meet him and Cienfuegos at the tomato processing plant on Wednesday night at 9 o'clock."

"Why there?" Chris asked.

"He said he'll have a new truck for me. It's got C&R's logo on the side, but it's not theirs. He said the owner is always busy on Wednesday nights, and won't notice the activity."

"We have to provide perfect backup," Kit said to Chris. "It's got to be perfect! And David, you've got to blow it off if they try to move the location."

He nodded.

"Let's go, then."

On the grounds of the tomato processing plant sat a small, one-story house. At one time, the plant manager had used it as a residence; now its main function was storage. Kit obtained permission from Sam Curtis to use it. He didn't ask for what, and she didn't tell him, but she did verify he'd be in church on Wednesday evening.

They'd had just two nights to set up the place for surveillance. To minimize their presence, they worked in the middle of the night using flashlights. Jason planted bugs in the processing plant itself. He would also wire David, so they'd be alerted in case Lopez and Cienfuegos tried to force a change in locations as they had before.

Meanwhile, Kit and Chris worked out contingency plans. They calculated the manpower they'd need, decided how the arrest would go down if David was in immediate danger, and had even asked for a member of the AUSA's office to be on call if they had a question about the adequacy of the evidence they were getting. They knew if they acted prematurely, they'd blow the case; if they waited too long, they'd put David at unnecessary risk.

"Any chance they'll check David for wires?" Chris asked.

"They haven't been that careful lately."

"Then certainly they won't check the building for bugs."

"No way. Besides," Kit said, "Jason swore they'd be invisible."

"Oh, did I tell you?" Chris said. "Steve is coming to watch this go down."

"No, you didn't tell me that. Why?"

"Why is he coming? The president is gone. I guess Steve has the time."

Kit didn't necessarily buy that.

For the rest of the afternoon, Kit worried. Why was Steve coming? She was the case agent, so why hadn't he informed her?

He did inform her . . . when he was on the way. She kept her irritation suppressed, her conversation crisply professional. But she dreaded facing Steve. Why did he have to come up now?

Sometimes she wondered why he had hired her. Had he been told by some higher-up that he had to take her?

She checked her watch. It was a quarter to four. David would be here soon to get wired up. She would have to be brutally professional with him. Cold, even. Hopefully, she'd have a chance to explain. Hopefully, she'd . . .

Her cell phone rang. She looked at the number. It was from the U.S. Fish and Wildlife Service. Ramsfeld?

Indeed. What did she want?

"Kit, I need to tell you something." Ramsfeld's voice was almost a whisper. "He creeped me out, I'm telling you. Really creeped me out."

"Who, Brenda?"

"Do you know that Coast Guard guy, Rick Sellers?"

"Yes."

"He approached me at the beach. Started asking all kinds of questions about you—did I know you, had I seen you, that sort of thing. I felt like he was stalking you or something."

"I assure you I haven't given him any encouragement."

"It's weird. Actually, it's more than that. Like when he asked me about this other guy, David, that you're seeing."

"What?"

"He seemed to know a lot about him, and a lot about you. Pressed me for what I knew. It was so weird. About your case, too. I'm telling you, he gave me the creeps."

"What did you tell him?"

"Nothing! Just that I knew you on a professional basis." Ramsfeld sighed. "You know he's friends with Joe Rutgers?"

Joe Rutgers? That was curious. They didn't seem to be anything alike.

Kit tried to blow off that phone call. She had other things to worry about. Still, Brenda Ramsfeld's words bothered her. What was the connection between Rick Sellers and Joe

Rutgers? Friendship only? And why was Sellers asking all those questions about her? What was he up to? Was it merely a personal interest in her? Or something else?

And if Rutgers was the white man who asked Martinez to hold the backpack with meth in it, was Sellers connected to that?

A sudden thought crossed her mind. Sellers had initially failed to tell her about the Coast Guard's use of IOOS, the current tracking system that could have told her approximately where the beach child had been dropped into the ocean. Later, he apologized and filed the reports she'd asked him to file . . . he'd even given her copies. A call to the Coast Guard's Search and Rescue headquarters in Norfolk would confirm whether he was being up front about that.

Curious now, Kit tracked back through the information on her Bureau phone, found the number of the Norfolk Coast Guard Office, and called. She'd left the copies of the reports Rick had filed at the cottage in Chincoteague, but maybe, just maybe, they'd have a way of tracing them.

A bored receptionist transferred her to an enlisted Coast Guardsman who listened carefully to her questions. "I'll check the status of those reports, ma'am, and call you back," he said.

⟡

The small house near the tomato processing plant would serve as a bunker from which she and her team would monitor David's meeting with Carlos Cienfuegos. She wondered why anyone driving by at 9:00 on a Wednesday night wouldn't wonder about activity in the plant. But David had said that Carlos had specifically picked that time, because he said the owner, Sam Curtis always attended church on Wednesday nights, and then he and his wife went with friends to a nearby diner for a late dinner. The routine stayed the same, week after week, and Carlos was going to take advantage of it.

The moon was up, a beautiful half-moon, silvery and shrouded by wispy clouds. Kit could see it through the trees, and she thought about how even now it was shining down on her grandmother's house on Chincoteague, and on the waves on Assateague, and on Bob Stewart's grave. The moon had been shining down on the little beach child, too, as the ocean gently rocked him until it laid his body on Assateague. Would she ever find out who had killed him?

She felt anxious, ready for this operation to be over. If David could get Carlos to say on the wire that the "cargo" David was to pick up in North Carolina consisted of people, the AUSA said he'd go to the grand jury with it. Get an indictment. Push the case against Hector Lopez and Carlos Cienfuegos.

Then the games would begin. Turning one suspect against the other. Getting witnesses to confirm what they'd suspected. Negotiating plea bargains with some of the underlings so they could nail the suspects they really wanted to nail: Cienfuegos for trafficking, Lopez for Bob's murder. And someone for the murder of the beach child.

Tonight could be the beginning of the end of her case. Oh, Kit was ready!

"Everything's all set," Chris said, coming up behind her. "It won't be long now."

Absolutely, she thought. This had to end soon.

❦

Jason and his recording equipment filled one small room in the house. He'd be monitoring the wire. The small transmitter on David was very short-range—the radio signal would only carry about one hundred feet. Plus, Jason had other bugs in the building itself, cleverly hidden in light fixtures, heat ducts, and behind vents.

Roger stood right next to Jason. Kit would be listening with headphones, too, so she could give the go-ahead once they had what they needed. Chris and Steve and six other agents completed the team in the house.

Of necessity, the group had to keep the house completely dark, working only with tiny red lights. Any appearance of activity could alert Cienfuegos to their presence. They had to be very careful.

At Kit's insistence, they had practiced what they were going to do early on Sunday morning at the offsite. Although David had teased her, she was determined to do everything she could to make tonight go well. If that meant pushing the team, that was fine.

They'd even constructed a list of admissions they needed him to get out of Cienfuegos and/or Lopez. There were four of them, and she'd made David memorize them.

Kit looked at her watch: 8:55 p.m. Any moment now . . .

"All set?" Steve Gould appeared at her side. He had parked with the others, a mile away, at the old church, and Chris had driven him in, and hidden his car behind the house.

"Yes, sir."

"Nervous?"

She swallowed. "We've worked very hard to get this right, but yes, sir, I am."

He nodded.

Kit's bureau cell phone vibrated. She answered it. It was the Coast Guardsman from Norfolk.

"I don't see those reports, ma'am. I've looked everywhere."

"Nothing on the body found on Assateague?"

"No, ma'am. Not a thing. I'll keep looking, but I went through all of our files. Nothing from CPO Sellers. Nothing at all."

Had Sellers lied to her? Kit pursed her lips.

But there was no time to worry about Sellers now. Headlights in the drive leading up to the tomato processing plant announced someone was arriving. Kit trembled in anticipation.

⟡

David pulled his SUV into the parking lot of the tomato processing plant and parked it nose out, about thirty feet from the building. Staging his car for a quick getaway remained an old habit. He wiped his hands on his jeans, pulled the key out of the ignition, and stepped out of the car. He glanced toward the house where he knew Kit was working.

The night sky was nearly dark. A half-moon, shrouded by clouds, hung overhead. From somewhere, an owl hooted. Then David heard another engine and Lopez pulled up in a box truck with C&R's logo on the side. Was it Bob's truck, now disguised? He suspected it was.

"Buenos noches," Lopez said, leaving his vehicle. He grinned like a cat standing over a fresh kill, and David wondered for a second if he was being set up.

But no, he reassured himself, Lopez was just like that. He nodded in response, and breathed a silent prayer. *Please, get me through this one more meeting.* Lopez made his skin crawl. David touched the iPod in his pocket and prayed that the transmitter would not fail. That Jason would record what they needed. That tonight would be the last of it.

Cienfuegos arrived at 9:13 p.m., driving a pickup truck, not his Escalade. David had never seen it. He parked the truck, acknowledged David and Lopez, and then Cienfuegos unlocked the door, and the three men walked in, their boots loud on the concrete floor. Cienfuegos wore jeans and a white Western shirt and black, alligator skin Western boots. Not the sort of thing you'd wear if you were going to do something messy, like kill somebody. That reassured David.

They walked through the building to the area where the tomatoes were sorted. There, Cienfuegos stopped, leaned up against a conveyor belt, and smiled. "So, Señor Castillo, you have been doing a good job?"

"You tell me," David responded. The white cinderblock walls and strong overhead lighting made the sorting shed as bright as noonday. He smelled a faint odor of bleach. Stacks and stacks of empty packing boxes lined the walls. In the back corner, a faucet with a hose connected was dripping . . . dripping.

Cienfuegos kept talking. He had a gun in his belt. "You do a good job. You get the trucks back, you not get stopped, you not ask questions . . . we like that, eh, Hector?"

Hector Lopez grinned and spit off to the side.

"So now, we make you another offer. A bigger job. For bigger pay. How you think about that?"

"You tell me what it is. And I'll tell you if I'll do it."

❦

In the house, Jason pressed the audio headphones to his head, and concentrated on what he was hearing. The transmitter remained at full strength. He gave a thumbs-up to Kit, who nodded. She had just one headphone pressed to one ear, so she could hear Roger or Chris or Steve if they said something. Chris was doing the same thing. Together, they'd decide when they had enough information to make an arrest.

❦

"My job is to help farmers get workers for their fields," Cienfuegos said, continuing, "and to help poor Mexicans get dollars to send to their families back home. It is a public service, really, a good thing. Bringing workers and work together. But sometimes, you know, the red tape, it keeps the good from being done. I have some workers coming to North Carolina from Mexico."

"They're illegal?"

"They need to come here. To work. For that, I need a driver I can trust."

"What do you want me to do?"

"Take a load of tomatoes to Norfolk. Then keep going, to North Carolina. And bring back my load of people."

"In the truck?"

"Sí, yes. Without getting stopped, you know?"

"What about the weigh stations."

Cienfuegos smiled. He rubbed two fingers together. "You know the right people, you find out when they are closed. I get you that information."

David shifted his weight on his feet. "These people, they are men, eh? Pickers?"

"Some, some . . ."

"Women, too?"

"We supply a lot of different kinds of labor, no? Field workers, domestic help, cleaning people. There are lots of needs in America."

"No green cards? Passports?"

"Some have passports."

"Where in North Carolina?"

"What does that matter?"

David narrowed his eyes. "I got reasons not to go in some parts."

Cienfuegos nodded, accepting his answer. "Hickory. In the Western part."

"And where do I bring 'em to?"

Hector Lopez grinned. "Casa Cienfuegos."

Carlos frowned and looked at David. "We have rooms for them."

"And where is that? Around here?"

"Yes. Close by here. You take the job, I tell you where."

David rubbed the back of his neck. "How much?"

"$5,000."

"Man, I get caught, those are federal charges."

"Don't get caught."

David paced away, frowning. Then he turned quickly and looked at Cienfuegos. "I read in the paper, when that cop got shot, they found a broken-down white box truck."

Cienfuegos cursed. David's statement had caught him off guard. "That driver was stupid, eh? You, David Castillo, are a smart man. That would not happen to you."

"5K isn't enough. They'll be looking at white box trucks."

"All right, then, seven."

"Make it 10K and I'll do it."

Cienfuegos looked at Hector Lopez. "This man drives a hard bargain."

"Let's just kill him."

Cienfuegos laughed. "No, no. I said he is smart. So OK, Señor Castillo, we pay you an outrageous 8K."

"I want the money up front."

"Half up front, half when you deliver."

David nodded. "When do we do it?"

Cienfuegos's eyes sparkled. "Now!"

27

KIT LOOKED SHARPLY AT CHRIS. THEY'D BEEN MONITORING EVERY WORD. "Do we have enough? Can we move?" she asked him.

Steve Gould was standing at a small window nearby. "Kit, who's this?"

She got up, set down her headphones, and joined him. She could see vehicles using only their parking lights approaching the other end of the building. Her heart began beating hard. "I don't know!"

"It looks like law enforcement."

"Roger . . . do you guys have anything going on tonight?"

"Nothing that I know of."

Chris joined them at the window. Men dressed in dark clothes began tumbling out of a large truck. They were carrying rifles and wearing ballistic armor. "It's either the sheriff's office or the state police. Look at that! They've got a ram."

"We need to intercept them!" Kit said. "Jason! Do we have a common frequency with local law enforcement?" Before he could answer, they heard the boom-boom-boom of flashbangs.

"Too late!" Chris said.

When David and the two men heard the flashbangs, they all reacted, turning toward the noise. "*Andele!*" Cienfuegos said, cursing, and he headed for a nearby door.

David followed. He didn't have a choice. He knew that if he didn't, Hector would simply shoot him ... and enjoy doing it.

As a door opened at the end of the room, Hector opened fire.

⸰━━◆━━⸰

"ERT—that's the sheriff's office," Steve shouted, looking through binoculars.

"Roger, call local dispatch. Tell them to stop the raid at C&R!" Kit shouted.

"They're coming out!" Steve said as a back door to the processing plant flew open and Cienfuegos ran out, followed by David and Lopez. The three men began sprinting across the parking lot, taking fire from men who had appeared at the door of the processing plant.

Kit grabbed a shotgun. "Let's go!"

Chris stopped her. "No! You'll be right in the line of fire!"

"We have to help him!"

"Let him run with them. We'll follow."

"He's right," Steve said. "Stay here."

⸰━━◆━━⸰

David ran out into the night, following Cienfuegos toward the woods. Hector ran right behind him. Once in the dark woods, David figured, he could lose them.

But about one hundred feet from the building, David felt a burning blow to the back of his leg, the rush of red-hot lead tearing into his flesh. His whole body jerked and he cried out, fell to the ground and grabbed his leg. The night seemed to explode in a thousand orange and yellow shooting stars and the moon above turned blood red. Lost in pain, he felt himself being jerked to his feet, supported between Cienfuegos and Lopez, and thrust forward, into the forest.

Watching from the house, the agents saw David fall.

"He's shot!" Chris said.

Kit's heart nearly exploded, and before either man could stop her, she was gone.

Kit left the house just as Lopez and Cienfuegos picked up David and disappeared into the woods. She focused on that spot. Bullets whizzed from behind her, and somewhere in her mind, she heard Steve and Chris shouting, "FBI! FBI!" Still, she ran, her feet trying to find traction on the uneven ground. She jumped over a log and a branch whipped her face. She dodged tree trunks as underbrush snagged her legs. She thought she saw movement ahead, and then she didn't. She raced on. Then her eyes saw a light—the dome light of a car. She ran faster, desperately, her breath jagged and sharp, and then, just as headlights split the night, she tripped. Fell. Her gun flew out of her hands and her face hit the dirt. She looked up just as a white Escalade spun gravel and tore off into the night. She clenched her fists, gripping dirt and leaves and twigs, and dropped her forehead to the ground. "Oh, God!" she cried out. "Oh, God!"

Moments later, in shock and disbelief, Kit pushed up off the ground. She found her gun, and began retracing her steps back to the tomato processing plant, numb with fear. Pressing the button on her communicator, she said, "Chris, it was a white Escalade, late model. It was a backup! He had it stashed in the woods."

She heard no response. She broke into a half-run, tears blurring her vision.

Steve Gould met her. "That was stupid! The dumbest move ever. You could have been shot! It's bad enough to lose an informant, but you could have been killed!"

Kit gritted her teeth.

"Poor judgment! Very poor judgment." Steve's tongue-lashing continued as they jogged back to the clearing. His words fell on her shoulders like a whip. She was impulsive. Reckless. She'd put herself and ultimately Chris and him at risk, because they had to run out and get the ERT to stop firing in her direction. What was she thinking?

Kit took his anger, absorbing it like a sponge. He didn't understand. How could he understand?

Chris met them at the clearing along with a sheriff's deputy. "The sheriff's office had a warrant for Lopez. He's a major meth distributor."

Kit spoke. "So, let's go. Who's chasing the Escalade?" she asked.

The deputy looked blank. "No one. We were told to stop the operation."

Kit's temper flared. "Are you kidding?"

"No ma'am."

"Did you establish a perimeter?"

"Not in that direction," the deputy responded.

She fought for control. "All right, we have the GPS." She grabbed her mike. "Jason, what's David's position?"

There was a moment's hesitation. "I don't know. One GPS transmitter is in the parking lot . . . that's the one in his truck, I guess, and the other one . . . the other one is about thirty yards from you, due north. Away from the building."

"Right where David fell," Kit said, peering into the dark.

"Hold on," Chris said. He jogged across the grass and came back a minute later with David's cell phone and a transmitter in his hand. "The cell phone must have pulled the transmitter off when he fell."

"So there's no backup?" Steve Gould said.

"We had a backup—two GPS trackers!"

"That aren't any good now!"

Kit felt her face grow hot. She was a heartbeat away from saying something she'd regret later when Gould interjected, "Chris, you take over."

A flash of indignation poured through her. "Why?"

"Impulsivity won't cut it."

Kit narrowed her eyes. "I'm not impulsive. I object to your decision."

"You foolishly endangered your own life—and mine."

"You made the decision to run toward the ERT."

"Because you were running into their field of fire!"

"He'd been shot!"

"And you could have been killed."

"So no *man* has ever risked his life to save another?" Kit glared at him, her anger pounding in her head.

Steve opened his mouth to reply, but nothing came out.

"She's right, boss," Chris said. "She really isn't impulsive."

Kit's throat tightened. She and Gould stood toe to toe, the air between them thick.

"Every minute we spend arguing about it puts David's life in greater danger," Chris said. "I think she should keep the lead."

Steve shook his head and kicked a stone on the ground.

"Sir, if I blow this, I'll give you my creds and my badge," Kit said.

Steve looked at her as if calculating her worth. He shifted his jaw. "Fair enough."

"Thank you, sir." And she shot a look of gratitude at Chris.

David fought panic in the back of Cienfuegos's Escalade. His leg felt warm with blood, his jeans were soaked. In the darkness, he could not see much, but from feeling his wound, he couldn't detect any arterial bleeding. But it was like a fireball was burning under his skin. Had the bullet hit a nerve? It remained in his leg—he couldn't find an exit wound. When he'd been shot in the shoulder it hadn't hurt this much. What was going on?

Stop the bleeding, David told himself. Don't go into shock. Fight it.

He saw an old T-shirt on the floor, ripped it into strips, and tightened the material around his leg. Meanwhile Cienfuegos and Lopez were arguing in Spanish, their words flying too fast for him to understand. He saw Cienfuegos take out his cell phone. He called someone, someone named Consuela. And Cienfuegos was giving her a list of things to bring, and David realized they were going to be meeting her somewhere, sometime. Maybe he could talk them into letting her take him to a hospital. The minute that thought entered his mind he rejected it. No way. They didn't care about him that much and it would blow their position.

Kit convened the agents and the leader of the sheriff's ERT under a light outside the tomato processing plant.

"So we have no one in pursuit and no way to track them." She tightened her jaw, trying in vain to stop the trembling in her gut. She looked at the deputy. "We need to put out an APB for Cienfuegos's car, a white Cadillac Escalade. There are three men together: Hector Lopez, Carlos Cienfuegos, and David

Castillo. David's our confidential informant. He took a shot in the leg as they left here."

"Where are they going?"

"No clue. We have teams surveilling Cienfuegos's house, and Lopez's apartment and we have put them on alert."

"We need ground support watching these roads." Kit pointed out four arterial roads that could provide a way of escape. "Can we get air support?"

"I've requested our helicopter and Maryland State Police is responding from Salisbury as well," Roger replied.

"How about hospitals?"

"There's only one, in Salisbury."

"Emergency care centers?"

Chris frowned. "Do you really think they're going to get him medical care?"

Kit grimaced and took a deep breath. "You're right. Besides, if they did, they'd probably just go to one of Carlotta's clients." She pressed her hand to her forehead. "Chris, you have some of the suspects' financial records. I need you to contact the banks where they have accounts. Let's see if they use an ATM. Also, credit cards . . . track their credit cards."

A sheriff's car, lights flashing, came down the road at a fast clip and pulled into the plant's parking lot. The burly sheriff of Accomack County emerged and walked swiftly toward the group. His ERT leader had briefed him on the way over. "Who's in charge?" he asked.

Kit introduced herself.

"This is a bad deal," he said, shaking his head.

"Who tipped you Lopez would be here?" Steve Gould asked.

"A woman named Maria Salazar. We got her for dealing meth and she's working a deal with the DA."

Maria? David's friend? "What help can you give us, Sheriff?"

"Everything I got. We want Lopez about as much as you want your man back."

"One more thing," Kit said. "Give David's cell phone to Jason, Chris. Maybe Cienfuegos or Lopez's cell numbers are in there, and we can trace those."

"Gotcha." Chris looked around. "Where are we going to set up?"

"We're ten minutes from the offsite. Let's go back there."

At the speed Cienfuegos was traveling, every bump sent waves of nausea rolling through David's belly. He could smell the blood, his own blood. His hands felt sticky with it.

He leaned his head back and tried to think. What could he do? How could he get out of this? His cell phone! He reached for it, but the place on his belt where it should have been was empty.

"Estacionate!" Lopez said, pointing to a bank. Cienfuegos jerked the car to the right and pulled into the parking lot.

Cienfuegos turned and looked at David. "You have an ATM card?"

"No."

But Cienfuegos didn't believe him. "Where is your wallet?" he yelled. "Give me your wallet!"

David pulled his wallet out of his back pocket. All it had in it was his fake driver's license and a hundred dollars. Carlos took the money and threw the wallet back at him. Then he looked at Lopez. "Use your own card."

Seconds later, Lopez jumped back in the car. "$200," he said. "Let's go!"

Cienfuegos took off again, and that's when David realized they were headed north on Rt. 13, toward Maryland. There wasn't a lot of traffic at 10:00 p.m. on a Sunday night. If only he saw a cop! Maybe he could signal him.

He was freezing in the back of the car. Shaking. The two men up front were arguing again. David couldn't follow the conversation. Once Lopez turned around and asked him something. He muttered something in answer, and Lopez gave up. Thank God, he gave up. Because all the Spanish had left David's head.

28

Kit stood over the table at the offsite, staring at the map spread out on it. Her mind was working quickly. She fought to keep her emotions under control. She knew she had to find Cienfuegos. David wouldn't last forever with a gunshot wound. Maybe Carlos would dump him somewhere. Maybe he'd signal for help somehow. Maybe . . .

They had to find him. "All right, so we have Rt. 13 running north and south and that's covered, right, Roger?"

"We're getting people there now."

"They're not in place yet?"

"On the way."

"Is the chopper up?"

Chris moved by at a fast clip, a paper in his hand. "The bank's playing hardball. I'm going to meet one of the officers at the local bank site. He's not happy about being rousted out of bed. I'll call you if I get anything."

Kit nodded. "Right."

"What can I do?"

Kit turned. Steve Gould was standing on her right. The anger had left his face. She thought quickly but before she could respond, her cell phone rang. One of the members of the surveillance squad at Cienfuegos's house reported that the lights, which had been off, had come back on and there was activity inside the house. Kit clicked her phone off. "Steve, please go to Cienfuegos's house. Something's going on. Maybe he'll show up there."

"Late model Cadillac Escalade?" he said.

"Yes. White."

"Gotcha."

"Here's the address. It should come up on your GPS, but in case it doesn't," Kit scribbled directions on a sheet of paper, "here's how to get there. I'll call the squad," she took the paper back out of his hand and jotted down a name and cell phone number, "and tell them you're on the way."

"Thanks."

With both Steve and Chris gone, Kit felt a sense of relief. Now there was no one to look over her shoulder. Question her judgment. She stared at the map. "Jen!" she called out suddenly to one of the Norfolk agents.

She came over.

"I need you to go watch the shed at the live oak farm, right here . . . see it? If Lopez is running, he may try to retrieve his stash."

"Right."

"Take someone with you!"

⸙

David had his eyes closed, fighting nausea and trying his best to withdraw from the fire consuming his leg. But when he felt Cienfuegos suddenly swing the SUV to the right, he had to look. Cienfuegos turned onto a small side road, accelerated, then swung left into a parking lot behind an auto parts store, where a green Suburban sat idling. Cienfuegos threw the

Escalade into park and turned off the ignition. Lopez jumped out of the front seat, jerked opened the door next to David, and said, "Get out!"

Get out? How? David's right leg was immobile.

He tried to use his arms to push himself out but Lopez reached in, grabbed him and pulled him out of the car. Eyes tearing with the pain, David planted his good leg, and lurched to a standing position, his vision darkening momentarily. Then he leaned against the Escalade.

Cienfuegos came around to David's side of the SUV and cursed when he saw the blood left on the white leather seats.

"What are we doing?" David asked.

"Changing cars. That woman, she saw us leave in this one."

Woman? What woman? Kit? "Look," David said, "why don't you just leave me here? I'm just going to slow you down, man."

"He knows too much," countered Hector.

Before David could answer, they were interrupted by a woman's voice: "Carlos, I want to go with you! You promised!" and before the sound of her voice registered in David's mind, she rounded the vehicle. "David!" she exclaimed.

He raised his head. Maria was standing in front of him. Maria! Her tiny white tank top barely brushed the top of her low-cut jeans and her hair curled around her shoulders in soft waves. But she had a look about her that was different, a hollow, haunted look. Something about her eyes.

"You know him?" Cienfuegos said, his voice sharp.

"Yes," she replied, not taking her eyes off the wounded man.

"How do you know Castillo?"

Please, please, David's eyes begged her. Don't give me up. Sweat broke out on his neck.

Maria pursed her lips.

"Consuela!"

Consuela? Her name was Consuela? David's head spun.

The woman he knew as Maria turned toward Cienfuegos. "I want to go with you."

Lopez grabbed her arm, squeezing so tightly his fingertips turned white. "How do you know him?"

"You let me go!"

Cienfuegos motioned with his hand, and Lopez released her. He looked at Consuela. "How do you know him? You tell me the truth or I leave you behind."

Consuela tossed her head. "His name is David O'Connor. And he's a cop."

⌁

Half an hour went by—the most excruciating thirty minutes Kit could remember. But then Chris called. "OK, we have an ATM withdrawal by Lopez."

"Where?"

"The Shore National Bank on Rt. 13 near New Church."

"They're headed north, then."

"That's my guess."

Kit clenched her fist. "I'll tell the chopper."

"You want to go?"

Did she ever. "Yes."

"Wait for me."

No sooner had she hung up with Chris than her phone rang again. This time it was Jen, the Norfolk agent watching the shed. "It was so dark and quiet," the agent reported. "I decided to check the shed. It's empty, Kit. Nothing there. Whatever stash it held is gone. Someone removed the lock, too."

They'd missed them! "Good work, Jen." At least she hadn't sat there for hours watching an empty building. "Come back here, quick as you can."

Chris arrived moments later. "OK, I have an agent working with the banks . . . there's two of them, one for Lopez, one for Cienfuegos. We're live on their ATM cards."

"Great. Roger is going to stay here and coordinate information. Steve is at Cienfuegos's house. Let's you and I take two more agents and a second car and head north. That way we'll be close when we locate them."

⚬══◆══⚬

"Look," David said, mustering all the strength he could. "It's true, I was a cop in D.C. But I shot a kid and I'm off the force and I needed the money. That's what I was doing. I didn't care what you were running. I just needed the money. Haven't you ever heard of a bad cop?"

Cienfuegos's eyes fell on David's iPod wires, which were protruding from his pocket. He jerked the wires, and pulled out the iPod. Then he held his hand out toward Consuela and snapped his fingers. She looked confused at first, then retrieved her purse, and dug her own iPod out of it.

David felt suddenly dizzy. They were the same model, and Cienfuegos was comparing them. He closed his eyes.

Cienfuegos cursed loudly. David's eyes flew open just as the Mexican threw his iPod onto the ground and stomped on it. Lopez moved forward and grabbed David by the throat. He began squeezing, cutting off his air. David gasped desperately for breath.

He looked into Lopez's eyes. They were cold, like a snake's eyes, and David saw his pupils enlarge and his face relax in pleasure. An icy cold chill raced through David's veins. His knees grew weak. Lopez tightened his grip. Consuela watched, her arms crossed. Then the edges of David's vision began to grow dark. Oh, God, he thought. Oh, God!

"¡Alto!" Cienfuegos said, jerking Lopez out of the way. David's throat ripped open and he began to cough. But Cienfuegos threw David back against the car. "Who are you working for?" he demanded. "Who?"

David didn't answer. Cienfuegos cursed again and drove his fist into David's jaw. Then everything went black.

⚬━◆━⚬

"Look, there aren't that many roads," Kit said, looking at a map while Chris drove the black SUV north on Rt. 13. "Not until we get to Salisbury, anyway."

"My guess is they'll head straight north, to Philly or New York. They won't risk crossing the Bay Bridge. The toll takers could ID them."

"You don't think they'll just hole up somewhere?"

Chris should his head. "They want to get off this peninsula as quickly as they can."

Kit settled back in her seat, her thoughts racing. "So at Pocomoke, they can go Rt. 13 or 113."

"They'll go 13. It's much quicker."

Kit nodded. The lights streaked by in the dark night. The dread she'd been avoiding now gripped her. She stared at the road ahead. The dotted centerline flashed by like a strobe. Her head pounded. She glanced at Chris. "How long . . ." her voice stuck in her throat.

Chris flexed his hand on the steering wheel. She saw his jaw shift. "It all depends on where he took the shot. If an artery got hit . . ." Chris's voice trailed off. He cleared his throat. "Think positively. With just a flesh wound, he can last a long time, especially if he can put pressure on it." He nodded his head, as if affirming his own thinking. "David's smart. He won't panic. He'll take care of himself."

Kit bit the corner of her lip. Her cell phone rang. She picked it up. "Yes? Yes . . ." She gestured for Chris to speed up. "Good! We're on the way." She looked at Chris. "Maryland State Police chopper has a white Escalade on the bypass around Salisbury."

"All right!"

⚬━◆━⚬

When he woke up, he could tell he was in a vehicle but he had no idea where or when or how he got there . . . he tried to move, and realized his hands were bound behind his back and there was tape across his mouth. Anger flashed through him. The thin stream of air he could take in past the tape wasn't enough. He began fighting, then realized quickly it was fruitless. Heart pounding, he began reciting the alphabet backwards in his head, a technique he'd perfected as a boy facing a drunken stepfather and trying to survive. Gradually, like a slowly melting glacier, his anger began to disappear. His heart rate slowed. His throat relaxed a little. He could breathe better. And his trembling became sporadic.

Where was he? In the back of a car. With something over him. A blanket. He moved his head around until his face emerged, and he pulled in a grateful breath of cool air. *Please help me, please help me, please help me,* he prayed silently.

An occasional flash of light helped him get oriented. He was on the back seat of the Suburban. He could hear Lopez and Cienfuegos up front. Where was Consuela? And where were they going?

The men were speaking Spanish. David forced himself to concentrate, and slowly he began to catch snatches of their conversation. He heard the word "Consuela" and then the word *"barco"*—boat. He heard Cienfuegos laugh softly and then say, in English, "We'll be halfway to Miami."

279

The FBI vehicles screamed up Rt. 13, lights flashing, jockeying through traffic and blasting across intersections. Kit, her stomach tight, stayed on the phone, listening to the Maryland State Police narrate the apprehension of the Escalade.

"How much farther?" Chris asked her.

She glanced over at the GPS unit. "About twelve miles."

"Ten minutes then." He glanced over at her.

Kit pressed the phone to her ear. The state police had pulled the Escalade over. She held up one finger, asking Chris to wait. She frowned. "One occupant," she said, looking over at Chris.

Her partner grimaced. "Wrong car?"

Nine minutes later, Chris pulled their SUV up behind the cluster of cop cars surrounding the Escalade in the parking lot of a bowling alley. Red and blue lights flashed so brightly Kit could hardly see around them. She jumped out of the Bureau car before it came to a complete stop, and raced toward the Escalade, flashing her badge. She looked inside, and fought nausea when she saw the blood all over the back seat. "Where's the driver?" she asked a cop nearby.

He motioned toward a state police car. Kit approached it. A state trooper looked up at her. "You Agent McGovern?"

"Yes." She flashed her creds.

"The young woman there was the only occupant." He nodded toward a Latina.

Kit shielded her eyes from the flashing lights. Did she know her? Was it . . .

"Car's registered to a Cienfuegos."

Chris suddenly appeared at her side. "Who is she?"

"David's Maria," Kit said softly.

29

LOOK, MS. ESPINOZA," KIT SAID, PACING IN THE INTERVIEW ROOM AT the state police headquarters, "the amount of meth we found makes you eligible for a nice long sentence in federal prison. You want to spend the rest of your life in jail? Never get married? Never see your family?"

Consuela Espinoza, AKA Maria, twisted her hands in her lap. She wouldn't make eye contact with Kit. "No comprende," she said over and over, shaking her head.

Sure, Kit thought.

But Chris was right on it. He leaned over Consuela, his arms braced on the table. And he spoke to her in Spanish, explaining her situation firmly, and pressing her again about where Carlos Cienfuegos was and what she was doing with his car, about her relationship with him and how long she had known him.

Kit studied the young woman as Chris questioned her. She was beautiful, with long, dark hair and dark eyes. Slim. Attractive. But there was a hollowness in her cheeks that caught her attention. Was she on meth? Is that what it was? Then she noticed something else. The woman kept touching her belly, almost cradling it, as if it were tender, as if . . .

"Consuela," Kit said suddenly.

Chris turned toward her in surprise.

"Do you want your baby to be born in jail?"

The woman looked at her, shocked.

"We need to know where these men are. You help us and we'll help you." Kit softened her voice. "Consuela, it's not just about you any longer, is it? It's about doing what's best for that baby. Will Carlos take care of you? Or will he dump you like he's dumped other women?" Kit saw a shift in Consuela's eyes, a bit of uncertainty. "Maybe he's already dumped you."

"He protect me . . . from Hector."

Ah, yes. Consuela/Maria had seduced Cienfuegos, Hector's boss, to keep Hector from hurting her again. Smart move. Still, Cienfuegos was using her. Kit felt sure of that. She pressed the woman. "Where exactly did he tell you to drive to, Consuela? With David's blood all over the back seat of your car? Knowing we were looking for a white Escalade?"

Tears came to the woman's eyes.

"Do you really think he's coming to meet you?"

Chris picked it up. "Tell us as much as you know, Consuela, and we'll help you out."

Time seemed to crawl. Kit's heart was beating hard. Then Consuela looked at her.

"He tell me," the woman said hesitantly, "he tell me drive north on Rt. 13 to Elkton, and he meet me there. Tonight."

"Where? Where exactly?"

She gave them the name of a motel. Chris turned and left the room to notify the Maryland State Police.

"What else?"

"He have me bring things to him."

"Like what?"

She described a suitcase, a large plastic container, and some personal things: toothbrush, toothpaste, clothing, money, food, and rope.

"But these things aren't in the Escalade."

Consuela shook her head.

"So you gave them to him."

She nodded and described the Suburban.

Kit had one more question. "Consuela, we know David was shot. How was he when you saw him?"

The woman stared at her blankly, her mouth a thin line.

"Consuela, he was your friend!"

Then the woman broke down. She buried her face in her hands. "He is bleeding everywhere. And I told them, I told them!"

"Told them what?"

"That he is a cop!"

⚓

Ciefuegos and Lopez jerked David out from under the blanket that covered him, through the back door of the Suburban, and into the night air. They pulled him to his feet. Eyes wide, he looked around. They were in a marina. The night sky stretched above them like a black cape. Hundreds of boats sat bobbing in their slips. The metallic clank of halyards against masts and the creaking of docklines were the only sounds. What time was it? David had no idea.

The men leaned David against the Suburban. Lopez pulled out a huge knife and showed it to him. "You make one sound," Cienfuegos said, "and my friend here gut you like a fish. Comprende?"

David nodded. With one swift move, Cienfuegos ripped the tape off David's mouth. "Can you walk?"

David shook his head. When they pulled him from the car, he had broken into an instant sweat and now a chill swept over him. What were they going to do?

"Let's dump him," Lopez said in Spanish.

"No. We keep him until we are out of here. Then we have plenty of ocean to put him in, right, Hector?"

Lopez didn't acknowledge the reference. "Look at him! He's dead soon!" he said, gesturing toward the blood.

"We keep him for now!" Cienfuegos snarled.

The two men got on either side of David and half-carried him down the main pier and onto one of the docks. Each time David's right leg hit the boards it sent a jolt of pain through him and he bit his lip to keep from crying out. How much blood had he lost?

They went past sailboats, trawlers, and powerboats. Some had small lights on inside, indicating someone might be on board, and David prayed someone, anyone, would just look out and see them. He knew that, if confronted, the men would make up a story: David was drunk, he was hurt . . . whatever. That's why they'd taken the tape off his mouth, to remove obvious signs he was being abducted.

But no one seemed to be out in the marina, and since David figured it was late, that seemed normal. He felt dizzy. The moon danced in the night and the stars swayed. David squeezed his eyes shut and opened them again, focusing on the pier. He could hear the occasional gurgle of a bilge pump. The smell of diesel and fish filled his nose. They walked down the C Dock and stopped in front of a big, sedan-bridge cruiser.

"In there," he heard Cienfuegos say, and they stepped onto the boat's swim platform, and then onto the boat.

Kit turned Consuela over to a female state trooper and emerged from the interview room, nearly bumping into Chris as she did. She looked at her partner. His eyes held more energy than she'd seen in days. "I've got the Maryland and Delaware State Police responding ..."

"They're not going to Elkton," Kit said, interrupting.

Chris looked at her quizzically.

"She's the decoy. The men either went south or ..." Kit hesitated, unsure of herself, "... or maybe headed east."

"East."

"Toward the boat."

Chris frowned. The harsh lights of the hallway intensified his expression. "What are you thinking?"

"I think they set Consuela up. They knew we'd be looking for that car. Cienfuegos's boat is fifty-two feet long and plenty sturdy enough for ocean travel. It may be the boat that's been running people up and down the coast." Kit put her hand to her forehead. "Boats like that may carry, say, five hundred gallons of fuel, plenty enough for a long trip." She looked up, her eyes imploring Chris. "Look, I know this is a long shot, but there aren't too many roads on the peninsula. Cienfuegos knows he's limited to Rt. 13, basically, if he wants to leave, and so, why wouldn't he think of an alternative escape route?"

"The boat."

"Right. Something that would keep him off the roads. It's a big ocean out there, and who'd be looking for them there? In the middle of the night? He doesn't know that we know he has a boat. His odds of getting away are a lot better out on the Atlantic." Her breathing was shallow. "Besides, remember what Consuela said she took to him? Rope? What's that for? A boat?"

She watched Chris for his reaction. He put his hands on his hips, walked away three paces, touched his chin, furrowed his brow.

Then he looked at her. "It's crazy, but I think you could be right. Where is it?"

"The boat? Ocean City."

"Let's go."

⚬━✦━⚬

The trip from Salisbury to Ocean City would take at least thirty-five intense minutes. Kit stayed on the cell phone and the radio, calling ahead to the Maryland State Police, coordinating with Roger, and double-checking the boat's location and slip number. She also called Steve, who decided to meet them at the marina. She clicked off her phone and wiped her sweaty hands on her khakis.

Chris sped through the dark night, his lights flashing. Kit could see the concentration in his face, the intensity in his eyes. Most women would find him attractive, but his intensity only reminded her of David.

David. Had she met him only to lose him? He'd stirred up feelings in her she thought were dead, intense longings she thought she'd never experience again. What's more, God had used him to challenge her thinking, to force her to confront her lack of forgiveness for Eric. So was that all God had had in mind? David was a momentary catalyst for her spiritual growth?

Oh, please, no . . . no . . . no . . .

Tears came to her eyes and she turned to look out of the window so Chris wouldn't see them. *Please God,* she prayed silently, *protect him. Please help me to find him. Please, God . . .*

Her cell phone rang. The Ocean City police were at the marina. A plainclothes officer had strolled down the dock and found slip 1430 empty. But over on the C Dock, a big Sea Ray had its motor running.

"What's the name?"

"Pleasant Dreams."

Wait. "Roger said Cienfuegos's boat was named 'Night Magic'."

"Boat names can be changed . . . easily."

Kit took a deep breath. "Odd time of night to have a boat warming up."

"Too early for fishing," the cop agreed, "and too late for cruising."

"If it starts to move out, call me right away. We're maybe ten minutes out." She snapped her phone shut and turned to Chris. "The name's wrong on the boat."

"Names can be changed."

"That's what the cop said."

Chris pressed on the accelerator and took the SUV up to eighty-five mph. "I'm going with your instincts." He nodded toward her cell phone. "Call the boss."

"You don't think that's premature?"

"Call him and tell him what you just found out."

So she did. Steve said he was on the way, with reinforcements. "Set it up before you move," he warned Kit.

"Yes, sir."

⚓

The Fair Winds Marina sat just west of the Ocean City Inlet, an opening into sheltered waters from the Atlantic Ocean, on the south side of Ocean City. One of the largest in the area, the marina was home to over three hundred pleasure and charter boats of all shapes and sizes. Ocean City is famous for sport fishing: marlin, tuna, bluefish, and shark teem in the waters offshore. Kit had been there as a child, surf fishing for flounder and sea bass. And she'd played at the beach. But Ocean City was a busy, commercial, touristy place, nothing like Chincoteague. It had never captured Kit's heart.

Because Cienfuegos was holding David, it was important that he not be alerted to police presence until Kit's team was ready. She'd toyed with the idea of requesting the Hostage Rescue team from Quantico, or the Norfolk SWAT team, but either group would take a minimum of two hours to get to the scene and Kit wasn't sure they had that much time. David had been shot, and the amount of blood she'd seen in the Escalade had convinced her time was short.

Instead, she had decided to rely on the Ocean City police chief's emergency response team—and whatever agents and state police she could collect.

Presuming, of course, her hunch was correct, and the Sea Ray warming up belonged to Cienfuegos, and that David was on that boat. And alive. Which was presuming a whole lot, she knew. They could have dumped him anywhere. Why would they want to keep him with them? They could have let him bleed to death. They could have . . . she stopped herself from pursuing that line of thought. There was no point to it.

The police chief, Dan Gunner, suggested they gather in the parking lot of a miniature golf course three blocks from the marina. When Chris pulled up, Gunner was already there, with thirteen of his people dressed in SWAT gear. Kit pulled on her ballistic vest for the third time that night. She exited the car and approached Gunner. Tall, around 6-foot, and blond, he looked very Germanic, with a square face and strong jaw.

"Thank you, chief, for responding," Kit said, and she introduced Chris and the other two agents, who had been following them in their own vehicle.

"We want as low a profile as possible," Gunner responded. "This is the tourist season and the last thing we need is a major incident."

Kit nodded. "I understand." Then she sketched out the basics of the case and fought to keep her throat from closing up as she told him about David. Just as she finished, a black Lincoln Town Car pulled up and a tanned, sandy-haired man got out with a rolled-up sheet of paper in his hand.

Chief Gunner nodded toward him. "Here's the marina owner, Sonny Foster."

"You called him?"

"He's a friend of mine." Gunner introduced Foster to the others. "You've got a map?"

Foster nodded. "Which boat are you interested in?"

Kit told him. "The owner's name is Cienfuegos. I thought the boat name was *Night Magic* but the boat that has the engine running is *Pleasant Dreams.*"

"He renamed it," Foster explained. "Not three weeks ago. Had the work done in our boatyard."

Kit's eyes widened. She looked at Chris, whose face looked intent.

"Tell us about Cienfuegos," Chris said.

Foster shrugged. "We got over three hundred boats here. I don't really know much about him. He just moved his boat here in the last couple of months. Must like to go night fishing, 'cause I've seen him coming and going at odd times. Other than that . . ."

"Did you ever see him with a lot of people on board?"

"Once. I thought the man must have a big family."

"Show us on the map the boat's location."

Foster spread the rolled up map out on the hood of a car. He pointed out the long pier, and the multiple docks that came off of it like fingers, the fuel dock, the marina restaurant, bathroom facilities, office, pump-out-station, and the access to the ocean. "The boat that's running is right here," Foster said, pointing to the very end of the C Dock.

"What kind of cover is there?" Kit asked.

"Well, you've got these other boats, and some lockers sitting on the dock itself. There's not much mass to them, though."

"Fiberglass boats and dock lockers won't stop bullets," Chris said.

Foster stroked his chin. "Here's a thought. The dockmaster's office is here, at the end of the E Dock." He pointed to a place on the map. "It's small, but it might help you a little."

Kit frowned. "How small?"

"About big enough for two people."

"Should we approach him by boat instead?" Kit asked, looking at Chris. "What do you think?"

"You got Coast Guard here?" he asked the chief.

"Sure."

"No, wait." Kit swallowed hard. Her gut was tight. "No Coast Guard." Who knows what connections Rick Sellers had, or to whom he'd been talking? "How about the marine police?"

"I have my own unit," the chief said.

"Can we use them?"

"Sure. I'll have them within range in 15 minutes."

"So let's set it up both ways, Chris," Kit said. "You and I will be in the dockmaster's office, and we'll have the marine police unit in the channel."

Chris nodded. "I'd like to go take a look at this marina."

"I'll come with you." Kit looked at Gunner. "Could you please get your unit ready but ask them to stand by, well outside the marina, until we're ready?"

Gunner agreed.

"What about my live-aboards?" Foster asked. "Are they in danger?"

"How many are there? And where are they?"

"Right now, I got maybe half a dozen. Let's see, I know I got one here, here, here, and here." He pointed to slips on the map.

Chris asked, "Is there any way to contact them?"

"We have their cell phone numbers. But they're at the office."

Kit shook her head. "There's no time for that. No time. We're just going to have to trust they'll be smart enough to keep their heads down."

The two agents drove to within a block of the marina, and covered the rest of the distance on foot. Staying behind the buildings on shore—the bathroom facilities, marina office, and restaurant—they crept onto the E Dock, staying low, using the docked boats for cover. The marina seemed full, a good thing. Silently, they watched for signs of life on Pleasant Dreams. The rumble of the boat's engine was the only sound. Then Chris touched her arm and pointed as a man appeared on the C Dock, carrying something which he placed on board. The other man emerged from the salon area and took the duffle bag, stowing it below. "They'll have really good vision from up there," Chris whispered, pointing to the sedan bridge.

Kit nodded. She'd been on a boat like that once, and knew you could pilot it from up there. The extra eight feet or so in height gave anyone on the bridge a strategic advantage.

"Look," Kit whispered. "What if we stage the police boats there," she pointed toward the access channel to the ocean, "and we stay here and call them out?"

Chris nodded. "And bring the others up there, behind the office." He glanced at Kit. "I'm still concerned about the people on these boats. We may need to evacuate them."

"We don't have time!" Kit nudged him. "Look!"

A man emerged from *Pleasant Dreams*, moved swiftly down the dock to the main pier, and crossed to the parking lot. He took two duffle bags from the Suburban parked there, shut the door, and made his way back to the boat.

"That's Lopez," Kit whispered. "He's shorter and older. And he limps."

"It looks like they're packing a lot in that boat, like they're planning a long trip."

"Let's go back. We can take a look at that Suburban on the way out."

"All right!"

Crouching, the two agents ran back down the E Dock, dashed behind the bathrooms, and circled around to the far side where the Suburban was parked. Chris stayed, watching, as Kit ran up to the SUV and shined her flashlight into the interior. It was empty, but the blood in the back seat made her stomach turn. Catching movement again on the C Dock, she slipped back toward Chris.

Then the two agents saw Lopez moving back toward the parking lot. He got in the Suburban and started the engine. Then he drove back through the parking lot, and stopped.

"He's at the boat ramp!" Kit whispered, and then she and Chris watched in amazement as Lopez stepped out of the Suburban, which was still in gear, and let the car drive itself down the ramp and into the water.

⚬════◆════⚬

He was a little boy, scared to death, hiding behind his bed while his stepfather raged. He could taste blood from a blow to his face, and feel the ache of his bruised arms and back. But he was used to pain—it was the screaming of his mother that most frightened him. The cruel anger in his stepfather's voice, the terror in hers,

*gripped him. His world felt out of control and he wanted to fight
. . . fight.*

David tried to move, felt the constriction of his bound
hands, and fought to get free, but he felt drugged.

My son, get up!

He forced his eyes open. What? Where was he?

The room was pitch dark, except for a small strip of light
creeping under the door.

My son, get up!

Who was that? Did he hear something?

He fought his way back to full consciousness. Then he heard
another voice and his heart began racing. Kit! Kit's voice!
Through a bullhorn . . .

"Carlos Cienfuegos, come out. This is the FBI . . ."

Kit! She was outside! David forced himself into a sitting
position. Where was he? Where? Oh, yes, on a boat. He heard
Kit's voice again. Emotion surged through him. His head
began to clear. Kit! Kit!

Cienfuegos. Lopez. He had to get away. To keep them from
getting to her. Or using him as a shield. He moved and felt the
searing pain in his leg. He couldn't stand, not on that leg. He
needed his hands to move but his hands were bound behind
him.

So David began groping in the dark for something, anything, anything sharp. His hands touched the cabinet under
the berth and he pulled open the door. But everything he felt
in there was soft, like towels or something. He could hear
Cienfuegos or Lopez shouting. He moved again, and that's
when his hands felt the edge of the cabinet door itself. It was
sharp. But sharp enough?

David began sawing the tape binding his hands against the
edge. "God, help me!" he whispered. "Please help me!" Sweat
began rolling down his temples and pouring out of his hair. He

sawed and sawed, changing angles and working, working until suddenly he felt a flood of relief as the tape gave and his hands were free. Free!

⊶———⊷

"Carlos, we want to talk. We know you have David Castillo with you and we want to negotiate. You're outnumbered, Carlos, talk to us." Kit crouched behind the dockmaster's office on the E Dock, bullhorn in hand, with Chris right behind her. All of her attention was focused forward, on Carlos Cienfuegos. He stood on the sedan bridge of his boat, at the controls, and Lopez was on the starboard deck.

"Carlos has a rifle," Chris whispered, pointing. "They probably both do."

"Put down your gun, Carlos. Let's talk."

The answer came back from the boat. "You let us leave. Then we give you Castillo."

"No good, Carlos. You give us Castillo first, then we'll let you leave."

"And the Coast Guard will be waiting, no? You think I am stupid?"

"No, Carlos, not stupid. But you are surrounded." Kit thought quickly. "We've been talking to Consuela, Carlos. We know what you're up to. We know about Lopez and the meth. We're onto you, Carlos, and there's no way you're going to get out of this clean on your own. But you give us Castillo and we'll talk. We'll cut a deal, Carlos. Make things easier on you."

Lopez shouted back, cursing in Spanish.

"C'mon, Carlos," Kit said. "You're a reasonable man."

"What do you say we get a phone to him?" Chris said. "Cut Lopez out of the decision-making?"

"David thinks Lopez is a psychopath."

"So let's cut him out of the conversation."

Kit nodded. She put the bullhorn up to her mouth. "Let's talk by phone Carlos. What do you say? Let us bring you a cell phone."

But Carlos' response was to have Lopez move on deck. "He's disconnecting shore power," Chris said. The boat went dark. "The next step is casting off."

◦━━╋━━◦

Through a port, David saw Lopez on the deck disconnecting shore power. He saw the lights go out, and felt the boat move. Were they casting off? Adrenaline coursed through him. He had to get off! No way was he going out to sea with these guys. Reaching out in the dark, he groped for the door handle, found it, and opened the door a crack.

Only a few battery powered interior lights were on. The salon was dim. To the right was the head. To the left he saw the galley and then the salon. The sliding door which led to the aft deck stood open. All he had to do was get through the salon, out to the aft deck, and over the rail without the men seeing him. The darkness gave him cover; now if only he could move.

The salon was empty. David could hear someone up on the bridge. Cienfuegos, probably.

That left Lopez, the more dangerous man, still on deck somewhere.

David closed the door again. He had to think. How could he get himself off of this boat? And how could he distract the men, and keep them away from Kit?

Chris would be with her. Chris and a bunch of others. She wasn't impulsive. She wouldn't have come to the marina alone. Still, David wanted to minimize her risk, if he could.

He reached up as high as he could, found a shelf of some sort, and grabbed it to pull himself up. But the shelf broke and he fell back to the floor, pain flashing through him.

⚓

"Light up the police boats!" Kit said into her radio. "He may be preparing to cast off."

The chief got his men on the radio and three boats turned on all their flashing lights and moved to the middle of the channel, blocking Carlos's exit route.

"Keep him there. But we don't want to escalate. Hold steady."

"Will do," Gunner replied.

Kit squeezed the trigger on the bullhorn again. "You're going nowhere, Carlos! Talk to me . . ."

⚓

David fought the pain, trying to gather himself again for another try. He heard a noise in the salon, and it jolted him and he sat listening, his heart pounding, while someone walked past the berth where he was. *Don't stop, don't stop,* he said silently.

The footsteps receded and soon David could open the door a crack again. When he did, he heard Kit's voice on the bullhorn, calling out to Cienfuegos.

He had to get off of the boat. He had to keep the men away from Kit. There was no way he could fight them. But he could draw them off.

David reached up, this time gripping the door frame, and pulled himself to his feet. His head spun with the effort and he rested his head against the doorframe until the spinning stopped. Then he opened the door and listened. Cienfuegos was on the bridge, yelling. Lopez was speaking, too, but in a lower voice, as if his words were directed at Cienfuegos. David could tell Lopez was on the foredeck.

He opened the door and stepped out of the cabin. The pressure on his leg was painful but he had no crutches and a crawl was too slow. As quietly as he could, he moved through the salon, bracing his hands on the walls, half-lifting himself along. He saw a gun and picked it up. It was a flare gun. He took it anyway, shoving it inside his shirt. Then, impulsively, as he passed the galley, David switched on the propane stove. He knew the heavier-than-air gas would seep into the salon and drop into the bilge. Maybe a spark from the bilge pump would set it off. Lots of boats had gone up in smoke that way. Ten more feet. Kit and Cienfuegos were still shouting at each other. The sliding door stood open. David checked. Lopez was nowhere in sight, and Cienfuegos would be looking forward, at Kit. He hobbled through the door, crossed the aft deck, picked up a flotation cushion, and let himself down onto the swim platform, just a few inches from the water. Pulling the flare gun out of his shirt to keep it dry, he held the gun above his head, and rolled slowly into the water, minimizing the splash.

The cold, dark water felt so good on his leg, so good he almost gasped. *Thank you, thank you!* he prayed silently. He released his grip on the swim platform, slipped further into the water, pushed off against the hull of the boat, and he was clear.

○═══╪═══○

"Chris, what are you saying?" Kit asked, her eyes wide.

"I'm saying I'll trade places with David. Let them take me."

"No! They'd kill you."

"Maybe, maybe not." Chris's eyes were shining in the light of the marina. "Honestly, Kit. David's not going to survive a long trip with them. I'd at least have a chance. You can get the Coast Guard to deploy, or maybe I can talk them into just letting me off somewhere."

"That's crazy."

"I can do this, Kit. I want to do it."

"Chris . . ."

"It's his only chance, Kit. David's only chance."

Would Cienfuegos trade David for Chris? That would be totally against bureau policy. Still, the fact that Chris suggested it struck her as kind, noble even.

"Give me the bullhorn." Chris took it out of her hand. "We've got to do this before Steve gets here." He lifted the bullhorn and spoke into it. "Carlos, we have a deal for you. This is Special Agent Cruz. I will go with you in place of Castillo."

"Why? Why would you?" came the shout back in the dark.

"Castillo is hurt. He needs medical attention. Come on, Carlos. You don't want a murder rap, too."

Silence. Cienfuegos must have been thinking. "How we do this?" he asked, finally.

"You put David out on the dock. Then I will come aboard."

"No guns."

"No weapons of any kind, Carlos. I'll be clean. You can put me off in Miami."

Kit could hear sharp words, as if Cienfuegos and Lopez were arguing.

Then Cienfuegos called out. "You come down the dock. Then we talk more. No tricks, or there is a bullet in your head, comprende?"

"Got it."

Kit looked at Chris, who stripped off his weapons as they spoke. "I don't want you to go up there a second too soon. Wait until they have David on the dock, OK? I don't want both of you taken. And keep your vest on."

"Right." Chris put his gun and holster on the dock. He pulled the knife out of his boot, and the back-up weapon out of the small of his back.

"We'll be tracking you. I'll have a Coast Guard chopper waiting offshore. Don't worry, Chris, we're not going to . . ."

"What's going on?" Steve Gould appeared out of the darkness.

Chris and Kit looked at each other.

"Sir, we . . ." Kit began.

Chris interrupted her. "We're trading hostages. Me for David."

"No. Absolutely not."

Kit's heart sank.

"He'll die, sir, without medical care, and I'll . . ."

"You're a trained FBI agent and I am not going to lose one of my people . . ."

Suddenly someone whistled. And whistled again. Kit looked at Chris. "What's that?"

Loud cursing in Spanish erupted from the boat. Cienfuegos shouted and pointed off the stern on the starboard side. She saw him pick up a rifle. Chris began grabbing his weapons again. Simultaneously, she shouldered her own rifle.

"Make sure you have justification for deadly force," Steve warned.

Shots rang out.

"What's he doing? What's he shooting at?" Kit said. She moved to the other side of the dockmaster's office, where she could see better. Lopez was firing toward the stern of the boat, away from the agents.

"He's firing off the stern. What's there?" Kit exclaimed. Then she saw a light, like a flare, arcing through the sky in a reddish blaze. "What . . . ?"

Instantly, an enormous explosion rocked the night, and *Pleasant Dreams* blew apart into a million pieces.

30

GOOD GRIEF!" CHRIS STOOD UP AS BURNING FRAGMENTS OF BOAT FLEW into the sky, bright orange embers and flaming pieces, like fireworks against the black night.

"David!" Kit cried out. "Where is he? Chris . . ."

But Chris was on the radio to Chief Gunner. "Get the fireboat up here, now!" There was a garbled response. Then Gunner's voice came back: "We saw a flare gun fire from the water near the B Dock just before the boat blew."

"From the water?" Kit looked at Chris. "Who could have . . . David? Was it David?"

They both took off running back to the main pier, past the restaurant and the marina office, and then down toward the B Dock. Steve Gould ran right behind them. Kit's heart pounded. The marina glowed orange with the light of the burning boat and an acrid smell filled the air. David . . . David . . . David . . . ?

And then she saw him. Or what she thought could be him. She saw a white cushion in the water just off the end of the dock, and a figure clutching onto it. She stripped off her ballistic vest and took her gun off her belt as she ran. Reaching the end of the dock, she put both down, quickly pulled off her shoes, and jumped into the water.

The cold took her breath away. All around her, reflections from the fire danced on the water. Here and there a piece of burning boat floated. But as she surfaced from her jump, and shook the water from her eyes, she saw the miracle: it was David, David! He was grinning at her and gripping the cushion. Within seconds, she arrived at his side.

His eyes were wide. "Kit!"

"Oh, David!"

"I got 'em."

"That was you?" Kit nodded toward the burning boat.

He grinned. "Yeah. I got 'em."

"You need help?" Chris called from the dock.

"Get the medics!" Kit looked back at David. "I'm going to pull you over to the ladder on the dock. Can you hold onto the cushion?"

He nodded and she grabbed the strap on the cushion and swam to the ladder attached to the side of the dock. Then she had David hook his right arm over a rung.

"Any chance you can climb out?" she asked.

"No way." He shook his head.

"Where are you hurt?"

"I took a shot in the leg."

"Where else?" She had her arm around him, gripping the back of his jeans with one hand and the ladder with the other. They were face to face in the water, so close she wanted to kiss him. Burning debris floated around them and smoke hung in the air. Her heart was trembling. She'd almost lost him, and now here he was, again, alive, and so close.

"Is he conscious?" her boss called out from the dock above.

"Yes!" Kit could see the firelight dancing in David's eyes. "What's hurt besides your leg?" she asked him again.

"My leg is killing me. Lost a lot of blood."

"Anything broken?"

He shook his head. "No, no."

"Can we pull him up?" Chris called down.

"No. He's got an unstable shoulder. We'll need a rescue basket."

David leaned his head against hers and sighed. "Never mind. Tell them they can leave me right here. Forever. I don't think my leg hurts anymore."

He was joking, she realized. Joking! "That's because it's frozen," she retorted.

"I don't care."

She felt his breath on her face, and the stubble of his beard, and caught the faint smell of his now-familiar shampoo, and she relaxed as his arm drew her closer still. "I love you," she heard him say, and he kissed her neck.

Steve had just leaned over the dock. He looked sharply at Chris. "She's in a relationship with a source?"

Chris shrugged.

⸎

Minutes later, David was up on the dock. The medics began cutting his wet clothes off, wrapping him in blankets, and one of them was preparing to start an IV. "We're going to Medevac him to Salisbury," the chief medic said to Kit, who was standing about ten feet away. "Chopper's on the way."

Chris looked at her. "You go with him. I'll finish up."

Kit thought about that. She wanted to go. She desperately wanted to go. She pulled the blanket an EMT had given her closer. Then she shook her head. "It's my case, Chris." Her heart wanted to go. Her head knew she couldn't. "We'll send someone else with him."

He nodded.

"Who is Kit?" one of the medics near David shouted.

"Me."

"He wants to say something to you."

Quickly Kit went over to the stretcher. David's eyes were wide open. She touched his face. "You'll make it, David. You're going to be OK." Was that hope or faith? She didn't know.

He blinked. "Lopez and Cienfuegos, they kept talking about Sandy Point . . . something about Sandy Point. A school or something. I couldn't quite catch it." David's voice was shaky. "Check it out, Kit."

"I will, David. You take care of yourself." Then she touched him again.

⊶━✦━⊷

Kit collected her vest and gun. David had said Sandy Point. Where was Sandy Point? Her cell phone rang. She heard the sound of rotor blades spinning and looked up as the Medevac chopper took off from a nearby parking lot, its blades beating the air furiously, dust kicking up from the ground. "Hello?" she said, pressing the phone to her ear. Her eyes stayed fixed on the chopper.

Roger had information for her. Two minutes later, she snapped off the phone and turned to Steve. "Carlotta is leaving her house. Roger's following her."

Chief Gunner appeared. "We've pulled two bodies out of the water. Want to take a look?"

There was enough of Cienfuegos and Lopez left to identify them. Kit, slightly sickened, turned away and looked at her boss. "Just a hunch here, but if Carlotta is headed toward Sandy Point, wherever that is, I want to go there."

"Where is it?"

If Steve's jaw were any more square he'd be a Lego, Kit thought. The more intense he got, the more angular his face became. "I don't know . . ."

Chief Gunner had joined them. He interjected, "It's south-west of here, about forty-five minutes, unless you're running Code 1."

"Find out." Steve nodded toward her cell phone.

She called Roger, snapped the phone shut, and nodded. "She's headed in approximately that direction."

"Let's go!"

Steve opted to ride with her rather than take his own vehicle, a fact which would have been disconcerting on any other night. She'd left Chris in charge of the FBI's interests in the Ocean City crime scene and was now gunning down Rt. 213 toward Sandy Point, her boss beside her. The roads were empty, the night sky black, the moon a white marker, like a chip a gambler had left on the table.

Steve cleared his throat. Kit braced herself. Was she going to get a lecture on impulsivity? On maintaining professional distance from informants? What? She shivered in her still-damp clothes.

"You did a good job back there."

Kit raised her eyebrows and glanced toward Steve.

"You had it organized. You worked well with the locals. And when you needed to take action, you did."

Kit felt her pulse quicken. "Thank you, sir."

"You can explain your relationship with David to me afterwards."

"I assure you, sir . . ."

He waved her off. "Later." Then he leaned forward and tapped the dashboard. "Let's pick it up."

Lights flashing and sirens sounding, the drive took less than thirty-five minutes. Steve remained on the phone with Roger much of the way. By the time Kit was ready to turn off 213 and onto Sandy Point Road, Roger reported Carlotta had, indeed, driven to an old school building, that there were lights on and activity throughout the place. "Wait for us there," Steve commanded.

The old school building actually looked like a big, oversized house with a cupola on top. Kit figured it was over a hundred years old, built in the days when travel was difficult and multi-grade schools were sprinkled about the county as close to the children they served as possible. Tonight, the old building looked lit up, like a Christmas tree, and inside, Kit could see lots of activity.

"The sheriff's emergency response team is getting ready," Roger told them as they watched the house from the woods nearby. "Carlotta's got two men with her. I suspect they're armed."

"One of them drove the second van?"

"Right."

The sheriff joined them. "We're ready."

"You have a perimeter established?" Kit was taking no chances this time.

"Yes, ma'am."

"OK," Kit said. "Let's watch and see what they're doing. Right now, we don't have any justification for going in. But if they try to move people . . ."

"Then we've got exigent circumstances."

"Right."

A man carrying a large box exited the house and put it in the back of a van. Then the second man did the same thing. When two women and some sleepy-eyed children appeared on the front porch, Kit said, "That's it."

"You lead," Steve said.

Kit saw the sheriff frown, and a slow smile turn Roger's mouth up. She knew exactly what they were thinking. The locals might resent following a Fed, much less a woman. Another time she might have made a point of it, but not tonight. There was too much at stake. "The sheriff's men are used to following him," she said evenly. "How about if you direct the team," she said to the sheriff.

He nodded vigorously. She could see the relief in his eyes. "Here's the deal: we don't want those vans to leave. And we don't want anybody hurt . . . especially not those children. I think we're dealing with trafficking victims. They'll be terrified. They may even be uncooperative. But they're victims. Carlotta and the men . . . those are our targets."

"Got it."

"Your team goes in first, we follow one minute later."

After they made sure their radios would work together, the sheriff disappeared into the night. Kit found herself praying silently. *Please let this go well. Please keep anyone from getting hurt* . . . She could hear Steve breathing at her side, feel the tension in the air, as she kept her eyes fixed on those vans.

Ten minutes later, the sheriff radioed that his team was in position. Five minutes after that, when Kit saw another woman being ushered down the steps toward the van, she signaled them to go.

Three deputies in cars converged on the vans. Three more emerged from the woods to cover the back, and more deputies followed until they'd surrounded the entire house. Flashbangs detonated inside. Women and children screamed. Kit could hear deputies shouting, "Get down! Get down!" She saw people raising their hands in surrender and others dropping to the floor. One woman fell onto her knees, hands raised in supplication, as if she were praying. Within forty-five seconds the whole scene was under control. Or so it seemed. "Let's go!" Kit said, and she and Steve and Roger began jogging toward the vans and the house.

Steve cut to the right. That's when Kit saw a dark figure angling away from a shed just to the left of the large house.

At first, she wasn't sure what she'd seen, but the sweep of a deputy's flashlight caught a white shirt and Kit broke into a run. "We've got a runner!" she yelled.

The night flashed by in a blur. Kit's eyes were fixed ahead, although the fugitive had been swallowed up by the forest. She entered the woods and briars snatched at her legs. A low-hanging branch lashed her face. She could hear two others running with her, just behind her. The beam from her flash-light triggered odd shadows and more than once she dodged a nonexistent foe.

But then she saw a figure clearly in a patch of moonlight filtering down through the trees. "Stop! FBI! Stop!" The figure glanced back and then kept running.

Kit increased her speed. Her breath was coming hard now and her arms were pumping. She stepped in a marshy area, jumped over a log, and raced through underbrush. When the figure glanced back a second time, they were closer together. Kit could see the fugitive was a woman. She guessed she was unarmed. And she knew she could catch her.

A minute later, just as the woods broke into an open field, Kit launched herself into the air and tackled her.

"Ah!" the runner said, thumping facedown onto the ground with Kit on top of her.

"Give me your hands! Your hands!" Kit yelled, and she grabbed Carlotta's arms and pulled them behind her. She struggled with her momentarily, but then the woman gave up.

"You OK?" Steve asked, arriving on the scene completely out of breath.

"Yes," Kit said, and the rasp of the cuffs closing around Carlotta's wrists emphasized her statement.

By the time they got back to the old schoolhouse, the two men had been cuffed and placed in cruisers, and the sorting-out process of the others present had begun.

"You've got to see this," Roger told Kit and her boss.

She handed Carlotta off to a deputy, and then she and Steve followed Roger into the house. Her eyes widened as she took in the scene.

There were fifteen, maybe twenty Hispanic women and children huddled in the largest room. They looked at her with big, questioning eyes. Some of them were crying. All of them looked terrified, casting sidelong glances at the deputies dressed in SWAT gear who stood around the room. Kit knew they had no idea what was going on, or what was about to happen to them.

"Look in here," Roger said, and he led them back to the kitchen. Huge padlocks hung on the handles of each cabinet door and the refrigerator as well. A nearby pantry was secured the same way. "They weren't allowed access to food. Not even the children."

Trash littered the floor and Kit wondered when the place had been cleaned last. The area near the back door was filled with bulging black trash bags. The whole place smelled of garbage and dirty diapers. "Oh, gag," Kit said softly, unable to contain her disgust.

"Come upstairs." Roger led her up a back stairwell. On the second floor of the house, there were four large rooms, former classrooms, two on each side. They served as dormitories. Dirty mattresses covered the wide plank pine floors and clothes were heaped in piles.

Kit stood in the doorway and counted: each room could hold eight to ten mattresses. "They could pack like . . . twenty people in each room!"

"That's not all . . . there's a third floor." Roger nodded toward a small door, secured by a lock. Just then, a deputy with a huge bolt cutter came up the stairs. He placed the jaws of the cutter on the hasp of the lock and snapped it off. "Thanks," Roger said. He turned on a flashlight.

Kit followed him up the small staircase. Part way up, Roger found a light switch and flipped it on. "The office," Roger said, as he reached the top of the stairs. "We'll need a warrant to go through this, but can you believe it?"

Kit couldn't believe it. The place was a virtual slave quarters. That far out in the country, the victims had no chance to get help. They were completely at the mercy of Carlos, Carlotta, and Hector Lopez.

As Kit came back downstairs, Steve met her. His face had softened, the angles were all relaxed, like a soldier at parade rest. And his eyes, his eyes were creased at the edges, more like he'd been playing with his grandson than looking at a crime scene. "Kit," he said, "good job."

She felt her face redden.

He gestured around the room. "They were using these people as slaves. Renting them out as domestics, ag workers . . . using them to clean office buildings. Paying them nothing. No medical care, time off, nothing."

Kit's throat tightened. "Where are they from?"

"Mostly Mexico. That woman over there," Steve motioned toward a young woman in jeans and a white shirt, "she told me Lopez took their passports. Wouldn't let them make phone calls. Go anywhere on their own. Lopez was the enforcer. He terrified them. They were trapped." He shook his head. "Immigration is on the way and so are Social Services and crime scene techs. We need to get warrants to take the computers and so on."

"Yes, sir." Kit spotted a young woman, sitting in the corner alone, rocking. She wore a tattered pink dress, and her arms were scored with cuts. Had she been mutilating herself? "What's with her?" Kit asked, nodding.

Steve looked in the direction Kit was indicating. "I don't know." He caught the eye of the woman in jeans, the one he'd pointed out before, and she came over to where the two agents were standing. She moved gracefully, like a model. "Kit, this is Adriana." He looked at the Latina. "Can you tell us about the young woman over there?"

Adriana stiffened as she followed his gesture. She had wide, brown eyes the same color as her hair, which was long and lustrous. Her nose had a slight arch, her skin was the color of caramel, and she had the kind of allure that even dire circumstances couldn't extinguish. "Is there a place we can talk?" Adriana said in a heavily accented voice.

"The kitchen?" Kit suggested.

"Sí. All right."

<hr/>

A few minutes later, Adriana walked in, her arm around the waist of the young woman with cuts on her arms. "This is Isabella," she said.

Isabella's long dark hair strategically fell over part of her face, like a curtain behind which she could hide. Parallel lines scored on her arms betrayed the anguish in her soul.

Wisely, Steve remained quiet, letting Kit take the lead. "Isabella, my name is Kit. We've come to help you." The woman glanced at her as Adriana translated, then her eyes dropped again. "Can you tell us what happened?"

It would take more than that invitation to get her talking. It would take a cup of tea, and some small talk, and an unrelated conversation to create an atmosphere safe enough for Isabella to open up.

Though tired, Kit remained patient. Steve stayed in the background, leaning casually against a countertop, his expression vague. Kit was frankly surprised at his ability to downshift that way. But despite his low-key demeanor, Isabella still kept glancing at him nervously and finally he caught Kit's eye and indicated he was leaving the room.

That broke the ice. Hesitantly, like a child confessing a misdeed, Isabella began telling her story.

She had come from a poor village in Mexico, she told Kit through Adriana. She had married young, had a child, and then her husband had become very ill. They had no money for medical care, and no hope, so when a friend told Isabella about this man named Hector who could get her a good job in America she jumped at the chance.

"He bring me in a truck with many others," she said, lapsing into broken English, "me and my son."

Kit's heart skipped a beat. "Your son?"

"I have nowhere to leave him! No one to take him. I come here to work and send dollars home to help my husband. Only . . . only . . ." Isabella began to cry.

Kit reached out and took her hand. "What happened?" She kept her voice soft.

Isabella began speaking again in Spanish, her eyes full of tears, her voice filled with anguish. Kit's eyes remained on Isabella as she listened to Adriana's translation of her words. "She came with many others in a truck. Hector took her passport, saying he needed it to get her work. Soon she found herself in a tomato field, picking from early in the morning until late.

"At first, it was OK. Her son, Jorge, could play nearby. There were some other children, too. It was hard work, and Hector, he not pay her what he promised. Carlos and Carlotta charge her rent. And for food. The money she had to send back to her husband, it was not enough. One day, she get word, he was dead.

"Then Isabella, she want to go back to Mexico, to her mama. To take her son back. She very, very sad. Very sad. But Carlos say she need to work to pay off debt: debt for the truck, the rent, the food . . . too, too much money she owe. He not let her go. So Isabella take Jorge and try to run away. She get caught. The next time she try that they say something very, very bad will happen to her. She scared, then, very scared. Sometime later, then, this man, Lopez, he catch Jorge playing in a shed. He very, very angry. Why? No one understand! Isabella try to stop him from hurting Jorge. Lopez hit her, he beat her. He tell her to keep her kid away from that place! But Jorge, he love his mama, and he try to protect her.

"That night, Jorge is gone. Isabella look for him all over. In the house. Outside. In the fields, the woods . . . she not find Jorge anywhere. And she cannot eat, she cannot sleep, she just look and look.

"Later, Lopez come to her. He say Jorge run away. But Isabella, she know her boy not do that. Lopez, he took him. She knows that. But where? Her heart not rest, she say, until she know what happened to her Jorge."

"How long ago did this happen?" Kit asked.

Adriana translated and Isabella shook her head. Then Adriana looked at Kit. "She doesn't know exactly. A month ago or more. When it was hot, very hot. And the tomatoes were ripe."

Kit's throat was tight. "How old was Jorge?" she asked, barely getting the words out.

The grieving mother understood that question. "Seven. Almost eight." Isabella responded.

Tears filled Kit's eyes. At last, her beach child had a name.

Epilogue

KIT JOGGED SOUTH ON ASSATEAGUE BEACH, HER BARE FEET GRIPPING THE cool sand, her arms and legs relishing the September breeze. The sun was bright, though lower in the south, and before her the sandpipers skittered as waves swept up onto the shore. They wouldn't be here for long. It was almost time for them to move south.

In the distance, on the beach, she could see a figure standing . . . a man, dressed in navy blue sweats and staring out at the ocean. Curious, she picked up her pace. Two surfers walked past her, headed north, wearing wetsuits and carrying their boards. She ran faster, her breath coming harder now, and she raised her hand to her brow to shield her eyes from the sun. Something was different . . . something was odd . . . something was . . .

The man had crutches. He was standing on the beach, propped up by crutches! Kit pressed forward, her heart pounding, and then her face broke into a wide grin. "David! David! David!" The refreshing air felt cool against her teeth.

David turned toward her, smiling, and as she drew near, he dropped his crutches and swept her into his arms. She nearly knocked him over, elation propelling her. "Whoa, whoa!" he said, laughing as he fought to maintain his balance. "Be easy on the crippled guy!"

"When did you get here? How long . . . why didn't you call me?" Instinctively she grabbed her cell phone. "You were supposed to text me at least!"

But David ignored her. Gently pushing the cell phone away, he cradled her face in his hands, laced his fingers into her hair, and kissed her. As his mouth touched hers she trembled. He kissed her again, and the rush of a thousand everafters raced up and down her spine.

"How did you find me?" she asked, looking into his face. His eyes were dancing.

"Are you kidding? Everybody on Chincoteague knows where you are. All I had to do was drive into town and ask the first person I saw." David grinned at her. Here on the beach he looked thinner, and he had lost some of his tan. *A month in the hospital*, she thought, *will do that to you.* "You are famous, girl."

She picked up his crutches and handed them to him, and slowly they made their way back over the dunes. She peppered him with the thousand questions she'd thought of since she'd seen him last, until he finally laughed and told her the inquisition was over because he couldn't use crutches and think at the same time.

David had parked his Jeep next to her Subaru. He opened the lift gate. Two cups of somewhat lukewarm coffee waited for them. "Sit down," he said, gesturing, and then he sat down next to her, where they could watch the sun set over Tom's Cove.

The air felt cooler now, and different birds filled the landscape. The fragile warm-weather species had made their way south, while others were coming down from the north. Ducks, loons, geese—the waterfowl found the richness of Assateague a sustaining pleasure. Soon, too, the snow geese would arrive, skein upon skein of them spiraling down from the sky, noisily descending like silvery ribbons on the brackish ponds of the island.

"So how are you?" Kit asked him, sliding her hand into his.

"Better. I'm starting to get my strength back."

"You look good."

"Naturally!" he joked.

"What happened with your boss?" She knew he'd had a meeting with him.

A slow grin spread over David's face. He shook his head. "He was so mad that I was working with you guys without permission. So he fired me. Then, he felt sorry for me because I'd lose my health insurance, so he rescinded that and put me on administrative leave again. With pay. For six months."

Kit smiled. "He must think a lot of you."

"He says I'm more trouble than any cop is worth." David laughed. "How about you?"

She knew he meant the review her boss had performed on the handling of her case. "I survived. I'm not sure I would have, though, if we hadn't found those people." She took a sip of coffee. "It was really dicey for a time." The sun resembled an orange lozenge hanging above the horizon. A "V" of geese flew past it, creating a postcard image. "I think Steve and I understand each other better now. And that's a good thing."

"And what about Carlotta and the others? The victims?"

"We took care of all of them, you know? We are putting several of them, including Jorge's mother, in witness protection. We're prosecuting Consuela and Carlotta . . ."

"Carlotta turned out to be his sister, right?"

"That's right. Cienfuegos's sister. Masquerading as his wife. And they had a lot of money stashed away. A lot."

"And Consuela?"

Kit looked at him to see if there was anything in his eyes, any regret or anger. There was not. "Conspiracy. Plus, she's here illegally. And pregnant. It's not a very happy time for her. She may be deported. I'm not sure yet. We're trying to help her, a little anyway, for giving us some information about you."

David nodded. "And Sellers?"

"We got him on drug trafficking. We found all the paperwork in that old schoolhouse. He was a meth dealer. Got his stuff from Lopez. He used a fake ID but we were able to identify him anyway. He tried to run but we caught him. It's a shame: at least four teenagers are hooked on meth, thanks to him."

"I knew he was bad the minute I saw him."

Kit turned to him. "Oh, did you?"

"Yeah. I saw the way he was looking at you. I almost punched him out right then and there."

Kit laughed. David put his arm around her shoulders and drew her close as the sun began to drop below the horizon. "So what's next?" she asked him, resting her head on his shoulder.

"I've got a job interview."

She turned to look at him. "Really?"

"My boss called a buddy of his and recommended me for a job at a police training academy."

"In D.C.?"

"Norfolk." David smiled at her.

"Oh, David!"

"There's this lady who lives down there I'd like to get to know better." He kissed her ear. "I don't know, though. She's kind of tough. She may be too strong for me."

Kit smiled. "I don't think so, Ironman."

She felt his soft breath on her cheek as he nuzzled it, and she turned her face toward him, and the feel of his skin and the taste of his lips were like nourishment to her. "I love you," he whispered.

"I love you, too."

In the west, the sun had dropped nearly below the horizon, turning the sky scarlet, pink, and a deep purple. Blue clouds streamed like banners on either side, and a solitary heron lifted off from the shallows of Tom's Cove, proclaiming the end of the day, the end of the summer, and the beginning of a brand new season of her life. Kit rested her head on David's shoulder and watched the receding tide as it streamed out to sea, leaving mud flats rich with marine life. In her mind's eye she could see her anger streaming away, too, her anger toward Eric, her anger toward her mother. She nestled closer to David and, silently, she thanked God.

Discussion Questions

1. Kit has retreated to Chincoteague after a difficult divorce and a job change. Once the home of her now-deceased grandmother, Chincoteague represents peace, rest, and nurturing to her. Do you have a place that is a home for your heart?

2. After Kit finds the body of a little boy on the beach, she abandons her plans for a vacation and begins to discover what happened to him, even over the objections of her boss. What do you think triggers Kit's intense interest in the case?

3. Read Micah 6:8. Kit has a passion for justice. What justice issues are near and dear to you?

4. David was involved in a shooting in which a teenager was killed. Have you ever known anyone who has experienced post-traumatic stress disorder? Depression? How might you encourage that person?

5. As Kit and David start working together, what is their relationship like? What strengths and weaknesses do they reveal? If you were a close friend of Kit's, how would you advise her if she told you about David?

6. Both Kit and David have experienced trauma at the hands of others. Have you had something happen to you for which you have found it hard to forgive someone?

7. David says that he's discovered that "unforgiveness is a poison you drink hoping someone else will die." What does that statement mean? Do you think it's true? How has unforgiveness affected you?

8. What does Kit find particularly hard about forgiving Eric? How might Ephesians 4:32 apply? Of what has God forgiven you?

9. Connie makes a remarkable statement after the death of her husband. She tells Kit not to give up the "fight

for joy." How in the world can anyone reconcile the death of a loved one and joy?

10. Kit's perseverance pays off in the end. What obstacles did she overcome? Over what, in your life, have you had to persevere?

11. Kit's personal pain goes back past her divorce to the abandonment by her mother at age eight. What attempts did Connie make to stir that pot? If Kit were your friend, how would you advise her to deal with her abandonment?

Want to learn more about author
Linda J. White and check out other great fiction
from Abingdon Press?

Sign up for our fiction newsletter at
www.AbingdonPress.com/Fiction
to read interviews with your favorite authors, find tips
for starting a reading group, and stay posted on what
new titles are on the horizon. It's a place to connect
with other fiction readers or post a
comment about this book.

Be sure to visit Linda online!

www.lindajwhite.com